BRUTE FORCE

His anger flashed like a gas explosion. He stood up, grabbed the plate and hurled it across the kitchen, the food scattering in the air and the plate crashing down and breaking.

"I try to do things for you!" he yelled. "I try to help you! You don't appreciate it a damned bit!" His raving was almost incoherent.

He grabbed the portable TV he had given her, lifted it above his head and smashed it to the kitchen floor.

"I don't need this in my life! Get the hell out of here!" she shouted at him.

He charged at her, sending her to the floor on her back with him on top of her. He beat her with his closed fist, smashing it down again and again into her breast. His fist sank deeply with each impact, sending white-hot pain through her. She was sobbing and screaming as he rained blow after blow, his face twisted with rage.

The terrifying thought that he was not going to stop flashed through her head. Her young daughters would find her dead on the floor.

REAL HORROR STORIES!
PINNACLE TRUE CRIME

SAVAGE VENGEANCE (0-7860-0251-4, $5.99)
By Gary C. King and Don Lasseter
On a sunny day in December, 1974, Charles Campbell attacked Renae Ahlers Wicklund, brutally raping her in her own home in front of her 16-month-old daughter. After Campbell was released from prison after only 8 years, he sought revenge. When Campbell was through, he left behind the most gruesome crime scene local investigators had ever encountered.

NO REMORSE (0-7860-0231-X, $5.99)
By Bob Stewart
Kenneth Allen McDuff was a career criminal by the time he was a teenager. Then, in Fort Worth, Texas in 1966, he upped the ante. Arrested for three brutal murders, McDuff was sentenced to death. In 1972, his sentence was commuted to life imprisonment. He was paroled after only 23 years behind bars. In 1991 McDuff struck again, carving a bloody rampage of torture and murder across Texas.

BROKEN SILENCE (0-7860-0343-X, $5.99)
The Truth About Lee Harvey Oswald, LBJ,
and the Assassination of JFK
By Ray "Tex" Brown with Don Lasseter
In 1963, two men approached Texas bounty hunter Ray "Tex" Brown. They needed someone to teach them how to shoot at a moving target—and they needed it fast. One of the men was Jack Ruby. The other was Lee Harvey Oswald. . . . Weeks later, after the assassination of JFK, Ray Brown was offered $5,000 to leave Ft. Worth and keep silent the rest of his life. The deal was arranged by none other than America's new president: Lyndon Baines Johnson.

Available wherever paperbacks are sold, or order direct from the Publisher. Send cover price plus 50¢ per copy for mailing and handling to Kensington Publishing Corp., Consumer Orders, or call (toll free) 888-345-BOOK, to place your order using Mastercard or Visa. Residents of New York and Tennessee must include sales tax. DO NOT SEND CASH.

SHOP OF HORRORS

Bill G. Cox

Pinnacle Books
Kensington Publishing Corp.
http://www.pinnaclebooks.com

PINNACLE BOOKS are published by

Kensington Publishing Corp.
850 Third Avenue
New York, NY 10022

First Printing: April, 1998
10 9 8 7 6 5 4 3 2 1

Printed in the United States of America

DEDICATION

As always, this book is dedicated to my dear wife Nina, for her love, patience, and help—with this book and the others, and my life, which badly needed all the help it could get.

Introduction

What makes a good cop turn bad?

There always have been bad cops, but the last decade or so seem to have spawned more of them than ever before—on every level from small-town cop to the more sophisticated federal agencies.

At best, a cop's life is stressful—and always on the line. He knows he may lose it any moment. It's the nature of his work, and he lives with it or breaks under it. Cops probably have more than their share of broken homes, substance abuse problems, and temptations from every direction than most any other profession.

The majority hold up under the strain of battling the endless war against crime. Most of them are dedicated men and women. But those who fall make the biggest and blackest headlines, and regretfully, all law enforcement suffers a black eye when it happens.

As a young man during the 1950s I read and was intrigued by a pulp novel written by the late Jim Thompson. It was *The Killer Inside Me.*

The main character was a good-old-boy Texas deputy sheriff who underneath his dirt-kicking, drawling, and good-natured personality had the soul of a sadistic, psychopathic killer.

Over the years the novel has become a classic in its genre. Warner Brothers made the book into a movie by the same title in 1975.

The book lived on in my memory. As a newspaperman and freelance writer covering the police beat and trial courts over many years, I encountered one or two real law enforcement officers along the way who reminded me of Thompson's fictional character.

The few bad ones I knew demonstrated both latent and actual cruelty and sadism.

Those were the days before the Civil Rights Movement, and it was difficult at times to tell the difference between a cop who took knocking people around as a granted tradition of the profession, and one who actually got his kicks beating up prisoners, slapping women silly or forcing sexual acts on them because of the power and control a badge afforded.

But not until I heard about the deplorable murder of lovely Deborah McCormick and the sadistic sex attack on a young Vietnamese girl in Houston, Texas, in 1994 did I come across what I consider the closest living specimen of Thompson's deputy sheriff, Jekyll-Hyde killer.

For me anyway, the pulp novelist's imaginary deputy sheriff became a reality in the man who committed the brutal sex attack and murder of Deborah McCormick and a subsequent rampage of sexual violence and attempted murder. (Technically, he was an ex-lawman at the time, having only a few weeks earlier been fired because of abusing his wife.)

All of the officers who investigated the McCormick murder and brought the killer to Texas's death row were revolted by the tarnished badge image left hanging over all police officers by the atrocious acts of one of their own, even though he wasn't wearing a badge when it happened. He had been a cop for nearly twenty years—and a good one—until a few weeks before he crashed.

But even while a good public cop, his tendencies of violence toward women were displayed at home in his fanatic desire to control and dictate, terrorize and beat up his wives and girlfriends. He could beat a woman almost to death, and then act toward her like nothing had happened.

Fortunately, the killer cop or killer ex-cop are only a tiny blemish in the countless ranks of good, very good, cops. The homicide detectives and others who worked the McCormick case are examples of some of the best.

I am indebted to them for their help with my book research and for the insight they gave me into this bizarre case of one of their own gone off-course on an out-of-control tangent.

I also salute Jim Thompson, who died in the 1970s, for his book that will forever be among the top of all crime novels written in that wonderful era of pulp fiction.

But sometimes, the true facts can be more horrifying than any of the nightmares that emerge from the minds of the writers of fiction.

I found the terrible murder of Deborah McCormick in Houston, Texas, to be one of those cases.

Chapter 1

The large man knew she was there now, inside the flower shop.

He was oblivious to the swoosh and hum of the early morning rush-hour traffic along the busy street behind him.

The luscious redhead—pretty as the red roses she sold—was at work already in the shop that sat back some distance from the street.

Now. It had to be now.

He felt a stirring in his body.

She would admit him, he was sure of that.

He knew that the shapely beauty and her mother kept the front door locked even during business hours if only one of the women was there.

On those occasions of solo duty, they let inside only people they knew and trusted. And both women knew and trusted him, of all people. They knew what he had done for a living, what they assumed he still was doing.

He moved forward, feeling sure of himself.

Impeccably dressed in starched, button-up Western shirt,

trim jeans, shining cowboy boots, he always made a good impression, especially with women. He knew how to play on a woman's emotions like tuning a fine musical instrument.

He knew all about the locked-door routine of this place, was confident of getting inside.

He knew what he would do.

He had the butcher knife with him, out of sight under his shirt.

Glancing up and down the street, he walked to the front door, slowly up the steps.

He was calm, but his excitement was building . . . a tingling.

As a pleasant, clear day spread over the city, Mary Ringer had arrived for work at 7:45 A.M., her day beginning early as usual. She pulled into the parking lot and parked her Suburban in front of the building bearing the large sign, Always & Forever Flowers.

This Monday, October 10, 1994, Columbus Day, would not be as busy as Valentine's Day or Mother's Day or Easter, but Ringer knew well that business was brisk on any day at the unique floral shop in the northwest section of sprawling Houston, Texas.

Unique in that Always & Forever not only sold flowers, plants, and funeral floral arrangements, but also hosted weddings and wedding receptions in its pretty Wedding Chapel with the columns on each side of the entrance; the chapel was next to the flower shop and the wedding reception hall.

The reception hall, furnished with tables and chairs and a serving table, was located between the two buildings at the back of a quaint, landscaped courtyard.

Young brides and grooms loved it—and the services were priced so that they could afford it. That had been her daughter's intent when she started the business over twenty years ago, to give less affluent people a nice wedding and reception at reasonable rates.

Couples could do it all here: buy the floral arrangements, get married in the chapel, greet well-wishers in the reception hall, take photographs in the courtyard.

Ringer was sorting out the invoices on the counter and preparing for delivery of the day's floral orders when her daughter, Deborah Jane McCormick, arrived at 8 A.M.

Deborah, a stunning beauty at forty-four, was strikingly attired in a pink knit pullover sweater, pink stretch-type stirrup pants, and gold slippers. She was wearing gold earrings. The ensemble was set off by her long, dark reddish hair and a voluptuous figure.

Proudly, Ringer thought Deborah was pretty enough to be a cover girl on a fashionable magazine rather than the hardworking mother of two grown daughters, aged nineteen and twenty-two, that she was.

Ringer herself was highly attractive, a youngish grandmother. In her early sixties, she looked far younger and her sparkling and outgoing personality added to the youthfulness. On the phone and waiting on customers, she mostly called everybody "darling."

People sometimes mistook them for sisters. And not surprisingly, they had almost a sisterly closeness and relationship.

Bustling about the flower shop, the two women chatted intermittently, conversing as they hurried about their respective tasks to get the flower deliveries on the road.

"We need some helium balloons and toilet paper," Ringer said, as she turned and picked up her purse. "I'll run to the store, unless you want to go."

"No, go ahead, Mom. I want to finish this arrangement I've got started . . . Oh, and get some orange juice, will you, please?"

As she started to leave, Ringer mentioned that the regular deliveryman had called in sick and would not be at work today. "But I called Charlie, and he said he probably would be in," she added, referring to the part-time employee who worked as a deliveryman when needed. Ordinarily, the regular deliveryman already would have been at work by now.

Picking up her purse, Ringer went out the front door, making sure to re-lock the door that was covered with security bars, as were all the windows. The "burglar bars," as they were called, were decorative in design but impenetrable. They were on the outside of the door and the windows.

Regular customers already knew that the front door always was kept locked when only one of the women was in the shop.

Most of the business transactions were conducted on the telephone anyway—floral orders and requests for the wedding chapel and reception hall being called in—and when a regular customer did show up, the door was opened after either McCormick or Ringer, if only one of them was there, looked out and made sure who it was.

There were good reasons for the precautions. In past years, the floral shop had been robbed twice and also hit several times by burglars. Then, too, the shop frequently was targeted by vagrants seeking a handout.

At about 8:15, when Ringer drove away in her Suburban bound for a retail discount drugstore, the traffic flow still was heavy.

She had to wait in the checking line at the discount store longer than she had anticipated and did not get back to the floral shop until 8:45 A.M.

As she drove back Ringer was irritated because the delay put a crimp in the always rushed-for-time, early-morning preparation of orders.

She alighted from the Suburban, gathered up her purchases, found the key on her key ring, and turned it in the still-locked door.

Debbie was not in the front when Ringer returned. Setting the orange juice and toilet paper on the counter and releasing the helium balloons, Ringer noticed some red roses wrapped in protective paper to prevent the buds from opening on the front counter.

The flowers had not been there when she left. Apparently Debbie had had an early customer, but where were she and the customer?

Maybe the customer had a change of heart and didn't buy the roses, Ringer thought. Debbie probably had gone to the storage room in back to get something.

"Debbie, I'm back, honey," she called out.

No answer.

Ringer walked to the back storage room. Not there either. Where is that gal, she wondered. Returning to the front area, she glanced down the short hallway that led to the wedding reception hall at the end of the twenty-foot corridor; the corridor itself was dim in the shadows.

The light was on in the reception hall, which was unusual. But Debbie might have gone to the refrigerator in the reception room to get a soft drink.

Heading down the hall, Ringer called Debbie's name again. Entering the reception hall door, she glanced to the left.

She screamed and her hands flew to her mouth.

Debbie, nude from the waist up, covered with bright red blood on her chest and stomach, was sprawled on her side on the floor near a curtained window in a back corner of the large room!

Her frilly white bra was down around her waist. Pink sweater in a heap on the floor . . . a pool of blood spreading out . . . terrible, gaping stabs and slashes on her chest, her stomach . . . unmoving, mouth open.

For a second, the room reeled and Ringer grabbed the doorway for support. Stumbling forward, she dropped to her knees beside the silent form, gasping out words.

"Debbie, oh Debbie, honey, what happened? Oh my lord in heaven, oh Debbie darling!"

Must do something . . . oh God, got to do something . . . help her. She pressed her mouth against her daughter's mouth, at the same time squeezing her nostrils closed, blowing into her mouth. Nothing, no response to CPR . . . no good, not working.

Sobbing, stained with her daughter's blood, Mary rose and ran to the telephone at the front.

She dialed 911, cried hysterically: "My daughter has been murdered! My daughter has been cut! Send someone, please! She's been stabbed and cut!"

She managed to give the address on Mangum Road before dashing back to Debbie.

DaLynda Wilker—everybody called her Dee—always went to the office in a jump suit.

For good reason. At any moment before her shift was over, she might be crawling in the damp and spider-infested space beneath a house, or digging through a rank garbage heap, or working with bloody clothing and bloody bodies.

She had been with the Houston Police Department for twenty years—fifteen of them spent in the homicide division's crime scene unit. It was Wilker's job to secure and control a crime scene, make sure that only authorized people entered, that the all-important scene was not violated in any way by messing up possible evidence.

At 9:15 A.M. on this Monday she was dispatched from her office in central Police Headquarters on Reisner Street close to downtown Houston to the northwest side to "catch a scene," as going to a homicide scene was known in the parlance of those who worked them.

The address, Always & Forever Flowers, had for a few seconds jolted Wilker's habitual equanimity. It was in the same area where she herself lived and it was a business address with which she was long familiar.

She knew the flower shop owners well, bought flowers and plants there on holidays. The mother and daughter who owned and worked in the floral shop were awfully nice people. The last place in Houston she had ever expected to work a scene was Always & Forever Flowers.

The traffic still was thick enough that it took Wilker almost thirty minutes to get there in the crime van that carried her working equipment. As she parked in front, she saw that two police patrol units and a funeral home's body car already were there.

One of the patrolmen, Officer D. R. Vasicek, who had been the first "silver badge," or uniform officer, to arrive, led her into the shop and down the hall to the reception room.

"It's a bad one. A half-naked woman, cut up bad, dead when I got here. Her mother found her."

When she walked through the door, Wilker recognized the bloody, mutilated body on the floor as Deborah McCormick. It hit her like no other scene had. During Wilker's visits to the shop as a customer, she had become friends with McCormick.

Automatically she noticed a helium balloon, string attached and dangling, nestled against the ceiling above the body.

Wilker knew the pretty victim as one of her favorite people, a happy, always eager-to-help individual. She felt shock and a rising anger at whoever the brutal killer might be.

Wilker quickly regained her professional reserve. The on-the-job nature honed by years of experience of encountering every imaginable form of violent and sick things that humans can do to each other took over.

She was all business as she placed the scene off-limits to everyone except the most immediately involved investigative personnel. She began making a video "walk-through" tape of the crime scene and flower shop and reception room areas.

Detective Robert E. "Bob" King was at his desk in the homicide office located in a district station in far-flung southeast Houston, where it had moved temporarily because the former site downtown was being remodeled for an administrative building.

Day shift duty Lieutenant Guy Mason notified him of the homicide across town at Always & Forever Flowers. Under the method of assigning breaking murder cases to detectives on a rotation basis, King and his partner, Detective Sergeant Hal Kennedy, who was out working leads on an old case, drew the assignment.

King headed for the address, knowing that his partner would join him shortly, as soon as he could be advised.

Chapter 2

King and the other homicide men were somewhat unhappy about how long it took to reach scenes in Houston's far outreaches from the southeast district station.

This time, for example, he had to drive clear across the breadth of the big city to get there, southeast to northwest; coming from the former homicide office downtown would have taken much less time, he mused.

It seemed like an eternity negotiating through the morning traffic. Actually, when he glanced at his watch as he pulled up at Always & Forever Flowers, it had taken thirty-five minutes to go the twenty-three miles.

King noticed it damn sure had taken so long that every TV station in town had its news crews already there, shooting footage and milling about; the crime scene van was there, along with a couple of uniform cars, an investigator from the medical examiner's office with a doctor who was on rotation in the M.E.'s office, and Alvin Wright of the police department's media relations office.

A bunch of spectators were gawking from behind the yellow crime scene tape that roped off the slaying site.

And, finally, King fretted to himself, here he was at last.

About the time that the detective arrived, the victim's father, Billy R. Ringer, who had rushed to the flower shop after a heartrending call from his wife, was talking to the TV reporters.

After going into the room where his daughter lay dead, the grieving father told the newspeople that McCormick had been robbed, stabbed, and apparently raped. With tears rolling down his cheeks, Billy Ringer recalled that McCormick in 1973 had persuaded him to help start the flower shop and later build the wedding chapel.

"She decided they didn't have things for people who couldn't afford big weddings. She just wanted to bring happiness. She was a bright, vivacious person." His voice cracked with emotion. "I don't know what kind of crazy did this. I guess he just decided she was by herself and took advantage of the situation."

Sergeant Kennedy arrived, as did Lieutenant Mason. After learning the known details, Mason called for two more homicide detectives, Sergeant Billy Belk and Investigator Tommy McCorvey, to help canvass the neighborhood for persons who might have noticed the killer entering or leaving the flower shop or had any kind of information that might help.

Another veteran investigator, Detective Jerry Novak, showed up also.

King and Kennedy, assigned as the lead investigators, divided their work: Kennedy would oversee the processing of evidence on or around the body and in the reception hall, King would interview potential witnesses and oversee the rest of the crime scene area.

King met briefly with relatives and friends who had gathered in the wedding chapel. Mary Ringer told him of her trip to the store for supplies, of locking the front door when she left, and of finding her daughter's horribly stabbed and cut, partly unclothed body when she returned.

She remembered, like a scene in a haze, that as she made

the 911 call for help from the phone in the front, she saw her and McCormick's purses open, apparently rifled, and three small coin purses of McCormick's on the floor near her purse.

The only known property loss was $400 in cash that Ringer had stuck in a blue makeup bag and put behind two cans that held scissors and other working tools on a shelf in the area where flowers were cut, pared, and arranged, Ringer reported. The makeup kit was open.

Ringer explained that before going on her errand, she had counted out the money from her purse to leave for her nineteen-year-old granddaughter to buy insurance for a car the girl had purchased recently.

The cash had been part of a customer's down payment for a wedding. Ringer had received the payment on Saturday after it was too late to deposit it in the bank, she said.

King listened with growing interest as Ringer told him the front door always was kept locked if she or McCormick were alone in the shop. The door was never opened for anyone unknown, the distraught mother said.

This meant that McCormick probably had recognized her killer and allowed him to come inside, King realized. Which meant that the list of known customers would have to be explored thoroughly. On the other hand, the killer just as easily could have been someone known to the pretty florist through other social contacts or relationships.

''Deborah definitely would not admit anybody who she did not know,'' Ringer said.

The detectives agreed that the wrapped roses Ringer had discovered on the counter indicated the killer at least had made a pretense of buying flowers.

By the time King took his first look at the body, a preliminary examination by the medical examiner's people had revealed McCormick had been stabbed several times in the chest and abdomen and fewer times in the back. The medics and detectives speculated that the woman first was stabbed from the front, and the back wounds were inflicted after she fell.

The absence of any extensive blood spatter indicated to King that the killer repeatedly thrust the knife into the helpless florist as she sprawled on the floor after she was dropped by the first savage stab.

Two small cuts on one hand appeared to be defensive wounds; she seemingly had resisted her armed assailant at some point.

There were unanswered questions as to the nature of a sexual assault that might have occurred. From all appearances, McCormick had not been raped—her pink stirrup pants and her panty hose were undisturbed. But the sweater and the bra ripped from her upper body had all the overtones of some kind of an attempted sexual assault, maybe kinky sex—of that the investigators felt certain.

The victim's bra, still fastened in back, had been jerked downward below her waist with such force that the left cup was ripped; the sweater also was torn and had what looked like a small hole from a knife stab on the right front, with a slight stain around it, revealing she first had been stabbed before the sweater was yanked off.

A false thumbnail was missing from the right thumb of the victim. When the body was turned over by the medics, the severed nail was found underneath, adding to the physical evidence of a struggle.

But the jewelry worn by the victim had not been disturbed. Besides the set of gold earrings McCormick was wearing, she also had two gold rings on her left hand, and on her right hand were a large diamond ring and a diamond tennis bracelet around the wrist.

The killer obviously had other things on his mind besides taking the expensive jewelry.

That there had been a struggle was indicated by an overturned crystal candy dish on one of the tables and a blood-smeared corner of the tablecloth that was pushed up.

In most cases, fingerprint work is done by the crime scene techs at a scene, but the area where prints might be found in the flower shop was so extensive that King and Kennedy requested additional help from the latent fingerprint unit. The unit sent three technicians, led by Ralph Saldivar, to go over the scene.

King and Kennedy took the print men on a walk-through of the crime scene and into the reception hall. What looked like partial bloody hand impressions on the victim were noticed by Saldivar. Using a relatively new technique, he sprayed a dye stain called amino black on the body to try and bring out possible fingerprints on the skin. Recovery of such body prints were extremely rare, but he did not want to overlook any chance. No prints were found.

The investigators recalled that Mary Ringer had given CPR to her daughter, becoming bloody in the process; the impressions, although not identifiable, were thought to be the mother's, left as she frantically tried to give aid to McCormick.

Dusted for possible fingerprints were the front door, the front counter and area, the women's purses and the makeup kit, one of the flower coolers that was partly open, and various locations and surfaces in the reception hall.

From talking to Mary Ringer, Detective King was able to put together a tentative time window in which the murder could have happened. Ringer had left the shop at 8:15 A.M. and returned thirty minutes later.

Before leaving for the store, Ringer had phoned a part-time employee, Charlie Rawlins, and asked if he could work in place of the ill deliveryman, she recalled.

At that time Rawlins couldn't tell her for sure. He said he would have to check with his wife on her schedule for the day, and his wife had just left to take their child to school. He promised to let Ringer know as soon as possible.

As King continued to look around the crime scene, a man who identified himself as Charlie Rawlins approached him, saying another officer had told him to "stick around" until detectives could talk to him.

The detective thought the part-time employee seemed nervous; he was sweating and firing up one cigarette after another.

Rawlins related that it had been 8:30 A.M. when he had called back in response to Ringer's earlier call. It had been McCormick who answered, he said, and he told her he would be to work at 9 A.M.

When he arrived, he didn't find the usual quiet workplace to which he was accustomed. Police cars, paramedics, and a fire truck were parked around the floral shop. He was intercepted by a uniform officer.

After he had identified himself and explained that he was reporting for work, Rawlins said, he was told not to leave until detectives could talk to him.

Rawlins's account sounded straightforward enough to King. The emergency personnel confirmed that the deliveryman showed up after they had arrived. That didn't mean the fill-in deliveryman couldn't have been there earlier than he claimed, but King thought it unlikely. However, he wasn't through checking out the highly anxious employee's story.

King told Rawlins he would want to take a statement from him later in the day. He made a note of the employee's home address and allowed him to leave.

If Rawlins had talked on the phone to McCormick at 8:30 A.M., as he claimed, it further narrowed the time period in which she was slain to fifteen minutes instead of a half hour.

Although no weapon was found during the initial search of the murder room and the rest of the floral shop, wedding chapel, and surrounding premises, the detectives noticed a variety of knives and scissors on the work counter and wondered if one of the flower-cutting tools had been wielded by the attacker.

When asked about this possibility, Ringer said she did not think any knives or scissors were missing or out of place, and those in the containers bore no tell-tale evidence of having been the lethal weapon.

King and Kennedy thought it likely the killer had brought a knife with him and undoubtedly took it when he fled, planning to get rid of it as soon as possible.

Dee Wilker had made the video of the crime scene and also took numerous color photographs of the body, the reception hall interior, and the front area of the shop where the wrapped roses lay on the counter.

She made a crime scene sketch showing various measurements and evidence locations. Later, this information was turned into a computer-generated crime scene diagram.

As she examined the body for preservable evidence, Wilker noticed that three smears of blood on the left leg of McCormick's stirrup pants, next to the seam, looked like swaths made by a knife blade wiped downward across the area. Looking closer, she could see tiny globs in the smears that she realized were fat tissue.

The killer had callously cleaned his murder weapon by wiping the blade across the woman's pants leg, Wilker believed.

She wanted a close-up, actual-size picture of the bloody swipes. For this purpose, she needed a special camera with a built-in measuring ruler; she called her office requesting the camera, and within a short time Officer John Goodfellow delivered it.

While examining the exposed areas of the body, Wilker spotted several loose hairs. Under a magnifying glass, the crime scene expert could see that they appeared to be foreign hairs, not the color of McCormick's reddish hair, but darker, almost black.

She carefully collected the hairs and placed them in a plastic evidence envelope for later examination in the crime lab.

It might well be that they had lucked out, that the vicious knifer had left behind evidence that would link him to the crime.

Three tiny white beads found on the floor next to the body

by the crime scene analyst appeared to have been pulled or somehow separated from some other unknown article because of white threads or fibers that were attached.

Later the tiny pearls were identified by Mary Ringer as decorations being sewn on a white satin bridal purse with a shoulder strap that McCormick had been working on as a gift for one of her friends who was getting married.

Wilker saw that the purse had the same type of pearls already sewn on the outside and also inside the purse flap. The detective took the purse to be tested by the crime lab for blood or any evidence that might be found.

Before McCormick's body was taken to the morgue at the medical examiner's office where an autopsy would be done, Wilker carefully "bagged" the victim's hands, placing brown paper bags over them to preserve any forensic evidence that might be present; with the false thumbnail broken loose, it might be that she had scratched her assailant. If so, the blood or skin tissue of the killer might be found under her fingernails.

This done, the body was released to the body car, and Deborah McCormick, who had loved the floral shop-wedding chapel business she founded more than two decades ago when barely out of her teens, left it for the last time.

The detectives doing the neighborhood canvass knew their job would not be finished on this first day of the murder probe—there were far too many businesses and nearby apartment complexes to visit. And always with such searches, there were many tenants who were not home. In the time they had been knocking on doors or dropping into business places, Detectives Belk and McCorvey were coming up with zip information, as far as having any value to the hunt for the killer.

They talked to employees at the service station that was adjacent to the Always & Forever Flowers and Wedding Chapel and moved on to the nearby strip of businesses—a food store, an upholstery shop, a bar and grill, and other small independent establishments.

They weren't all that surprised by the poor results; the time of morning when the murder was believed to have happened was the busy rush hour along Houston's freeways and arterial streets, with motorists speeding to their jobs, paying little attention to anything except the endless stream of bumper-to-bumper traffic.

After the murder hit the newspaper and TV, someone might remember seeing something or somebody and get in touch with police.

King talked again with Mary Ringer. The tearful mother reiterated that McCormick would not have admitted any stranger while Ringer was gone. That was definite.

"She had a single key to the front door that she kept with her," said Ringer. "She also had a door key on her key ring, but she kept this single key separate and within handy reach. She would have re-locked the door after she let someone in. She always left the key in the lock to open the door again when the customer left."

At King's request, Ringer looked in her daughter's purse and around the counter area, but could not find the single key she had mentioned.

It was her opinion that the killer, when he fled the scene, had taken the key from the inside lock, re-locked the door from outside, and pocketed the key or disposed of it.

Family members later checked McCormick's home, just on the chance she might have accidentally left the key behind that morning, but the key could not be found.

It was never located.

King was standing outside the wedding chapel when a youth, who was a boyfriend of McCormick's nineteen-year-old daughter, approached and told him a woman who worked in an office of a small business directly east of the floral shop had some information. He pointed to a woman standing nearby.

When the detective questioned the witness, a secretary in one of the small firms, she said she was working at her desk when through the window she saw a small white pickup truck turn in from Tulsa Street and speed through the driveway that ran between the string of offices.

It had been shortly after 8 A.M. After the truck sped by, she had looked out the door to see where it was going and saw the vehicle turn west where the drive changed directions. She thought no more of it until she heard about the murder of McCormick.

"I didn't see what the driver looked like," she told King. "The only thing I noticed was that the truck had some kind of emblem on the side, like the star that is on city park and recreation trucks."

King knew it would be impossible to trace the truck with so little information, but he told the woman if she saw the truck again in the area to call the police.

The detective felt pretty sure of what the truck driver had been doing. He theorized the driver turned off Tulsa, an east-west street south of Always & Forever Flowers, to take a shortcut and avoid the construction in progress on Mangum Road.

Turning into the drive that ran through the small group of businesses and in front of where the woman worked, he continued north to another drive that ran into Mangum Road, thus exiting onto Mangum Road past the construction tie-up.

Besides the city parks vehicles, the Houston electric power company trucks also bore a star emblem, which meant there were dozens of pickups on the streets that would match the meager description. King included the information in his incident report anyway.

Another tip came to the detectives from a motorist who, when driving down Mangum Road that morning, had seen a man running from the direction of the flower shop toward the small business strip at 34th and Mangum. The runner was either a young black man or a dark-complected Hispanic, the witness thought.

Again the informant did not have enough of a description to do any good, and people familiar with the area said numerous people on foot were not uncommon.

It was mid-afternoon before King could leave the murder scene and go talk again with Rawlins, the part-time deliveryman. At his residence Rawlins agreed to accompany King to the homicide office to give a statement about talking to McCormick on the phone at 8:30 A.M.

When King later drove Rawlins back to his house, Mrs. Rawlins had arrived home and the detective talked to her briefly. She confirmed the account given by her husband, that he had phoned the flower shop at 8:30, after which she had driven him to the shop at 9 o'clock.

Detective King drove back to the flower shop to canvass more businesses for possible witnesses. He was especially interested in checking with some of the businesses that might have security cameras that would have recorded activity in the area that morning. It was past 6 P.M. and some of them were closed.

The security cameras were a far shot at best, and King found nothing that might be a lead to the killer. Cameras at several businesses were out of order.

The detectives were gathered in the southeast side homicide office hashing over what they knew from the day's work at the McCormick scene. They still had no idea of the identity of the brutal slasher, but a theory of the events that took place in that vital fifteen-minute period was shaping up.

Detective Novak, a veteran of murders that were sexually motivated, thought the killing of McCormick definitely fell into that category of homicide classifications.

"Look, this is what I think happened," Novak said. "The

place was robbed of $400, but I think that was incidental. I think the killer had sex in mind when he went in there. He probably knew Deborah, from what her mother said about keeping the door locked and not letting anyone inside when just one of them was there.

"The victim was a beautiful woman, and the guy may have had her on his mind for some time. I think the killer marched her at knife-point to that reception hall . . . it's not used much except at special times . . . Her blouse [sweater] was removed. It was torn on both sides of the neck and at the shoulders. The killer may have jerked on it and pulled it off himself or made her take it off.

"Then her bra was pulled down to around her thighs. Then I think she was made to kneel and perform oral sex on this guy. Something set the killer off at this point, and he started stabbing her. Might be that she bit him."

None of the forensic tests that could determine whether the murder victim had been raped, or sexually assaulted in any manner, had been made at this time, but there had been foreign hairs found on the woman. And from the position in which the body was found, it was thought by the detectives that she might have been kneeling when the vicious stabbings happened.

Novak, with his years of investigating every variety of sex crime known to the human race, believed the assault had been in the perverted or kinky category, especially since neither the victim's stirrup pants nor her panty hose had been removed or even disarranged. The seasoned homicide investigators knew that a killer in this vein made a woman get on her knees with one twisted purpose in mind: to make her perform fellatio on him.

The veteran detective believed that she had been stabbed in the back first, when something set the man off as she kneeled, then was stabbed repeatedly in the chest and stomach after she fell backwards.

His preliminary reconstruction of the sequence in which the

knife thrusts were inflicted would be proven incorrect by the latcr autopsy findings.

From what they had observed, King, Kennedy, and the other sleuths did not disagree with Novak's astute perceptions. However, King wasn't sure about the sequence of the terrible wounds.

For one thing, he remembered the small hole in the woman's sweater and from that alone, he felt the killer had stabbed her first to make her disrobe and get on her knees, stabbed her that one time while she still had the sweater on.

Chapter 3

Outside it was another pleasant autumn day for Houston. It was 6 A.M. on Tuesday, October 11, 1994. In the Dr. Joseph Jachimczyk Forensic Center on Old Spanish Trail, at the edge of Houston's sprawling medical center south of downtown, Dr. Tommy J. Brown, assistant medical examiner, and Pamela McGinnis, a forensic chemist in the crime laboratory of the M.E.'s officc, both had arrived early for the autopsy on Deborah Jean McCormick. Present also was Det. Sgt. Hal Kennedy.

The forensic center is named after Harris County's legendary coroner, Dr. Jachimczyk, who after becoming coroner in the 1950s modernized the badly lacking autopsy facilities. Previously, all autopsies had been done in the basement of the county hospital.

Dr. Jachimczyk, a feisty, outspoken pathologist, is credited with bringing the medical examiner's facilities up to state-of-the-art. He is remembered fondly as the coroner who, tired of trying to answer lawyers' questions about autopsy results, went back to school and obtained a degree in law. He became a doctor-lawyer who really knew what he was talking about on the witness stand, one of the nation's top and most respected medical examiners.

Although the weather outside was warm and clear, the temperature and atmosphere in the morgue on the ground floor of the multi-storied building that houses the medical examiner's office and facilities is always the same: cold.

The room, surreal under the glaring bright lights, exudes a certain sterility fitting for the dead and the work at hand. There is a smell, too, long undetectable by those who work at the shining metal tables and are unaware now of the indescribable odor that prevails.

One pathologist who tried to describe it called the smell "unique, inescapable, and unforgettable." Detective Bob King has described it as "somehow antiseptic but filthy." "Cloying and pungent," a reporter said. Perhaps a combination of all the factors—chemicals, the sterile, shining tools, the disinfectants. Seldom the odor of decaying flesh, unless it happens to be a body that wasn't discovered for a long time.

Even though the autopsy room shined and sparkled with modern science's most refined technical equipment, and those there to do the work were the most respected of medical and forensic specialists, the morgue when viewed and smelled by the common man still would come across as a setting for some Frankenstein movie. Most detectives who had to sweat out an autopsy could be included in this "common man" bracket when it came to the smells and sights.

It was the work at hand that pervaded the room with an under-feeling—for those less accustomed to the procedures—of a setting for a science-horror film. But the two experts there to do "the work" were paradoxically down-to-earth with each other, relaxed in their long, everyday familiarity with the procedures that instill ordinary laymen with nightmares.

An autopsy is simply the cutting up and dissecting of a human body, outside and inside, using the shining instruments such as an electric saw for removing the top of the skull. As brief as it is, the saw's buzz is a sound that sends chills along a layman's spine when he gives thought to where the sawdust comes from. It is the only way to get inside and sec what happened, if anything, to the brain.

As a forensic chemist, McGinnis's specialty is serology: the testing of the bodily fluids—blood, semen, saliva, and urine—that might show up at a crime scene. From blood-filled vials, from cotton swabs swiped inside all of the body's orifices—mouth, vagina, and rectum—from slide smears stained and viewed under certain lights and high-powered microscopes, the serologist goes about her business.

That business is finding out what happened to the different parts of the body of a murder or rape victim; more specifically, as related to types of sexual acts that a human can perform on another human.

Deborah McCormick's body lay on a large, gleaming metal tray equipped with running water and drains. The body was in the same condition as when removed from the murder scene—nude from the waist up, still clad in the pink stirrup pants, panty hose, and gold shoes.

The body is not undressed until visual examinations are made by the serologist and the pathologist (in this case the assistant M.E.). The clothing and its condition are particularly scrutinized for evidence.

Almost immediately McGinnis, who knows as much about body fluid stains as cooks know about food recipes, observed stains in the crotch and on the left leg of the pink stirrup pants.

Dr. Brown also had noticed the stains. He had been alerted by the investigators that there was a question as to whether the victim had been raped, a question raised by what looked like stains other than blood on the woman's pants.

Brown asked McGinnis to use an alternate light source called a Poly Light to study the stains. Under wavelengths produced by the Poly Light, certain chemicals will fluoresce or glow, including seminal stains, saliva, and urine. The light test is not a definite identification of a stain, but it helps pin down what stains need specific chemical analysis.

McGinnis saw that the suspicious stains in the crotch and on the leg did fluoresce under the light. She next conducted an acid phosphate test on the stains and both tested positive. They were seminal stains. The chemical tests the amount of acid phosphate in the stain and acid phosphate is a component of seminal fluid.

McGinnis knew that semen is composed of two components. As she would explain it later in court: ''Semen is composed of spermatozoa cells [the prosecutor would call them ''those little squiggly things under a microscope'']. You have a pre-ejaculate. You could have acid phosphate that comes from the prostate gland and also a fluid from the seminal vesicles.'' What she detected on McCormick's clothing was acid phosphate.

The fluids and their stains would tell a story all their own about what the killer did sexually to Deborah McCormick.

With the examination of the clothed body and the photographs of the stains completed, Dr. Brown slipped on surgical gloves and began stripping off the clothing—the gold slippers, pink stirrup pants, and the panty hose. These items were put into a cardboard box, sealed and labeled, and placed in the morgue's cooler for later transfer to the property room at the Houston Police Department.

An identification photograph was taken of McCormick's face, with the morgue identification number of 947147 given to the case. Body measurements and weight were recorded: McCormick's body was five feet, seven inches in length, and weighed 130 pounds.

Now came the important job of locating, measuring, and photographing the stab wounds on the body, the ''external trauma,'' as the pathologists call it.

Brown found six wounds in the chest and upper abdomen—four of them located in the mid and lower chest in an irregular circle around the left breast; another large, gaping wound was directly below in the left upper stomach. The fifth wound was in her left side.

Next came the job of determining what internal organs had been damaged by the knife's thrusts. To do this, the pathologist made a long, Y-shaped scalpel incision extending from the victim's sternum bone down to her pubic area, laying open the front of the body.

The doctor began his examination, finding that three of the chest wounds did not penetrate the chest cavity; the blade had been blunted by the breast bone and ribs. Two of the savage stabs had plunged into her heart, one of these going completely through the heart and into the right lung. In one wound in the abdomen the knife blade sliced through the liver and into the right kidney.

The doctor learned that immediately following the deep heart wounds that resulted in rapid hemorrhaging into the sack around the heart and into the chest cavity, McCormick's life ebbed quickly. She probably had lost consciousness within one minute, the pathologist judged.

After turning over the body and examining the three back wounds, Brown concluded they had been inflicted as McCormick lay face down after collapsing from the frontal wounds. They were most likely made after she was dead or only barely alive, but the evidence was strong they were post mortem wounds; the margins of the back wounds were not as red as those in the front, indicating the victim's blood pressure was either diminishing rapidly or already had stopped completely—meaning she was almost dead or was dead when stabbed in the back.

On the top of the right hand Brown observed two small defensive cuts probably received as she struggled with the killer, raising her hand to ward off the knife. The broken-off fake thumbnail also indicated a struggle.

The knife wounds were photographed both before and after the body was washed.

The pathologist inserted cotton-tip swabs into the mouth, vagina, and rectum, two in each orifice, to check for seminal fluid which, if found, would reveal in what way the woman was sexually assaulted.

Removing the cotton swabs, the doctor rubbed the tips against glass slides to make smears that later would be stained with the proper chemical and examined under the microscope. The swabs also were preserved, placed in an evidence bag and sealed along with blood and other body fluid samples taken from the body. The swabs and fluid samples also went into the morgue refrigerator to be picked up later by police.

Later microscopic examination of the slides disclosed the presence of spermatozoa in McCormick's mouth, which confirmed the investigators' theory that she had been forced to perform oral sodomy on the killer.

But it left an unanswered question as to why sperm was found in her vagina also since the undisturbed stirrup pants and panty hose on the body indicated vaginal rape had not occurred.

Before the body had been washed, Brown had discovered a loose foreign hair on the right breast, which was placed in the evidence bag with the several foreign hairs found on her pants leg earlier by McGinnis. For comparison purposes, the pathologist extracted both pubic and head hairs from the victim.

Fingernail scrapings also were obtained, but later analysis of the samples did not show any blood or skin tissue, eliminating speculation that she might have scratched the killer while struggling with him.

The body examination also revealed a small bruise on the left side of the mouth, which could have resulted from the victim being struck in the face.

Routine tests of McCormick's blood showed there was no alcohol or drugs present.

All of the autopsy findings pretty well substantiated the theory of the investigators about what happened to Deborah McCormick during those horrible fifteen minutes or less in the wedding reception hall.

The temporary confusion from the vaginal test having shown the presence of sperm, was cleared up later when McCormick's long-time boyfriend stated that they had engaged in sexual intercourse on Sunday night, the night before the murder.

Chapter 4

Mary Ringer recalled the last hours that she and her husband had spent with McCormick on Sunday, the day before the family's world was destroyed.

It had been a happy time together, a lovely day. Sunday had been warm and sunshine-bright, a marvelous autumn day. The beautiful weather was a welcome relief from the heavy rain that pounded Houston on Saturday when a cold front moved through. Saturday had been dark and dreary and wet, as only this city on the Texas Gulf Coast can be when heavy weather sets in.

That Sunday, the Ringers and McCormick and her boyfriend, Tom Atwood, with whom she had had a marriage-like relationship for six years, drove to the Ringers' recently purchased lake home at Livingston, not far from Houston, to spend the day. It had been a quiet, relaxing time that ended with the four having a late-afternoon dinner together and then driving home to Houston.

McCormick was long-divorced from the father of her two daughters, and he had remarried. Their divorce had been an amicable parting. Ironically, Ringer recalled when recounting the comparably short, happy life of her daughter that McCormick and her ex-husband's new wife became good friends.

"Deborah was like that—she was good to everyone. She was a happy person who always was doing something special for someone, always thinking of little things to do for them."

In fact, the day that her former husband had phoned to tell his ex-wife that he was getting married, McCormick had asked him, "Do you have flowers for the wedding?"

The ex-spouse, a little startled, had replied that only "a simple wedding" was planned at the home of his fiancée's family.

Nevertheless, McCormick had prepared a floral arrangement for the future wife and also sent a boutonniere for her former husband.

"She wasn't being facetious or smart-aleck about his remarriage—it was simply an act of good will; that's the way she was, no animosity toward anybody that I ever knew about," Ringer recalled.

McCormick's relationship with Tom Atwood was a steady, mature sharing of life by two lonely people who, over the years of their being together, came to consider their romance to be that of the same emotional bond as a married couple, their friends and family members remembered.

"Tom and Deborah loved each other very much," Ringer said. "He was so good to her, took her everywhere on vacations around the country, always showed her a good time. Once, when they went to Disney World at Orlando, Florida, she had a trick photograph made showing her on the cover of *Cosmopolitan* magazine. It looked so real."

Truly, McCormick was pretty enough to have been a cover girl.

All of the family thought highly of Atwood. McCormick's life had been much happier after she met him.

In the days following her heinous murder, Atwood was so devastated by McCormick's tragic and untimely death that for a long time he could not even talk about it with the family members without completely breaking up.

He could not sleep, found it difficult to work at his job as a company executive. To him, it seemed his very existence, his own life, had ended with McCormick's violent death. Atwood grieved as deeply as members of the immediate family over the loss.

It had been Ringer who first brought McCormick and Atwood together with a somewhat unique introduction that she had been kidded about by her relatives and friends. Maybe it was appropriate that the proprietress of a floral shop-wedding chapel, a romantic business combination if ever there was one, would be adept at playing Cupid. Why not? as Mary often said wryly.

Billy Ringer, her husband, was a real estate inspector, and Mary frequently took calls for him from people wanting their homes to be inspected prior to sale. One day such a caller had been Tom Atwood, seeking an inspection for a house he was going to buy.

During the conversation, Mary asked Atwood for his wife's first name—part of the application form she had to fill out—and he said he was not married.

She learned he had only recently moved to Houston, having come from Louisiana to take a new job. It turned out he was employed with a company located on Highway 290, the highway that Mangum Road runs into, only a short distance from Always & Forever Flowers.

Highly impressed with his pleasant voice and personable manners on the phone and after learning his age, about the same as McCormick's, Ringer said, "Okay, now I'm old enough to be your momma, but I've got a gorgeous daughter who needs to meet someone that sounds as nice as you do. Why don't you two get together for a drink sometime?"

Mary Ringer is a very direct kind of lady in all of her dealings with people. She likes people and is a good judge of character. Friends believe that's why she is such a successful business woman—she's honest, caring, and above all, direct and to the point in her personal and business dealings. And people love her for it.

"That sounds like a good idea," said Atwood. "I would like to meet her."

Later, when she gave the appointment time for inspection of Atwood's house to her husband, Ringer said, "Billy, when you meet him, call me as soon as you can and let me know if he looks and is the extremely pleasant and nice fellow that he sounds like."

Her husband slowly shook his head and chuckled when his wife explained what she had done.

When her husband called later with a definite "thumbs up" rating, Ringer set up the get-acquainted date for him with her daughter.

From that beginning, the couple had been inseparable for six years, and their love seemed to grow stronger every day. Although they kept separate residences, McCormick and Atwood were together almost every night at one of their houses.

As far as Atwood was concerned, this lovely and vivacious woman was the one he had been seeking all of his adult years. McCormick felt the same way about Atwood.

From the time she was a child, Deborah Jean McCormick was something special in the eyes of her family and friends.

As her brother, Dr. Billy Raymond Ringer, Jr., a Houston plastic surgeon, remembered, "We were all very close. Obviously, being the older sister, she had the typical older sister syndrome. As we grew up, she always made sure that little sister and little brother had what they needed when they needed it. We were always dressed right. The socks matched, and we got the things we needed when your parents aren't around right then."

After growing up, McCormick had the same caring attitude when she worked for her brother as his office manager and also helped him in the operating room.

"She was very kind, gentle, loving, a sweet, giving, caring person," the physician recalled with tears in his eyes. "All my patients loved her. She was always there for my patients.

"She would be the one that came to me and said, 'Billy, this lady is really having a lot of pain,' or she's really upset about this or that or whatever. She'd ask me, 'Can I send her flowers in the hospital? Can we get some candy?' She would do sweet things like that for my patients. For people she hardly knew except just the interaction in the operating room or in the office."

The surgeon said that McCormick and their mother Mary were close, "like very, very close sisters because a lot of mothers and daughters don't have the blessing of being able to share as much time and as much love and as much of their lives together as they did."

McCormick was the heart of the Ringer family, in her brother's view. "She was the person in our family that planned every birthday party, who saw to it that every Thanksgiving the turkey was perfect, the stuffing, the green beans, the potatoes and everything were out and the rolls were just right.

"She was the one who always put together our family functions and made them happen, and we celebrated all those functions at her house, Thanksgiving as well as Christmas. Christmas meant so much to her. She was a very good Christian, and she loved celebrating the birth of Christ, and we celebrated it with great joy at her house."

The Ringer family came to Houston from Oklahoma City when McCormick was twelve years old.

McCormick was born in an Oklahoma City hospital on May 31, 1950. Her parents had lived in Oklahoma all of their lives until moving to Houston. It was a better job offer for Billy Ringer, Sr., that prompted the move from their native state.

In the Houston public schools McCormick did well. She made good grades and took part in a variety of school activities. Her artistic talent led her to join the school newspaper staff. She did all the artwork for the paper.

With her cheerful personality and ebullience, she was a natural leader and an organizer. As she would continue to do in her adult years, she planned the school parties, the decorations and the refreshments, the club meetings and activities—just about anything that needed to be done her classmates called on Debbie to do it.

McCormick always enjoyed doing things for other people, particularly for the handicapped and the underprivileged.

Her artistic abilities and caring attitude spilled over into her professional life when she opened Always & Forever Flowers in 1973. Her dad shared in McCormick's wish to own a flower shop and backed it financially.

Dr. Ringer recalled, "Debbie and Dad were very close, too. He spent all of his life doing whatever he could to make sure she had everything she wanted. She was his rose and life. As I remember, the flower shop was Debbie's idea. Between them, her and Dad, they came up with the name Always & Forever Flowers and Wedding Chapel."

Before opening the floral shop, McCormick took a course in flower arrangement and plant care at the Houston community college, and she taught the floral procedures to Mary Ringer when her mother joined her in the business operation.

The wedding chapel was started after McCormick one day delivered some flowers to another wedding chapel in town. She later told her father, "It was just an old house and it smelled. They don't have anything nice for people who can't afford big weddings."

Shortly after that, Ringer remodeled a building that he already owned and converted it to the charming wedding chapel adjacent to the floral shop. It became almost an immediate success.

By 1994, an estimated 20,000 couples had exchanged marriage vows there.

"She just wanted to bring happiness to people," her father told reporters on the day she was murdered.

After the opening of the floral shop, McCormick's children did not suffer any neglect in their home life because of their mother's new career. McCormick made sure that would not happen.

To accomplish this, she just put in longer hours during the day—at the shop and in her home—and necessarily sometimes into the night. She also managed to be active in her church, and in the Brownies and the Girl Scouts when her daughters were members.

While McCormick was raising her two daughters, her home over a period of time became a refuge for teenage boys and girls who were having problems with their own families or in school. Some of them had gotten on drugs.

McCormick took the youngsters into her home and treated them as her own children. They went to school every day with her girls. They were fed, clothed, and given the same loving care and attention as her own daughters. The cast-out kids responded to her love and they mended and did well. At one time McCormick had as many as six other teenagers beside her daughters living in the house.

McCormick loved animals, too. Once she had taken in eight stray cats who came to her residence over several weeks.

"Everyone loved Debbie," said Mary Ringer. "Debbie was always there, no matter what problem anyone had. And someone comes in and takes her life. It's just not fair."

Billy R. Ringer, Sr.'s desire to keep on living undoubtedly was gone. It died with McCormick, his "rose and his life."

It had left him even at the time he talked with the news

reporters right after viewing his murdered daughter inside the Always & Forever Flowers wedding reception hall.

Already it was gone as he said, "When I had cancer in February and the doctors told me I wouldn't live, she was always there by my side. It looks like I'm going to live, but now I've lost my daughter."

After fighting so hard, after meeting death's head-on challenge and seemingly winning an unexpected victory over the deadly illness, Billy Ringer, Sr., now gave up.

Life no longer meant anything. Why should he, an aged man tottering on the brink of the eternal abyss, be spared and his beautiful Debbie with so much more time ahead to enjoy life in all its fullness, be ripped from this world with such savagery and degradation?

Why?

There was no way in his tormented mind that he could balance the scales of heartless fate, or the will of the gods, or however anyone tries to reconcile the terrible things that happen to good people.

McCormick's father, his life unbearable, lived only a few weeks after her death. He died in January 1995, giving way without any further resistance to the ravages within of his own personal killer.

But as far as family members were concerned, Billy Ringer's death could be marked up to McCormick's killer. The doctors said in July 1994, a few months before that nightmarish October 10, that Ringer seemingly had "beat the odds" like no other patient his doctors knew.

His son, heavy with the grief of two family tragedies in such a short span of time, tearfully said:

> "After my father was diagnosed with cancer of the stomach and the esophagus in July [1994], Deborah spent every waking hour making sure he was comfortable, taking good care of him up to the time she was killed.
>
> "As I recall at that point he had beat the odds. The

doctors felt that he was one of very few, about seven percent in the world, that was going to actually survive that cancer.

"But when Debbie died, it killed him. He quit fighting and quit eating. He gave up. He wasted away. He became so emaciated he couldn't even lift his head hardly off the pillow. He finally got to where he couldn't prevent me from starting an IV [intravenous feeding] on him. I got him through Christmas [of 1994] with an IV hanging from the poles at my house and kept him alive for six weeks."

Through it all, her whole life falling apart around here, Mary Ringer somehow came through.

With the help of one of her granddaughters, she continued to operate Always & Forever Flowers and Wedding Chapel. She knew that was what McCormick would want.

"Life goes on," she said quietly, but the look in her eyes was one of someone who had been body-slammed, over and over and over.

Chapter 5

Detectives King and Kennedy had the M.E.'s autopsy report on Deborah McCormick. It verified how they believed the murder had gone down. Based on the wounds he viewed in McCormick's body, the pathologist said the murder weapon was a large knife, probably a kitchen butcher knife.

In his official report Dr. Brown attributed McCormick's death to "two stab wounds in the chest and one in the abdomen," and for the books, King noted, it was ruled officially to be "a homicide."

The detectives had gone over the known facts in the slaying again and again, and they had little doubt the killer was someone that McCormick knew. Most likely, he was a previous customer. She willingly let him in and he apparently ordered the roses found on the counter. But so far, they had not come up with any witness who had seen the killer enter or leave the flower shop.

On that Monday morning as McCormick's bloody, half-nude body lay on the floor, the large man left Always & Forever

Flowers, aware and angry that his favorite shirt had been ripped by her fingernails.

He got into his car and drove only a few miles to a car wash. He still had the butcher knife, under the front seat. He had wiped the blade on her pants leg.

He dropped a quarter into the public phone and dialed the number of a motel.

When the sexy female voice answered, he said, "I'm at a car wash getting the car washed and waxed." He suggested that she and her little five-year-old girl meet him at a restaurant for lunch.

He had met the beautiful, black-haired topless dancer only yesterday and they had checked into the motel. Her child was with a baby-sitter.

The call, as the woman remembered afterward, was between 9 and 11 A.M.

Later, at the bar and grill he had suggested, they had an exquisite lunch, complete with a bottle of good wine.

Then they went to a place that featured children's games and playthings so the youngster could play awhile. In the evening they went to another restaurant and from there to the dancer's home in Sugar Land, a community in southwest Houston. He knew he soon would be living there.

Detectives King and Kennedy, the primary case investigators, had been partners for some time and they made a good team.

King, forty-two, had graduated from high school in his home town of Austin, Texas, enrolled at Texas A&M at College Station in the Marine Corps platoon leader program, graduated with a second lieutenant's commission, and served his hitch in the Marines for two-and-one-half years. He knew he did not want a military career, as his ambition was to become a big city policeman. While assigned to the Marine base at Quantico, Virginia, King was intrigued by all of the police activity in nearby Prince George County, Maryland.

"There always was something going on: SWAT units in action, big arrests, good cases, it just got us fired up." King said a buddy in his platoon also planned to be a cop in Los Angeles when he got out of the service, following in the footsteps of his father and an older brother.

After King was discharged, he filed his application with the Houston Police Department (HPD). He was accepted and started as one of the new class of 70 trainees on January 17, 1977. Upon graduation that May, he went on the street as a patrolman, later served in SWAT (the police tactical squad), and had been assigned, after taking an examination for the job, to the homicide division in September 1992.

In appearance, the dark-haired, businesslike Robert King might have been mistaken for a junior law partner instead of a homicide detective. He was nice looking and well spoken.

His partner, Hal Kennedy, about the same age, was a sandy-haired detective sergeant who kept in top physical shape with regular weight lifting. Kennedy wore glasses for reading. In his manner of speaking, Kennedy reminded King of a "tough, old-time cop," not meaning that he had a pre-Civil Rights attitude by any means. Kennedy was just the opposite, personable, polite, by-the-book in his police work, but he could be tough if needed. He and King had been with the HPD about the same period of time, but Kennedy had been in the homicide division longer.

By now, the McCormick murder had hit the newspaper and the television newscasts. As expected, some tips started coming in to Crimestoppers Anonymous, the police program that routinely offers a reward for information leading to the arrest and conviction of offenders in major cases, with a promise that the informant's identity will remain anonymous.

In addition to the regular $1,000 reward offered by Crimestoppers, the Ringer family announced a reward of $10,000. Posters featuring a color photograph of Deborah McCormick with details of her murder were printed and distributed throughout northwest Houston and other locations.

The poster, under the words "Who Murdered Deborah McCormick," requested help on the homicide, urging anyone who might have information to phone either Detective King in homicide or the Crimestoppers Hotline, giving the numbers.

The day after the murder, a woman phoned and said she suspected her live-in boyfriend might be the killer.

"He works at an air-conditioning place near that flower shop," she said. "And he told me he done it."

The boyfriend was questioned. Somewhat sheepishly, he admitted telling his girlfriend he had killed "that woman in the flower shop," but said he had done so during the heat of an argument. He soon was absolved of any involvement when his alibi for the time when McCormick was killed was fully checked by the investigators and verified.

Another tip came from a homosexual who lived in northwest Houston. The tipster told a wild story about his boyfriend, who he said was an alcoholic. The informant said his boozed-out boyfriend recently pulled a butcher knife, tied him up, and threatened him.

On the day of the flower shop murder, the boyfriend had left their apartment, taking his butcher knife and vowing to pull some robberies at knife-point.

When the knife wielder was located and quizzed, he looked even better as a suspect when it was learned that he had walked very close to the Always & Forever Flowers at the estimated time of the killing.

But a thorough rundown of his activities that day eliminated him as a suspect in the knife murder.

On Friday, October 14, 1994, King was going through reports on the McCormick case. Four days of investigative work had turned up nothing but headaches from long hours.

They had run down the few screwball stories that turned out

to be false leads, but King and Kennedy had worked cases for far too long to get discouraged at this point.

On this day King was notified by Crimestoppers Anonymous that a man had called the Crimestoppers Hotline saying he knew someone who might have killed that woman in the flower shop. The caller had identified himself as Stephen R. Glassgow. He thought he might know something about the McCormick murder, but he wanted to make sure his name would not get out.

Assured that his identity would be protected, Glassgow said, "This guy I'm calling about was fired from the sheriff's department. We are partners in a janitorial office cleaning service.

"A week ago, on October 7, he went to the bank and cleaned out our business account, about $1,000. He's disappeared and nobody has seen or heard from him since."

At first, it sounded as if the caller was a disgruntled business partner who wanted to track down the withdrawn bank funds. But then Glassgow started giving reasons why he thought his partner might be involved in the floral shop murder.

"For one thing, he was a pretty good customer at the Always & Forever Flowers. And he used to live in some apartments on Watonga, close to the flower shop. I know that the sheriff's department fired him for beating up on his wife and girlfriends. A week or so before that murder, he beat up the last woman he was living with. Nobody knows where he is now."

"What's his name?" King asked.

"Mike Griffith."

"What does he look like?" King pressed.

"He's in his forties, a big guy, blackish-gray hair, looks sort of Hispanic. He was a deputy sheriff for a long time before they fired him for beating up women. Really a likeable guy, though . . . a hard worker, too. I wouldn't have ever thought he would empty the bank account."

King thanked Glassgow for his call and said he would be in touch.

"Be sure and call if you hear from him or find out where he might be," King added.

The detective turned to his computer and ran a record check on Michael Griffith.

The computer showed that Michael Durwood Griffith currently was wanted on an outstanding warrant charging assault in the beating of a woman on September 19, 1994. The records revealed he owned a car, a black 1988 Chevrolet Camaro bearing Texas license tag 784-WHO.

The last three digits were fitting, King thought. WHO, indeed. He wanted to know much more about who Michael Griffith was and his recent activities. The computer disclosed Griffith had been a suspect in two past incidents investigated by the Houston Police Department.

The first incident was on October 20, 1992, when police investigated a domestic squabble between Griffith and his wife, Laurene Tompkins, from whom he then was separated. She told police investigators that Griffith had taken about $1,500 she had just withdrawn from the bank and had thrown his flashlight through her car windows, breaking them. He had arrived in a car with a girlfriend, Stella Fletcher, just as Tompkins came home from the bank and drove into her driveway.

Tompkins, who also was employed by the Harris County Sheriff's Department, later had talked to the sheriff's department's internal affairs division about the altercation but did not file criminal charges, hoping that he would seek counseling.

The second report on file was about an incident that happened in January 1993 at Griffith's apartment.

He reportedly had terrorized Stella Fletcher, his girlfriend, and held her prisoner in his apartment on Watonga.

At that time, Fletcher—the same girlfriend who was with him during the earlier flashlight-throwing incident at his wife's home—was employed as a deputy trainee in the Harris County Jail, where Sergeant Griffith was a floor supervisor.

During the more than twelve hours she had been restrained in Griffith's apartment, he had repeatedly threatened to stab her with a pair of scissors.

The address was near the Always & Forever Flowers, King

realized. He dialed the latent fingerprint lab of his own department. Ralph Saldivar and W. Benningfield, another technician, were working late. King requested that they run a check of Michael Griffith's fingerprints, which were on file from his previous arrests, and compare them with any fingerprints found at the McCormick murder scene.

Saldivar called back with disappointing news. The ex-deputy's prints did not match with any of those found at the floral shop or the wedding reception hall.

Which didn't mean all that much, because King knew that an experienced law enforcement officer like Griffith would have been extra careful about leaving any prints.

Next, the detective phoned the records department and asked that a mug shot of Griffith, taken when he was picked up and questioned in the earlier incidents, be sent up.

When he got the mug shot, King agreed with Glassgow's tip that Griffith looked Hispanic. He appeared to be tanned, his clean-shaven face was beefy, and he had dark-grayish hair. He was a big guy, six-foot-one, and weighed 210 pounds.

Later, King called the phone number that Glassgow had given when he first called Crimestoppers. He wanted to ask the tipster if he knew the name of the girlfriend who was the latest beating victim.

A woman answered the phone. She identified herself as Glassgow's ex-wife. He had been at her house when he called Crimestoppers and left her number, she said.

King said he was trying to contact Glassgow to see if he knew the name of Griffith's most recent beating victim. The ex-wife replied that she knew the woman. Her name was Amanda Lopez and she was a hairdresser. She gave King the woman's phone number and address.

That evening, he was able to contact Lopez by telephone. They talked at length.

She had quite a story to tell.

Chapter 6

Amanda Lopez had been a hairdresser, working on both female and male customers, for some fifteen years. Now, in the spring of 1993, the strikingly pretty, black-haired woman knew she had to keep working, maybe even harder than ever before.

She had two daughters, ages eight and eleven, to raise by herself. She and her husband were in the process of getting a divorce. Whether she would even get child support was something that wasn't determined yet. She was just glad to have him out of her life.

One day a big, dark-haired man, clean-shaven and neatly dressed from starched shirt to shiny black cowboy boots, came into the beauty salon and wanted his dark brown hair dyed black. He probably wasn't much older than she was, Lopez thought, and he didn't like the gray in his hair.

His name was Mike, she learned, Michael Griffith. He was an awfully friendly guy and talked like he had an education. He appeared to be Hispanic himself, but said he wasn't. He complimented Lopez on her work and tipped well.

Starting to leave, he turned and said, "Could we have lunch together some time?"

Lopez smiled but shook her head. "No, I'm married, and getting a divorce, but with my little girls I don't want to be going out with anybody right now until the divorce is all over with, you know."

He grinned, too. "Sure, I can understand that. But don't forget that I asked."

Griffith was a regular customer after that. Even though they didn't go out, he sent her flowers regularly, sometimes red roses.

In time, they did begin dating, after Lopez's divorce was final. Sometimes now he stayed overnight in her home just off Highway 290. He always was nice to her girls, never getting out of line with her when the children were around.

In March 1994 Griffith moved in.

She had never seen a man so neat and clean—not only with himself, but he didn't mess up things around the house like most men did, Lopez noticed. She remembered the first time when he got out of the car, he reached down and pulled out the floor mat and shook it.

If ever there was a "clean freak," Mike was one, she decided.

Which certainly wasn't a bad habit, as far as a woman was concerned. She had never met a man as particular about cleanliness and neatness as Mike. Once he mentioned he had been in the Marines and was over in Vietnam. Maybe that explained it—service guys learned how to take care of their bodies and their living quarters. The way he kept his black boots shined, you'd think he was going to stand inspection.

There was something else: their sexual relationship was an active one—Mike had a sex drive that was unbelievable.

* * *

By late spring, Lopez noticed changes in Griffith. He was getting more possessive every day, keeping close tabs on her, expecting her to call him several times a day from work, tell him what she was doing. He said he would be worried about her if he didn't hear from her.

What did he think she would be doing at the beauty shop? Lopez wondered.

Griffith got mad at her, too, suddenly and over nothing. His temper could be like a lightning bolt from a clear sky. You could never see his cloud of temper forming.

One evening she and the girls were going over to her family's house for dinner. He didn't go with them. Lopez said she would like him to be there, but he said he knew her family didn't like him.

He stayed at home while Lopez and her daughters went to the family get-together. When they returned, the house was in shambles. There was broken glass everywhere, as if he had thrown things and busted them and stomped on them. They were bottles probably, because he had been drinking. Thankfully, Griffith was no longer there.

Another time they had been out to a club. An argument had started while they sat at the table. He lied about something she asked him. She was sure of that.

They still were arguing when they got home. He was mad, and Lopez was mad and was spitting words back at him.

Suddenly he slapped her in the face, hard. It made her ears ring and her mouth and head hurt. He had never done that before. Then it was over immediately. One of her teeth was chipped from the blow. He didn't apologize. He acted as if nothing had happened.

One time Lopez was with Griffith when he and his partner in their janitorial business, Steve Glassgow, were cleaning an office. Griffith got angry at Glassgow for not doing things the way he wanted them done.

There were words and he lunged at Glassgow. The startled partner backed away, obviously scared by the large man's furious temper that had flared without warning.

"You'd better get out of here," Griffith told him, and he left.

Lopez didn't know what to do. She just stayed quiet, fearful that Griffith might turn on her with his wrath.

But all that had happened to her was nothing in comparison to that terrible morning of September 19, 1994, when she thought she was going to die from him brutalizing her.

Summer was dying, but residents of Houston could not tell it. September in its ebbing days was a blast of furnace heat, and fall promised to ignore the calendar with its own soaring temperatures and steaming humidity. In the big coastal city, the weather seemed always on the brink of boiling over somehow, and so did Griffith, his girlfriend noticed.

On this morning of September 19, Amanda Lopez was hurrying, trying to get breakfast for the girls and get them off to school, and trying to get ready for the special beautician class in color she was taking. On top of everything else this busy morning, she had not finished her notes for class.

Griffith came into the kitchen and said, "Well, I'll help you write your notes down."

"Okay, thanks." She was through feeding the kids, and she heaped up a breakfast plate for Griffith. The girls waved goodbye and were out the door to meet the school bus.

Setting the plate on the table in front of him, she said, "Here, go ahead and eat and let me finish the notes." She needed to go over the notes anyway, to have them in her mind for the class.

Griffith ignored her. He kept writing, oblivious to her comment and the food.

"Really, I need to do that, Mike," she said.

His anger flashed like a gas explosion. He stood up, grabbed the plate and hurled it across the kitchen, its contents scattering in the air and the plate crashing down and breaking.

Lopez's eyes grew wide. "Mike, for heaven's sake, what did I do?" Her heart was pounding.

"I try to do things for you!" He was yelling. "I try to help you! You don't appreciate it a damned bit! You don't appreciate anything I do for you!" He was raving now, almost incoherent.

He strode into the bedroom, grabbed up a portable TV he had given her in August, lifted it above his head and smashed it to the kitchen floor. The set seemed to explode, shattering into pieces.

Now her own temper went off. Her voice rising, Lopez cried, "You know what, you need to just leave! You need to get out! I want you out of my house now! I've already been through this once with my ex, and I don't need this again in my life! You just get the hell out of here! Now! Find a place to go! You're not staying with me anymore!"

She didn't know how—they had been in the kitchen, but all at once they were in her daughters' bedroom. The raging Griffith had grabbed hold of her and was twisting her arm. She backed up, or tried to, wincing in pain.

Some flowers Griffith had given her were in a vase on a table, and she jerked them up and hurled them in his face.

"Get the hell out of here, damn you!"

"Well, you don't satisfy me anyway!" he shouted.

She came back with a remark that really set him off. He charged after her and from that point, she could not remember clearly what happened.

They were struggling, then she was on the floor on her back, him on top of her, beating her with his closed fist, smashing it down again and again into her breast, his fist sinking deep on impact, sending white-hot pain through her, flashes of light going off in her head. She was sobbing and screaming as the relentless pounding on her breast continued.

As he rained blow after blow, his face twisted with rage, and he twisted her arm cruelly behind her.

Oh God, he won't stop. He's not going to stop! That terrifying thought flashed through Lopez's head with each wave of intense pain. *He's not going to stop! My daughters are going to find me dead on the floor!*

The hurt knifing through her body, she screamed: "Michael, for God's sake, stop! Mike, oh please, God, stop!"

He stopped.

He let go of her arm, slowly moved off her and sat down on the floor. He grabbed his head in his hands, sat there silent, holding his head.

Lopez managed to crawl to the bed, get up and sit on the edge. She was hurting badly. *Oh Lord, please stop the hurting.*

She clenched her teeth, gasped out, "I can't believe you! You hurt me, hurt me bad! You need to go! Get out of here!" She was crying hysterically now.

Griffith stared. "Come here and sit down by me and let's talk."

"No, I don't want to get near you!"

They sat motionless, a frozen scene in a nightmare.

Lopez wanted to run, just get out, away from him, but she could not move. She was immobilized by brassy-tasting, stark fear, or maybe it was her blood she was tasting. She believed if she even moved he would grab her. He was sitting on the floor near the dresser, close to the door. She could never get by him.

She was dizzy and the room was whirling. She mumbled something nonsensical, like, "I guess I better go to class."

"You're still going to go to class?" he asked.

Everything blurred to almost darkness. The next thing she knew she was in the kitchen, and he was there, too. She said she wanted a Coke.

"You look tired," he said.

So tired, yes, so hard to stand up. "I am tired because I hurt so bad. I hurt in the back of my head.'' Griffith had hit her a hard, crushing blow to the back of her head.

''Why don't you go lay down awhile?'' He spoke quietly, softly.

She was afraid to move, afraid to try and run.

He was saying something. ''Come on and lay down beside me.''

He added something Lopez never had heard before. ''I'm sorry.''

She laid on the bed and he moved down beside her. He made her put her arm around him. He wanted to be caressed, but she didn't do that. She tried not to doze off, but she was so sleepy or groggy, all sound was fading out and blackness came.

Lopez woke up with a start. She managed to glance at a clock and saw it was 1 P.M. This all had started at about 8 A.M. Her girls would be coming home soon. She needed to get out of there, stop them before they came in.

Griffith also stirred.

She said, ''I need to go change my clothes. I guess I'm not going to class after all.''

She got up slowly, painfully, walked away from the bed, feeling he would reach out any second. She changed into shorts and a t-shirt.

Nothing was making any sense now.

They sat at the kitchen table and talked. She spoke quietly, like reasoning with a child: ''Look, Michael. You need to find a place to stay because you're not going to stay with me.''

She saw he had picked up the phone, heard him say, ''Let me call somebody.''

''No, don't use my phone.'' Even in her fear she resented his touching anything of hers. ''Go to the store and use the phone. Don't use my phone! Find somebody to stay with, get out of here!''

Griffith used the phone anyway. She had no idea who he called.

She said, "You know, I'm kind of thirsty. I think I'm going to get some Cokes," like it was the most normal of casual conversations, just passing the time of day while she was sure her life was hanging in the balance.

Griffith was on the other side of the table. He stared at her. Then he said, "Okay."

She eased across the kitchen, grabbed up her purse and left as fast as she could, afraid he would be after her. But he did not follow.

Lopez went to a friend's house. She was afraid to go to her family's home—they would be too upset by what had happened.

Finally she did go to their house. Her folks, seeing the bruises from the severe beating, told her, "You need to file charges."

Her sister came back with her to her house, to meet the girls and take them. Lopez called the sheriff's department, and a deputy came out to take the report.

Griffith had left, no one knew where.

For some odd reason, Lopez thought of something Griffith had told her. He said he had a weak stomach. He said certain things made him sick at his stomach.

The weird thought came to her, at this, of all times: He sure is picky.

Griffith stayed away. A warrant charging him with assault had been issued. He did not try to contact or see her again. He was probably in hiding.

Strange as it may seem, Lopez did see Griffith again. She sought him out, reuniting with this strange man who had been on the verge of beating her to death. It was one of those things that Freud and his ilk would have to try to explain, if it could be explained at all. Those who deal with the human mind and law enforcement officers who deal with the offshoots and twisted trails of the mental processes can never fathom why a woman so mistreated will return to her tormentor. It happens time and time again. As the moth is drawn to the fire.

Chapter 7

On the afternoon of Friday, October 14, 1994, the large man with the black hair parked his car nearby and walked to the savings and loan branch bank in the 5600 block of Westheimer. It was located near the famed Galleria skyscraper that features shopping malls filled with stores and restaurants on every floor. It was a few minutes past 2:30 P.M.

He had a revolver tucked under his well-starched shirt, in the band of his blue jeans. No knife for this job. Money, the need of it, was his focus right now. But something else might be possible, if the circumstances were right.

His excitement was rising.

The big man pulled on the front door. It was locked. A customer had to be admitted by a bank employee pressing a button.

He could see the attractive blonde looking at him. No other employees were in sight. She pressed the button and he entered. He walked toward the desk where she was, glancing at the rate board, his eyes sweeping quickly over the banking layout. There were no customers and the blonde at the service desk was the only employee visible in the front area.

She smiled and asked some questions: How could she help him, did he have an account with them, what kind of account did he wish to open—the routine patter. He moved in front of the desk and showed her the gray revolver.

"Give me the money. Keep quiet, don't punch any alarm. I know all about them."

The blonde turned pale. She reached into the cash drawer to comply and handed him all the cash from the top of the tray. She had a pretty mouth. He could put that to good use, if there was time, if she wasn't so visible to outside passing traffic.

"Come on, give me more money than that. You've got more in there. Don't give me the bait money."

He knew all about bait money, the cash that when picked up sets off an alarm in a security office that calls out the cops. The money also is traceable from pre-recorded numbers on the bills. He had had enough training in that kind of stuff.

He glanced around the bank and asked her, "Is there some place back there I can lock you up?"

"There's a restroom back there." She was scared. They were trained to keep their cool, comply with orders, get a description, don't resist. He wondered how much she would resist if he did his thing.

In spite of the attempt at calmness and cooperation, she was scared shitless, he could tell that. He had been around robbery victims before, talked to them after they were robbed, knew what they were going through.

"Let's go back there."

He waved the gun, and she turned and went through a door toward the restroom about fifteen feet away.

He was feeling the tension, the stirring inside him, but he was worried about those big windows through which passing motorists or people walking could see what was going on in the bank.

She took a few steps, was through the door, out of the view from the outside.

No time for anything else, he had to get out of here. He didn't want a witness to identify him. He hadn't bothered with a mask. He raised the gun and fired at the back of her head.

She screamed as the bullet hit her. He fired again. The blonde slumped against the wall next to the restroom and slid to the floor. Damn, she was still screaming.

"Lay down and be still." He turned and walked back toward the front, then started shooting at the overhead security camera near the front door. His shots did the job.

He left immediately, walked to his car, drove away. He didn't think he was noticed by anyone. He tooled into the traffic. No sirens, no flashing emergency lights.

He thought to himself that she would have been good, real good, if he had had the time and the place.

He drove only three blocks from the bank and pulled into a bar. He went inside and ordered a cold beer. He sat there calmly for some time, thinking back on the scene at the bank, again thinking of the pretty blonde and wishing he had had more time and more seclusion.

But he had some spending money anyway. He needed it to keep his women in a good humor.

In the back room of the savings and loan bank branch Sandra Denton opened her eyes. She could not see him anywhere. She was aware that she was bleeding. She had no idea how badly she was injured. All she could hear was the loud ringing sound that started the instant she was struck by the bullet.

The only first aid she could think of was to take off the jacket she was wearing and wrap it around her head.

She waited a minute. She decided to get up and go and try to get help. Moving in a crouched position toward the front where her teller station was located, she scanned the front area to make sure the gunman had gone. She entered the station and yanked out the bait money, setting off the alarm. She also pushed an alarm button, making doubly sure.

She went to the front door and looked out. She waited a minute or two to be sure it was clear. Her head was throbbing and the ringing noise continued.

Then she saw a police patrol car with emergency lights flashing pull into the bank parking lot, and she ran outside toward the police car.

"The bank's been robbed and there are two other employees inside!" she cried. She was not sure what their fate had been.

The patrolman got on the radio and called for an ambulance to take the wounded woman to the hospital.

Unsure whether the gunman still was inside the small bank building, officers called for a SWAT unit, the police tactical team that handles hostage situations and similar police emergencies and showdowns. The special weapons team encircled the building within minutes.

Other officers closed off Westheimer to the increasing rush-hour traffic so bystanders could be cleared and kept from the area where they might be hit if shooting occurred—as might happen if the robber were still inside, perhaps holding the other women employees as hostages.

SWAT negotiators managed to contact by phone the other employees who were hiding inside. The workers did not know whether the gunman had left the building or not.

About 4:10 P.M. the SWAT members stormed the bank, rushing in with weapons at ready. They quickly located the two frightened bank employees, one who was pregnant, and escorted them outside. A search confirmed the ruthless bandit who had gunned down the woman teller for no known reason was gone.

* * *

At the Houston hospital where Sandra Denton had been taken, doctors discovered her wound was not as serious as first thought when she was admitted. X-rays showed that the slug still was lodged in her skull but not in a dangerous location. The medics took four stitches in one ear that had been creased by the bullet. They did not try to remove the slug at this time.

Denton remained in the hospital about twelve hours before she was released. Somehow, probably because of her hair, the second wound, also minor, was not discovered until she went to her personal physician the next day.

She luckily had escaped with two minor wounds; either bullet, a few inches on a different course, could have killed her.

When robbery detectives were able to question Denton, she described the gunman with slicked-back black hair as in his thirties, about five feet, ten inches tall, with a stocky build and wearing a dark shirt, blue jeans, and black cowboy boots.

Denton said later that she, with other bank employees, underwent a simulated robbery training operation at least once a year, "and there are certain procedures that we are to try and follow, to go ahead and give the person the money and be safe after that."

But being shot from behind without warning or reason by a stickup man was not in the playbook.

"This guy is one ruthless SOB," one detective observed to reporters. "He didn't want to leave a live witness."

Detectives who canvassed the busy neighborhood around the branch bank didn't find anyone who had noticed the gunman or any speeding vehicle leaving the scene.

The interview with Lopez had given Detective Bob King an insight into what kind of character they were looking for as a suspect in the McCormick murder.

Amanda Lopez in her interview had convinced King that Michael Griffith had the psychological makeup to have committed the brutal killing at Always & Forever Flowers. He had a mean and dangerous temper that could send him off on a tangent at any time.

King personally was revolted at the idea that the perverted murderer of McCormick might be a former law enforcement officer. Cops are a closely knit brotherhood, but a cop that goes bad is more disliked by his fellow officers than any ordinary suspect would be. A bad cop has violated all the things that law enforcement stands for and gives the rest of the profession a black eye with the public that at times is hard to overcome.

It didn't take long to find out that Michael Griffith had disappeared from all of his past haunts. King and Kennedy talked to the former officer's friends and co-workers. They would get another name of someone "who might know something" from one witness and that person when questioned would mention somebody else who might know something.

But everyone they contacted had the same story to tell: Griffith seemingly had dropped from sight. There had not even been a sighting of his black Chevy Camaro, the license of which was on record.

The outstanding assault warrant in the savage beating of Lopez gave the investigators ample authority to hunt in earnest for the ex-deputy. However, so far the investigation and searching had failed to turn up any new leads on the McCormick slaying or the whereabouts of Michael Griffith.

The investigators realized that Griffith, who had been a lawman for some twenty years before he was fired from the Harris County Sheriff's Department on January 21, 1993, would know well how to avoid being picked up. He had enough "cop smarts" to avoid even smart cops.

Chapter 8

Winn Chen was a beautiful Vietnamese girl who was studying hard to become part of the American dream. Now in her second year of college at the University of Houston, she planned to enroll also at the Texas Chiropractic College at Pasadena, Texas.

The idea of this diminutive girl who stood four feet, eleven inches tall and weighed all of ninety-five pounds snapping in place the vertebrae of some big and hefty patient always brought amused reactions from her friends. But that did not influence her plans of becoming a practicing chiropractor as soon as she could complete her studies and get a degree in that field.

For about a year the energetic little coed also had been helping out part-time at a bridal and alteration shop located in the 12000 block of Bissonnet in west Houston. The combination bridal shop and dry cleaning plant was operated by a distant aunt of Chen's.

Chen had arrived in the United States from her native Vietnam in 1978 when she was only three years old. While studying hard in the public school system, the winsome Chen had been determined to make the most of the opportunities that America offered. Her life in the U.S. had been like a dream when compared to the nightmarish and critical times in her war-torn country.

Earlier on this day when Chen arrived, her relative had been at the store but left to run an errand, saying she would be back in a short time.

At about 4 P.M. on this Friday, October 28, 1994, Chen was alone and in charge.

The large man with the black hair was on the prowl again.

This time in west Houston, driving slowly along the streets and looking for a business that would meet his needs, to fill the urge that had been building in his muscled body and now was overpowering.

He was carrying both the gray revolver and the butcher knife that he had used before. They were concealed by the starched shirt he wore with his jeans.

He was needing money, as usual, but that really was secondary in his careful scrutiny of the business fronts along Bissonnet as he drove along the street.

The growing excitement as he prepared to do what he had to do was making his nerves jerk with the anticipation of his planned foray, his hunt for that certain type of female prey that could fill the aching sexual hunger in his own special way.

He pulled over and parked near the bridal and alteration shop that had the fashionably outfitted mannequin in the big front display window. The mannequin was wearing a bright red gown. Through that large window he had seen the pretty girl inside as he had driven by.

The hot afternoon sun of 4 P.M. reflected from his glass-bright, highly shined black cowboy boots as he got out and walked toward the shop's front door.

She wasn't in sight as he entered, but the sound of the door chimes brought her hurrying from the back of the shop. She smiled as she greeted him with the practiced politeness afforded to prospective customers.

He smiled back and said, "Do you have a white, silky tuxedo in stock?"

She said the shop did not sell that type of tux, but he might rent one and he could look in the catalogue to see if there was something he wanted.

There was something he wanted all right—wanted badly now—but it wasn't in the catalogue.

"I really need to get a white tuxedo as soon as I can. Could I talk to the manager, please, to see if you could get one for me in a hurry for special delivery?"

"I'm sorry, sir, but the manager just stepped out, but she will be back in a few minutes. You're more than welcome to look through the catalogue and wait for her if you like."

What a pretty face she had, so innocent.

"All right, I'll wait, thank you."

He walked back to one of two chairs in front of the window and sat down. His patience was running out rapidly, the intensity of his need inflamed by talking to her.

As he waited in the chair, another customer came in, a woman, apparently a regular, who asked for her dry cleaning. The girl brought it to the counter, said something about a zipper that had gotten messed up. The woman said she would go ahead and take the cleaning and see what her mother wanted to do about it.

The black-haired man coughed, and the customer glanced back at him. He didn't want this. He partly shielded his face with his hand and pretended to look at the catalogue.

The woman seemed to hesitate, as if trying to make up her mind, but then she left. He could see in the big mirror behind the counter that the woman sat in her car parked in front for a minute or two, as if she was still undecided. Then she drove off.

It was time to do it now, before someone else came in or the manager returned. He got up, walked toward the counter.

The girl looked up from a piece of material she was doing something with. He pulled the gray revolver and pointed it at her.

He kept the gun down low, next to his hip, where she could see it but the weapon could not be seen from outside through the window.

"Give me all the money in the register," he said.

The girl looked scared, the way he liked it. She fumbled in the register drawer and handed him the cash, about $60.

"All right, walk to the back now. I'm right behind you."

She walked ahead of him to the alteration workroom at the rear, which was shielded from view from the front part of the shop.

As they walked, he asked, "How old are you?"

"Fourteen."

"You're too young to die," he said.

He unzipped his pants. He was more than ready, throbbing.

When she turned around, he was fully exposed. He thrust himself forward, saying, "You know what to do."

"Please, don't hurt me," she was pleading now. "Just take the money and leave."

"Quit talking. Take off your shirt." She was shaking, obviously terrified, and she hesitated. "If you don't, you know what's going to happen to you!" He meant it to sound mean and threatening.

Slowly, she unbuttoned and removed her shirt.

"Okay, now, the bra. Get it off."

She again hesitated.

"I'm telling you for the last time, you know what's going to happen if you don't."

Closing her eyes, she unfastened and pulled off the bra, exposing her full young breasts. She now was nude from the waist up, like the other one had been, but younger, breasts not as large.

The telephone rang.

It was a bizarre tableau hanging in time as the phone rang again: the girl standing half naked, him standing there with an erection and the gun both aimed at her.

She asked, "Should I answer that?"

The phone kept ringing.

"Answer it, but don't let anyone know I'm here."

She picked up the receiver and answered with the name of the shop. After listening to the caller a few seconds, the girl said, speaking rapidly, "Yes, yes. There are lots of customers here waiting." He figured it might be the manager calling.

It sounded like the girl started to say something in a foreign language. He flashed the large butcher knife, pressed the blade lightly to her face where she could feel it, then started waving the knife in the air with a threatening motion.

He whispered hoarsely, "Don't say anything to let them know I'm here. You know what will happen."

She kept talking on the phone and he was damn fed up. "That's enough. That's enough. Get off that phone." He spoke it quietly but the words were full of anger.

"How long will it be before you get back?" the girl asked. She listened a few seconds, then said only, "Okay." She hung up.

He ordered brusquely, "Get down on your knees. You know what to do."

As she knelt he shoved forward into her face and said again, "Come on, you know what's going to happen if you don't."

Tears flooding down her cheeks, gagging, she took him into her mouth. He jerked involuntarily with the sudden pleasure of warmth engulfing him.

As she performed oral sex on him, he said. "You've done this before, haven't you?"

She did not answer, only turned from him suddenly and began to vomit on the floor.

Seeing her being sick and sobbing convulsively, he said, "Okay, okay. Hold on. Settle down."

She did not look up at him, continued to stare at the floor.

He began masturbating as she still kneeled with her head

lowered. Suddenly he gasped as he ejaculated on the girl's hair and upper body. She flinched and tried to turn away.

Then he commanded, "All right. Lay face down on the floor."

She turned over on her face.

He searched around the room briefly, then tied her hands behind her back with her bra that had been on the floor close by. He stepped away, again looking for something to finish tying her with. He came back with the cord from the vacuum cleaner.

He wrapped the cord around her wrists, then yanked her feet up and toward her bound hands and tied them together behind her back.

He told her, "Don't call the cops, and don't do anything, because I know where you're at and I'll come back for you."

He turned and hurried to his car and drove off into the roaring afternoon rush-hour traffic.

Fourteen, that's young, just a kid. He wondered if he should have killed her anyway. He had never hurt a kid, but he agonized now about not finishing her off. She was a live witness who could identify him. Just like the bitch at the bank. He had shot her, but he had seen in the papers she had lived through it.

Another live witness.

But for the present, his excruciating sexual desire was dissipated. He knew it wouldn't be for long. He already was thinking about making love to Amanda Lopez, who was coming back to him. She couldn't stay away.

Winn Chen lay unmoving on the floor, her trussed-up position adding pain to her terrible humiliation and sickness and the deep fear that the horrible man would come back, maybe to kill her after all. She gagged again and spit up on the floor. She was sobbing.

Her fear was incapacitating. She had thought for sure he was going to kill her before he left. She was afraid he might return any minute. She knew she had to do something, try to get free of her bonds.

The minutes dragged on in silence. She was alone.

She wanted someone with her, right now. She had to have help. He still could come back. He was crazy, crazy. He didn't care about anything, no remorse, no shame—only had one thing on his mind, the dirty filthiness.

Chen remembered she had set the phone down on a sewing table when he told her to hang up. With the phone's location in mind, she managed to struggle partly to her knees in her clumsy, bow-bent bondage and scooted, slowly and painfully, toward the phone.

It seemed to take her forever. Then she was there, but still unable to get her hands free.

For a few minutes she lay there and stared at the phone, wondering how she could use it. Help was so near now with the phone in front of her, but so far away because of her helplessness.

She shook at the thought that awful creature would return and find her trying to get to the phone. He had warned "don't do anything," and she knew what he would do if he caught her.

Finally, she made a desperate try. Using her mouth and butting it with her head, she knocked the instrument off the table on to the floor. She had to find a way to call for help.

Chen rolled over and turned around with her back toward the phone. Slowly—it hurt so much to try and stretch her hands—she inched them upward as high as she could and strained to move her feet up to give her hands more leeway.

With these acrobatic maneuvers, she was able to reach the phone dial. Slowly, gritting her teeth and counting the dial holes by feeling, she dialed the number of a male friend.

She laid the phone on the floor after dialing, inched her head close to the mouthpiece.

The friend answered. Chen was crying so hard that he could not understand her frantic words.

Finally she said, "I need for you to be here."

He didn't ask any questions. All he said was a quick okay, and hung up. He knew she was working at the bridal shop.

She twisted around to reach the phone dial again. This time she dialed the 911 emergency number. She knew she should have made that call first, but all she could think about was the comforting presence of someone she knew, who would understand this hideous nightmare.

The 911 operator answered, but then the line went dead. She did not know whether she had in some way caused the disconnection or if it had been at the other end. In a few seconds, the 911 operator called back and said that the police were on their way.

Now, Chen was worried about her partial nakedness. She did not want someone else to see her this way. Again using all her strength, she managed to wiggle around and edge partly upon a chair seat, concealing her naked breasts. It was the actions of a chaste young woman, embarrassed by what happened to her.

She was in that position, pressed against the chair, when a police officer showed up five minutes later and knelt by her side. He began to untie her and console her with assurances of, "Take it easy now. You're going to be all right."

At the same time the policeman came to her aid, the female manager also returned, breaking into tears when she saw Chen and apologizing for being so long in getting back.

Within minutes her male friend also burst in and joined in the effort to comfort the sobbing girl.

After that, it was a blur of detectives and crime scene people, asking questions, taking pictures, obtaining a description of Chen's attacker and quickly getting it on the air.

Later, when she was questioned in more detail, Chen told of how she had lied when the man asked her age. She said she had sensed that something terrible was about to happen, probably rape, and she had said she was fourteen in hopes that it might deter his obvious intentions.

Investigators said her action may well have saved her life, if the assailant had even a trace of decency left in him.

Chen, after receiving medical treatment and regaining enough composure to talk to detectives from the sex crimes unit, described her attacker as twenty-eight to thirty-two years old, five-feet-eleven to six-feet-one, weighing 220 to 230 pounds, clean-shaven, with short cut, black hair and brown eyes. She believed he was Hispanic. He had been neatly dressed in a shirt, jeans, and black cowboy boots.

She presumed he had been in a vehicle, but she had not noticed it. Detectives theorized he probably did not park in front of the shop.

The crime scene techs took possession of the pair of jeans that Chen had been wearing. The jeans appeared to be stained with semen. A swab was made from the spot on the floor where the assault victim had vomited to also test for semen.

The homicide division has a crime analysis section with data analysts assigned to both the sex crimes and the murder investigation units.

Detectives King and Kennedy had alerted the sex crime analyst to watch for any reported sex offense similar in M.O. to the Deborah McCormick sex-murder case.

Later, when Mena Kennison in sex crimes read the report of the perverted sexual assault on Chen, it suddenly had a familiar ring to it. The modus operandi, the M.O. of the attacker, was identical to the sexual assault committed upon McCormick, she realized. The attacks were glaringly similar also in that both women had been ordered to strip to their waist and to kneel to do the sex act.

Kennison pulled the report on the earlier case, the sex-robbery slaying of Deborah McCormick two weeks before across town in northwest Houston.

There was no suspect description available in the murder case, but the robbery and deviate assault on Chen sounded exactly like what the detectives theorized had happened to McCormick. But for some reason, this time the attacker had left his victim alive.

Kennison passed along the Winn Chen report to Pat Mathis, who was the crime analyst in the murder investigation unit. Mathis notified King and Kennedy.

After the name of Michael Griffith had surfaced as a possible suspect in McCormick's murder, Kennedy had put together a photo array of several mug shots that included one of Griffith. The other photos were of men of the same general description.

The photo lineup, as it is known, had been prepared to show to people who worked or happened to be in the area of Always & Forever Flowers during the crucial time period of the murder, on the remote chance that Griffith might have been spotted in the neighborhood that morning.

Spurred by this latest information supplied by the sex crime analyst, King, who still was at the homicide office, phoned his partner at home, though the hour was getting late. He told Kennedy of the close similarity of the attack on Chen to that of McCormick.

"The description that the girl gave sounds like Griffith," King said.

Since Kennedy had the picture lineup with him and lived not far from Chen, King asked him to take the photos to her house and see if she could make an identification.

At Chen's residence, Kennedy handed the girl the stack of assorted police mug shots and explained, "We may have a suspect, Winn. We may have someone in here, but we're not sure. Look through it slowly and carefully and see if you recognize a face. Try to identify anyone in there."

Within a few seconds, she exclaimed, "That's him! There is no doubt! That is him! I'll never forget that face!"

She held the photo of the ex-deputy sheriff, Michael Griffith.

The elated Kennedy phoned King at the homicide office.

"She picked out Griffith at first glance, and she's absolutely positive that he is the one, even though she says he looked younger in person,'' said Kennedy.

Now the investigators had sufficient evidence to obtain a felony warrant for the elusive murder suspect's arrest on charges of aggravated robbery and aggravated sexual assault in the Winn Chen attack. They could launch an all-out manhunt on the basis of the felony warrant.

They realized that if Griffith had pulled both brutal crimes in less than three weeks, he had become an exceptionally dangerous suspect who they had to nab before other women were attacked or murdered.

With this latest sexual assault, Griffith's suspected violent actions had fallen into the serial sex offender category, and it already was known that he had severely beaten several of his women in the past—Amanda Lopez's vicious beating being a prime example.

Griffith was a walking death threat to any woman he might encounter.

The sex unit detectives had quizzed the witness who had come into the bridal shop to pick up her cleaning while Chen's assailant, posing as a customer wanting a white tuxedo, was seated in a chair ostensibly waiting to talk to the store manager.

Mildred Beech had recalled the man in the chair in a vivid manner. Beech had aspirations for a career in the law enforcement field and was doing graduate work at Sam Houston State College to earn a master's degree in criminal justice.

About that afternoon in the bridal shop on October 28, she said later: ''When I entered the shop, I did not notice the man at first. Then he made a noise, kind of like clearing his throat or coughing, and I noticed he was sitting behind me in a chair.''

She said she could see him reflected in a long mirror on the wall behind the customer counter. While she was waiting for her cleaning to be brought up front, she watched the man in the mirror.

"He seemed a little bit nervous. It was like he was staring at me, maybe not for a specific purpose, but he was very concentrated on me, what I was doing. He did not seem to be very relaxed at all."

She observed he was "kind of slumped back in the chair . . . kind of pushed back like he was trying to conceal himself."

She had mixed feelings about leaving. She got into her car that was parked in front, but did not drive away immediately.

"I sat there for a minute because I still had that uneasy feeling that there was something wrong, and I contemplated whether to do something about it. I really thought about calling the police. I had this feeling he was either going to rob the place or hurt the salesperson, the girl. I can't explain why. It was just a feeling."

Beech could see only about half of the man's face from her car. As she lingered and wondered what to do, the man turned fully in his chair and looked directly at her for several seconds, almost as if willing her to leave. She saw his face clearly.

Finally, she decided not to call the police because "they would just think I was crazy and imagining things."

When detectives talked to her following the attack on Chen, she gave them a detailed description of the suspect.

Chapter 9

Erika Rutledge was both beautiful and smart. She had long, almost black hair with a reddish glint and a figure equal to any in *Playboy.*

She could have worked as a secretary or been a school teacher or held any number of white collar or professional jobs. But she could not make the money that she made as a topless dancer at a Houston club. For baring her breasts and doing a dance routine, she drew top dollars. Her measurements made her more than qualified for the job in that particular environment.

She was working at the club Sunday, October 9, 1994, the day she met the black-haired, good-looking guy who soon began to charm her with his conversation. He wasn't the usual try-to-grab gawker that frequent the topless clubs.

He had nice manners and was one of the neatest men she'd ever seen, from his starched shirt to his polished black cowboy boots. His coal-black hair matched his boots.

His name was Michael Griffith. He said he was a retired Houston police officer and now owned a janitorial office cleaning service. She noticed he carried a pager. Must be a busy guy with a flourishing business, she thought.

They hit it off from the start. That night they checked into a motel together. He had to go to his office the next morning, he said when he left, but promised to be back soon. She remained at the motel.

Somewhere between 9 A.M. and 11 A.M.—on Monday, Columbus Day—she got a call from him.

"I'm at a car wash getting the car washed and waxed," he said. "Why don't you pick up Tena and the two of you meet me for lunch." He mentioned a popular restaurant. Tena was her five-year-old daughter, who was with a baby-sitter.

She noticed he was wearing a different shirt when they met at the restaurant. He must have dropped by his apartment to change. His black Camaro was squeaky clean and sparkling from the wash-wax job.

From almost their first meeting, Griffith was a free spender. He gave Rutledge a lavish gift only three days after their first date. It was a stunning green emerald necklace that took her breath away. It matched the big green emerald and gold ring that he wore.

"Oh Mike, it's beautiful!" she exclaimed, throwing her arms around him and kissing him passionately.

They continued to see each other regularly. And the gifts did not let up. There was a bottle of her favorite perfume, Ysatis, and an expensive Dooney Bourke purse.

On the day that Griffith moved in with Rutledge and her daughter in their house on Highway 6 in the community of Sugar Land, he presented the dancer with two bottles of cologne, one in an exceptionally pretty bottle that drew her oohs and aahs—and more deep-throat type kisses.

Rutledge noticed Griffith did not have much extra clothing when he moved into her house. A day or so later he brought in a box of stuff from his car trunk, but he still had a sparse wardrobe.

He always kept everything clean and pressed. She knew he had been living in an apartment, so she asked him, "Mike, how come you haven't brought more clothes from your place?"

"It's a long story, but to make it short, my former girlfriend was crazy. She tore up all my clothes. She was crazy as hell."

One morning when she stepped out of the shower, Rutledge heard her washing machine going in the garage. A few minutes later, Griffith came in from the garage. She saw that he was angry.

"What's the matter, hon?" she asked.

He was carrying a purplish shirt wadded up. Tossing it into the trash, he said, "That looney bitch I told you about tore up one of my favorite shirts."

"Gosh, she must be crazy," Rutledge said.

Later, she retrieved the shirt and examined it. It was very pretty, she thought, but it had two tears in the front, upper area of one shoulder, like it had been clawed or something. Must have had a fight with his former girlfriend, she decided.

Griffith made it clear that the only way Rutledge could reach him when he was away was to call his pager. Never his business phone. The pager was the only way to get in touch with him, he emphasized.

He always was getting calls on the pager. He said some of the calls were "coded," which she thought strange. But she didn't ask any questions. He didn't like questions.

It was evening when Rutledge woke up from a nap on the couch. She went into the bedroom. The light was not turned on, but she saw Griffith scrunched up in a corner behind the bed talking on the phone.

This time she did ask a question, like it or not. "Hey, you have another girlfriend or something?"

Griffith said, "That was my crazy ex-wife. She keeps calling me. I don't want to talk to her, but she won't let me alone."

Rutledge did not believe the story. She was beginning to have doubts about him in other ways, and he was getting so possessive of her, so demanding.

He had started calling several times an evening while she was at work. Sometimes she would not call back because she was dancing or talking to a customer. If she could not talk right then and forgot to call back, he really was boiling.

He got upset about it, but she was upset herself, at his immature attitude.

"You should understand, Mike, if I can't call you, then I can't call you. I don't understand why you're so sore."

One night when she came home from work Griffith's car was not there. She went into her bedroom and into an adjoining bathroom. Then she saw the message. Written in lipstick on the bathroom mirror were the words, "I love you."

A sentimental gesture, she thought, but no mention where he had gone or when he'd be back. She looked through the house. Most of his clothes were gone.

The date was October 28, 1994, the day, unknown to her, that Winn Chen had been brutalized in the bridal and alteration shop.

Rutledge's affair with the ex-lawman had lasted 18 days. She had no idea that during their relationship Griffith had been two-timing her with his old girlfriend, Amanda Lopez, although she was suspicious that he was seeing other women.

On the other hand, Lopez did not know Griffith was involved with Erika Rutledge.

Steve Glassgow phoned Detective King to say he had heard something about Griffith's possible whereabouts.

"When I came in the office there was a call on the voice mail from a woman who asked for Mike," he said. "Said her name was Erika and left a phone number."

Glassgow had called the number and talked to her.

"She told me Mike lived with her almost three weeks, but that he left on October 28 and she didn't know where he was. She wanted him to call her. She said that he had a lot of cash on him when she met him. He bought her a high-priced purse, an emerald necklace, some expensive perfume. I don't know whether she was missing Mike or his presents."

Glassgow doubted it was his and Griffith's joint bank account cash that Griffith was using in the high living, the joint business fund that had been cleaned out on October 7.

"That would be long gone, I'm sure," Glassgow said.

He gave King the phone number the woman had left.

King talked to Erika Rutledge that same night. She did not know much about Griffith's background, she said. He had told her he was an ex-Marine and a retired Houston cop. He was generous and treated her and her little girl nicely. Except he was getting awfully touchy and possessive before he left, and demonstrating a temper.

"Do you know if he carried a knife?" King asked.

"Yeah, I saw it accidentally one time when we were in his car. It slid out from under the front seat. I thought it looked like a hunting knife. He said he carried it for protection."

Suddenly the stalled McCormick probe gained momentum. Everything was breaking loose at once, like a thaw after an ice storm.

Mary Ringer phoned Detective King on Tuesday, November 1 with a surprising development. She had received in the mail an invoice of charges made on her J.C. Penney's credit card for purchases on October 12 that neither she nor any family member had made.

Ringer told King the invoice showed that a pair of men's jeans and a shirt totaling $127.69 and "colored stones" in the amount of $325.83 had been charged on the card at the store in the Sharpstown Mall.

On the day of the murder Ringer had reported nothing but $400 cash missing. On that terrible day in the floral shop, Detective Kennedy, noting Deborah McCormick's purse opened and several cards spilled out, had asked Ringer if she knew of any credit cards that were missing.

At the time, in the shock of the tragedy, the mother said she did not know off-hand of any missing cards. But seeing the invoice jarred her memory of having loaned the Penney's credit card to McCormick so that she could buy her own expectant daughter some maternity clothes.

As soon as he could get in touch with the security supervisor at the mall department store, King asked him to locate the sales tickets signed by the buyer and preserve them so they could be checked for possible fingerprints.

King asked what the "colored stones" item would be.

"That would be something in the jewelry department," the security officer said.

A salesclerk in jewelry traced down the $325.83 purchase on that date and told King that it was an emerald necklace. The customer signed the name of Mary's husband, Billy R. Ringer, whose name was on the credit card.

The saleswoman remembered the transaction. She said the buyer was a "big, rugged-looking guy" with black hair.

"He was medium size, dark, a little on the heavy side, kind of Hispanic looking."

She remembered he was wearing a gold ring with a large emerald set and wanted to buy some emerald jewelry for a girlfriend.

"I asked him when her birthday was, I usually ask that when it's a man shopping. But he didn't know. I think it was a new girlfriend."

She showed him an emerald necklace priced at over $300 with the tax.

When shown the photo lineup which included Griffith's mug shot however, the clerk was unable to recognize any of the pictures. King and Kennedy figured that was because Griffith looked so much older in his mug shot than he did now with his hair dyed coal black, as Amanda Lopez had reported.

On November 2, Detective King was feeling the extra hours he had been working. He stayed busy long after the end of his regular shift. When something seems to be unraveling, you don't stop and finish it the next day.

At 4:05 P.M. he was driving home and looking forward to a restful evening when he was paged by Mary Ringer. He had left his pager number with her with instructions to call at any time if she needed to talk about the case.

King was nearly into Houston's downtown section after leaving the southeast homicide office. He pulled into the nearby central police building on Reisner to return Ringer's call.

She was excited when she answered. "Another credit card invoice came in the mail today. There are more charges on it that none of us made."

Mary Ringer said that the American Express Optima card issued to her husband had been used to buy gasoline one time at a Chevron station and six times at different Exxon stations. After getting the bill in the mail, Ringer had called American Express to report the card as stolen and was told that a charge had been made on the card as recently as October 31 at a restaurant—just two days before Ringer received the bill that had been printed on October 24.

Ringer recalled she had loaned the card to Deborah McCormick to purchase a water heater.

Saying she had talked to the American Express fraud investigators on the phone after making the report, Ringer gave King the phone number.

When the detective contacted the fraud department, he learned that the credit card had incurred additional charges after the billing statement was printed on October 24. They included gasoline purchases made at two service stations, a hotel bill, and the most recent charge at a restaurant on October 31.

The fraud investigator told King that he would have the "stolen" alert removed from the card immediately; the card had been flagged only a short time earlier when Mary Ringer notified the office of the theft.

With the "stolen" warning lifted, any user of the card would not be alerted if he tried to make other credit transactions. Any business to which the card might be presented would be instructed immediately: "Do Not Alert Presenter." Unless he had tried to use it in the last hour or so, the person with the stolen card would not know that it had been flagged.

A business receiving the card would be advised to call American Express, who in turn would call the 911 number to alert Houston police to send a patrol unit to the address in an effort to nab the card holder, King was advised. Also, the credit card company would page Detective King.

King's next move was to call Exxon headquarters to determine from the long coded numbers on the gasoline charge slips at what service stations the charges had been made.

After giving the Exxon officials the code numbers, the detective was told that the card had been used five times at a station located in the 8400 block of Highway 6 South, and one time at a service station in the 11000 block of Bellaire.

Knowing that all the gas stations maintain security cameras focused on the check-out area inside, King hoped that one of the two stations might have captured the card user on video.

He was disappointed when he called the stations.

As it turned out, the card user had paid for the gasoline at the pump, or by inserting the card in the computerized pay-out machine in the pump area, where there is no security camera.

Detective King's next phone call was to a bar and grill in the 6000 block of Richmond where the credit card had been presented on October 31, 1994, Halloween night. The restaurant manager told King he did not have the details on the transaction but would get all the information the next morning when the day-side people were on duty. He said it should be easy because Halloween day and evening had been a slow business day.

Once again, after doing as much as possible on this latest development, King headed for home. He was relaxing there at 10:45 P.M. when his pager went off again.

Calling was the American Express fraud investigator who told King that the card had been used only a short time ago at a restaurant in the 10000 block of the Southwest Freeway a few minutes past 10 P.M.

Unfortunately, there had been a delay in notifying American Express. The delay had been long enough that it would have been futile to send a police unit to the scene, the investigator said.

King hung up and dialed the restaurant. He first talked to the manager and was switched to the waiter who had served the man who presented the credit card.

The waiter remembered the customer. ''He was a big, stout-looking guy who looked Hispanic. I guess he was around six feet tall, probably weighed 220 pounds, had black hair cut short.''

The big man had been with a Hispanic woman. ''She probably was five-six, attractive, had long, black hair. She wasn't skinny, wasn't fat, just—you know—about right. I remember she was wearing some nice perfume and had on a black or navy blue dress. She was classy.''

The waiter said they had tipped well and remained in the restaurant for fifteen minutes after the man presented the card to charge the full course meal with wine.

Hearing the description of the woman with the big man, King wondered if it might have been Amanda Lopez.

She fit the waiter's description to a T.

Early the next day King and Kennedy drove to the beauty salon where Amanda Lopez worked. She was not there.

They talked to a relative who also was employed at the salon. She told them that Amanda had left her two young daughters with her mother and had run off with Michael Griffith! No one had seen or heard from her since she left; her children still were under their grandmother's care.

The detectives now added Lopez's description to the pickup bulletin that was out on Michael Griffith, as a woman who might be accompanying the murder suspect.

My God, King thought. *You could never figure out people. She gets throttled by this guy when they were living together—might even have been killed by him. She files the assault complaint for which the ex-lawman was being hunted before the felony charges in the Chen attack were lodged, and now, when he seemingly is a one-man crime wave, she's apparently gone back to him.*

Chapter 10

Amanda Lopez was confused.

She could not understand her feelings. She never would be able to explain how she was feeling to her family, her mother and sister who saw her battered condition on that horrible day of September 19.

Now, Lopez wanted to see Michael Griffith again, the man who she thought was going to beat her to death when he flew into a rage and pummeled her as she lay on the floor that awful morning. She wanted to see him again. Reasoning or logic did not enter into it.

At first she justified her changing emotional state by telling herself she was worried about him, only wanted to know if he was okay. Michael was strange, but then he also could be a wonderful guy. He always was nice to her daughters.

Lopez began trying to page him in mid-October 1994. She talked to him on the phone twice after that, and then they met, for the first time since their violent breakup, for lunch at a restaurant on the Southwest Freeway.

It was the beginning of their renewed torrid romance; soon

it was an almost dream-like existence of moving from one motel to another, a new one every night, eating at good restaurants, making love, shoving aside all reality or thoughts of anything or anyone except the immediate sensual world of the two of them.

The day that she left to be with Griffith, her daughters were with her ex-husband. It was his weekend to have them. She knew that when he did not hear from her, he would take the girls to her mother. She felt for sure they were with her mother now.

She did not call her ex-husband or her mother, though. No way could she do that. No way she could explain what had happened. No way anyone would understand, except maybe the girls when she hugged them to her and told them later all about it.

She had not been in touch with any member of her family since making the decision, had not even contacted the beauty salon where she had worked so long. She had dropped everything, given up everything, to be again with this man who had captivated her whole being.

They had decided to start a new life together, somewhere else, out of Houston where he said life had been so bad for him. They planned to go to Las Vegas, Nevada, to be married. Fun City, the Utopia for all those looking for a new start, running from the past, living for the present. She would leave the children with her mother until things settled down, until Mike and she knew for sure where they would be living.

Meanwhile, their week of nomadic motel living continued. She could not even go to the authorities and drop the assault charge against Griffith that kept him on the run. Too many questions would be asked—by the police, by her family.

She chose instead to run with him. After all, she was the one who had suffered the beating, who had filed the charge. If she was happy with him now, what did the past matter? She should be able to drop the charge if she wished. It was nobody's business but hers. But Michael did not want her to mess with it right now, saying it might wreck their plans for a new life.

Griffith still bought her presents. The first lunch they had together he gave her a pair of emerald earrings. They matched the emerald ring he wore. After lunch, when they went outside to her pickup, he tried to give her $200.

She did not take it, telling him, "No, I don't need it. You need it more than I do."

"No, here," he insisted, putting the money on the hood of her car. "Go buy yourself something, buy a new, sexy nightgown."

When she met him that first time, Griffith had wanted to leave his Camaro parked under the carport at the apartment complex residence of some friends. They rode in her car from then on.

Later they went to a place specializing in intimate lingerie and sexual enhancements. He bought her a beautiful, sexy gown and some sort of sexual ointment that was supposed to turn up the heat in their lovemaking.

They checked into a fancy hotel that evening, showered and made love again—and again. After that, they went to a nice restaurant for dinner.

Every night they stayed at a different motel. The nights, and sometimes part of the days, were for love. Other times they passed the hours by "just hanging out," like a couple of high school kids, walking leisurely in a mall or bowling or taking in a movie. It was almost like being teenagers again.

At one mall, they stopped in a store and Griffith bought two pair of blue jeans and two shirts. The store, for some reason, did not accept the credit card he offered, so Lopez paid for the clothing from her money. She had emptied her bank account of $1,500 cash when she went to be with Griffith.

Later, at the same mall, they went to a shop selling bath soaps, perfumes, oils and bubble bath, and similar items. He purchased a large basket of bubble bath, creams, and sprays for her, which they both used at the motels.

Griffith always charged everything on credit cards—with that one exception when his card was turned down—and he had a bunch of them in his billfold.

As she later would describe the week or more of living only for each other, Lopez said, "We just kind of did nothing. Just hung around and bought stuff."

They ate luxurious meals, steaks and shrimp, always with a good wine. They sat close together, held hands, kissed sometimes when they were eating at a place where the waitress or waiter was the only other person there at mid-afternoon.

On November 3, 1994, they checked into a Holiday Inn on Highway 290 at West Little York Road. It would be the last stop in Houston before they headed out west, to the glitter and glamor and a new life together. Tomorrow they were headed for new horizons.

But another feeling began to intrude into Lopez's days. She was feeling guilty about her daughters, about not seeing them or even checking on them. She finally told Griffith that she had to see them once more before they left, tell them that when she was settled someplace new she would have them with her again.

She picked up the phone to call the youngsters, but Griffith intervened.

"Don't call them right now. They're doing fine, they're with your mother. You can call when we get to Las Vegas."

But she called her mother's house on the night of November 3 and talked to the girls. She said that she was going to come get them tomorrow morning and take them to breakfast.

Griffith did not say anything then, but the next morning, as she dressed, he said he did not think it was a good idea at all.

"I have to see them, Mike," she said. "I can't just leave

them without saying good-bye and letting them know I'm going to be with them before too long."

At about 9:20 A.M., she phoned her mother's home and told the daughter that answered that she would be at the house in ten minutes to pick them up for the promised breakfast.

Griffith made his pitch as she started for the door. He sat on the bed, quiet but frowning. Then he said, "The only way I know you will come back is if you leave your money."

That was fine with Lopez, anything to get out of the room and on her way. She took the envelope of bills from her purse, the money from her bank account, and put it on the night table. She walked to the door. He was silent again.

For a few seconds, she felt a surge of the old fear, the feeling that he might drag her back into the motel and unleash that terrible anger and violence that she had known. Her heart in her throat, she reached her car and drove away.

As October turned to November, the men in Houston homicide had launched an all-out dragnet for Michael Griffith and Amanda Lopez.

Teams of detectives spread out to the city's motel strips, checking especially at the luxury motels that they knew Griffith favored. Quietly, they talked to motel clerks, showed the mug shot of Griffith, described the woman who might be with him. But they were having no luck.

They wondered how Griffith had been able to drop out of sight: the pickup bulletin described him and Lopez and the black Camaro that Griffith drove, complete with license number; all patrol units in the city were watching for the car and the suspect. It was obvious that Griffith had been laying low, on the run for two or three weeks.

None of his known acquaintances or former associates had seen or heard from him since he disappeared on October 7, after cleaning out the joint cleaning business fund.

The detectives decided that he must have ditched his car

someplace, maybe stashed it in a private garage. He was cop-smart when it came to eluding the law, and probably the first thing he had done was get rid of his Camaro.

Kennedy and King went to the restaurant on Richmond where the manager had promised to check with the day employees about the couple who ate there Halloween evening, the man paying for the meal with one of the stolen Ringer credit cards.

The investigators ate lunch there and showed a photograph of Griffith to the waitress who had waited on the couple on October 31 and when they came back to have dinner again on November 2.

She identified Griffith's photo as the man who had been with a pretty, black-haired Hispanic woman.

"She was very young, maybe in her late twenties, attractive. They were real nice and pleasant. They asked to be seated on the patio. They ordered everything I suggested. They left me a twenty percent cash tip, and I remember people who leave me a twenty percent tip," the waitress recalled.

The man had signed the card Billy R. Ringer, the name on the credit card.

The same couple returned on November 2, about the same time, she said. Again they were seated on the patio. The man asked if she could wait on them.

"I told him I couldn't because I was the manager that day. But I selected a good waiter and told him to take good care of them because he was going to get a good cash tip."

The man paid with an American Express Optima card bearing the Ringer name, as before.

On the evening of November 3, King received a phone call from Amanda Lopez's ex-husband. He had learned that Lopez had called her daughters to tell them she would pick them up the next morning to take them to breakfast.

"She said she would be at her mother's house at 9:30 tomorrow morning," the former spouse said.

He agreed to meet the detectives early the next morning to accompany them and point out Lopez's car.

Detective King organized the surveillance of the small, one-story wood-frame house in northwest Houston where Lopez's mother lived. He was not taking any chances on Lopez possibly showing up at a different time than she had mentioned. The surveillance units spotted up in the neighborhood at 5 A.M. on Friday, November 4.

Houston homicide detectives and officers from the Harris County Sheriff's Department joined in the stakeout. No one was more eager to get the former Harris County deputy sheriff behind bars than the newly elected Sheriff Tommy Thomas, who made no bones about his feelings.

He was thoroughly ashamed that a former deputy of his department might have committed the crimes he was suspected of doing. Even though he had not been the sheriff when Griffith was there, Sheriff Thomas was upset and had pledged his department's all-out help.

Other than Detectives King and Kennedy, the lawmen waiting in the pre-dawn darkness of early autumn included Sergeants D.D. Shirley, Danny Billingsley, John Denholm, and Jim Hoffman, all detectives from the sheriff's department; police Homicide Sergeant Gene Yanchek, and Lieutenant Jerry Driver of northwest patrol, along with uniform patrol officers Kenneth McDonald and Henry Chisholm.

It was a small subdivision with only three entrance streets. Lopez's ex-husband was in the car with Detective King.

King had talked to Lopez at length on the phone but had not seen her in person.

They were parked on a side street just off the Hempstead Highway. Dawn brightened the eastern sky. But it was not until shortly after 9:30 A.M. that the man beside King said suddenly, "There she comes. That's her Toyota Corolla."

King picked up his car mike and alerted all officers that Lopez had entered the neighborhood and was headed toward her mother's house.

As Lopez stopped in front of the house, King pulled up beside her. He stepped from his car, went to the driver's window, showed his identification and told the woman to get out. He asked for her driver's license.

She handed it to him. He saw that the attractive, dark-haired driver was Amanda Lopez.

King asked her, "Where is Michael Griffith?"

She did not hesitate. "At the Holiday Inn on Highway 290."

"Do you know the room number?"

"I think it is 162." As the detectives soon would discover, she gave the wrong room number, apparently not intentionally but because of her flustered state at the moment.

Lopez was not arrested, but King told her she would need to go to the homicide office to make a statement. The important thing at the moment, he knew, was to keep her in sight and prevent the possibility of her trying to tip Griffith that the police were closing in.

Lopez volunteered to cooperate fully, and said she would direct officers to where Griffith had left his black Camaro at a friend's apartment at the beginning of their week together.

As thought, Griffith had parked his car elsewhere than his own apartment for the obvious reason that he knew he was being hunted on the assault warrant filed in September by Lopez.

Lopez left in a patrol car to point out where she said Griffith's car was parked.

Chapter 11

After conferring briefly, the caravan of detectives drove to the Holiday Inn. They had quickly put together a plan. King and Kennedy would go to the motel office while the other investigators took up posts around the motel to await word from the detectives who would confirm that Griffith was there and in what room.

After identifying a photo of Griffith, the desk clerk checked the registrations and said the man was staying in Room 262 on the second floor under the name of Billy Ringer.

King radioed the room number to the other units. Kennedy was going to stay in the front office, give the officers a few minutes to get set up, then telephone Room 262 and tell Griffith to step outside.

As King drove around the motel to the designated room, he saw that several officers already were on the second floor landing on each side of Room 262. Detective Shirley was flattened against the wall and Detective Hoffman was on the other side of the door.

King stopped his car below the room and stepped out into

the parking lot. He saw Hoffman was knocking on the door. As King watched, he saw through an elongated window at the side of the door a man look out. The man looked right at him. King drew his gun, pointed it, and yelled, "Police! Open the door!"

On the landing, Hoffman also had called out as he knocked, "This is the sheriff's department. Open the door."

He saw a man glance through the window, then heard movement inside. The door was opened by a man in boxer shorts.

Hoffman said curtly, "You're under arrest. Turn around and get on the ground."

Griffith complied immediately, turning and sprawling face-down on the floor.

As Hoffman and other officers stepped inside, they had trouble getting Griffith's arms in position to handcuff his hands behind his back, and in doing so Hoffman somehow ripped the seat of his pants, much to his chagrin when he told about it later.

Down below, Detective King sprinted to the stairs and entered the room.

Detective Hoffman had advised the suspect he was under arrest on charges of aggravated sexual assault and aggravated robbery. Griffith had said nothing. Hoffman had the impression he was a little reserved, "like knowing he had finally been caught." The officers holstered their weapons after Griffith was lifted and placed in a nearby chair.

King read the suspect his legal rights from a blue card containing the Miranda warning that the D.A.'s office provides for all officers, although he and all the detectives have long known the words by heart.

King went through the full routine procedure, pointing out to the suspect his right to remain silent, to have an attorney present, or to waive that right if he desired, the whole doxology of Miranda.

Griffith, who had read the same legal warning to offenders, replied he understood and waived the rights.

King asked how far he had gone in school.

"Twelveth grade, high school," the suspect said quietly.

King asked if he would sign a consent-to-search form authorizing the officers to search his motel room. He nodded.

Detective Shirley asked him, "Who's room is this?"

Griffith said, "I don't know."

"Well, who is Billy Ringer?"

"I don't know," the suspect said.

King removed the handcuffs long enough for Griffith to sign the search form, which was signed by Detectives Denholm and Hoffman as witnesses. King then replaced the handcuffs.

"You need to get some clothes on—we're going to take you to the station," King said.

After Griffith dressed, Sergeant Shirley instructed Patrolman McDonald to take him to the homicide office at the southeast side station. McDonald knew Griffith from when he had been a deputy sheriff. They had worked some "extra" off-duty security jobs together. He led the handcuffed suspect to the patrol unit.

As they headed toward the police station, the patrolman could not resist asking, "What happened to you?"

Griffith replied, "After I lost my job, I just lost it."

Griffith also volunteered to show the patrolman where Griffith's much-sought black Camaro was parked.

McDonald got on his radio and advised he was deviating from the original destination to the apartment complex where Griffith said the car had been left by him.

Meanwhile, King began searching the motel room. On the dresser he found Griffith's wallet, which contained thirteen credit cards. Among them he saw the four cards stolen from the purse of Deborah McCormick at Always & Forever Flowers.

Also on the dresser was a gold ring with an emerald set, which was identified as Griffith's.

From the wastebasket the detective retrieved two receipts from another motel, signed by Griffith, and showing he stayed there October 28–30.

Raising the righthand corner of the mattress on the bed, King saw a large butcher knife with a black handle between the mattress and the box springs. The blade was about eight-and-one-half inches long, he estimated. He noticed the brand name of Good Cook on the knife.

He believed they had found the knife that took McCormick's life and threatened the Vietnamese girl in the bridal and alteration shop. It matched the description given by Winn Chen.

Next to the knife lay a folded envelope containing money, which when laid out and counted totaled almost $1,500 in bills.

Summoned to the motel to photograph the room and the evidence found in the search was crime scene unit technician T.Q. Williams. After taking the photographs, Williams took possession of the knife and other pieces of evidence for transfer to the police property room. Except for the knife, which would go immediately to the police crime lab for testing.

At the apartment complex where they had been directed by Amanda Lopez, the investigators, among them Detective Sergeant Yanchek, found Griffith's 1988 black Chevrolet Camaro parked under the carport. Lopez said the friends who lived there and had permitted Griffith to leave the car had the keys.

Within a few minutes, Patrolman McDonald and Griffith joined the others at the address. Yanchek again read Griffith his legal rights and asked him to sign a consent form authorizing a search of his car. He signed it.

While searching the vehicle, the officers discovered a sales receipt in the center console. It bore the name of Always & Forever Flowers and showed an amount of $81.10 paid for two dozen red roses. Later, Mary Ringer would identify the receipt as one given to Griffith when he had bought flowers at the floral shop at an earlier date, before the murder of her daughter.

Investigators now had the proof on paper that Griffith, as a previous customer, knew McCormick and without question would have been admitted by her to the locked flower shop.

This, plus the Ringer family credit cards stolen from the murder victim's purse and found in Griffith's wallet when he was arrested, left little doubt that the killer of Deborah McCormick was in custody at last.

The officers also took possession of a briefcase in the Camaro, but nothing was found in it relevant to the investigation.

After searching the Camaro, the detectives made arrangements for the car to be impounded for additional going over by the crime scene techs.

Lopez was at the police station for almost eight hours, giving a seven-page statement on what she knew about Griffith and their activities together.

The questioning of Griffith was done in an interrogation room measuring about seven by eleven feet. It had no window. The furnishings were simple: a table, three chairs, a computer, and a file cabinet.

Detective King talked to him first.

Griffith told King he did not kill McCormick and had no other statement to make. He did try to explain the stolen credit cards, claiming that he had found them in a garbage can in the restroom of a fried chicken restaurant located at Mangum and West 34th. He said he knew it was wrong, but that he had started using the cards.

He denied knowing anything about the McCormick murder or the attack on the Chen girl at the bridal shop. He was polite, saying "Yes, sir" and "No, sir," but he had nothing to say about the crimes other than his admission of using the credit cards.

When Detective Sergeant Novak took his turn quizzing the suspect, Griffith changed his story about where he had found the credit cards. This time he mentioned he found the cards at a different fast-food restaurant at 34th and Mangum.

Kennedy and Sergeant Wayman Allen also questioned the former deputy with the same results: nothing.

On Saturday morning, the day after the arrest of Griffith, Detective King arrived at the southside station early. It was about 7:15 A.M. when he went to see Griffith in his jail cell.

King advised the suspect he would be placed in a lineup at about 9 A.M. and he asked if Griffith wanted to waive an attorney or wanted to get a lawyer to be present. He told the suspect that he had about two hours to contact a lawyer and get him to the lineup.

Griffith lay down on a bench in the cell and looked as if he were dozing off.

At 8:40 A.M. King returned to the jail. Griffith said he had not been able to get an attorney. King decided to go ahead with the lineup, firm in his belief that the suspect had had enough time to get legal representation.

The detective started picking other jail inmates as "fill-ins" for the lineup. He picked men who were as near as possible to Griffith's physical description—in height and weight and hair color.

One of the inmates was shorter than Griffith—standing about five feet, four inches—but the detective chose him because he so closely resembled Griffith in spite of the difference in height.

The lineup was conducted in the "show-up" room on the second floor of the police station. It is a special room equipped with a one-way glass through which witnesses can see the subjects in the lineup, but the subjects cannot see the witnesses.

Mildred Beech, the customer who had been suspicious about a nervous-acting male customer in the bridal shop before Winn

Chen was attacked, was brought into the show-up room to view the lineup, which would be videotaped.

She stared intently as the men filed into view, turned sideways, then faced to the front. Within seconds she positively identified one man in the lineup panel of six as the one she had seen in the bridal shop on October 28, sitting in the chair.

She identified Michael Griffith as that man. She would never forget his face, she knew that.

Chapter 12

Being a homicide investigator is not always as glamorous and adventuresome as depicted on the TV cop shows, not by a long shot.

Detective Bob King had learned early in his career that there are some long, drab, sidewalk-pounding hours of seeking and running out leads that more often than not prove useless. And some of the real-life, or rather real-death, murder scenes are not what you would want to see on your TV screen.

A great deal of time is spent in endless paper work: writing incident reports, getting search warrants, filing complaints. There are the hours spent interviewing witnesses, going before grand juries, testifying in court at preliminary hearings and trials, not infrequently waiting long periods of time in courthouse corridors to testify.

Sometimes—just like the ordinary silver badges working the patrol units—you still have to collar a puking drunk.

On this Tuesday morning Detective King was on his way to the Harris County Jail to collect specimens of blood, saliva, and head and pubic hairs from murder suspect Michael Griffith.

He had gone before visiting District Judge Jimmy James in 209th State District Court and obtained a search warrant to require Griffith to give the various samples so that they could be compared in the crime lab to the crime scene evidence from Always & Forever Flowers.

Griffith would pluck and comb out his own hair samples, with King observing. A jail technician, Bertha Allen, drew two vials of blood from the suspect.

For the saliva sample, the tech opened a pack containing sterile gauze, being extra careful not to touch the gauze.

Griffith was instructed not to touch it with his hands, but to pick it up with his teeth, work it into his mouth, work it around thoroughly, and then drop it back—still with his mouth—into the gauze packet.

It was sealed for delivery to the police crime lab for testing, along with the blood and the head and body hairs.

All of Griffith's samples would be compared with the blood, semen stains, and hairs found on Deborah McCormick's body, around her on the floor, and on her clothing to determine if a match could be made. The blood and saliva testing would require the expertise of a highly trained serologist to seek out DNA readings. DNA can be obtained from blood, saliva or semen stains.

To get the necessary hair—some loose hair samples first—a clean paper towel was held in position to catch the falling hairs as the suspect ran his hand through his head hair.

Griffith then was asked to pull head hairs from in front, back, and on top. About twenty-five hairs had to be collected, preferably hairs with the roots still intact.

Next, Griffith had to hold another clean paper towel underneath his testicles and comb through his pubic hair so that samples fell on the towel. He then was required by the search warrant to pull buttock hair from all portions of the buttocks.

It's the down side of detective work, and King was glad when it was done.

With all of the samples placed in sealed containers, the

possible evidence that could tie Michael Griffith to the heinous murder was taken immediately to the crime lab, a trip of about ten minutes.

There it was turned over to Marita Carrejo, a forensic expert assigned to the serology section of the crime lab.

Some of the bloodiest work in criminal investigation in the burgeoning metropolis of Houston—a city known in past years as the ''Murder Capital of the World''—is done by scientists in smocks and surgical gloves. Lady scientists primarily.

Their world is one of molecules and microscopes, tubes and testing techniques, and complicated-sounding acronyms and formulas and data grouping tables. The end of all these means boils down to guilt or innocence of a suspected or accused perpetrator in rape and homicide cases.

The verdict starts coming in when the forensic detectives go to work. Their meticulously-arrived-at findings eventually can give lay trial jurors unbearable headaches when they hear the scientific explanations of the evidence.

No matter how patiently the intricate DNA procedures are explained by the experts, the prosecutors fear—with good reason—that no more than a glimmer gets through to most juries. Maybe if a juror has majors in physics, chemistry, and biology he or she might get the general drift.

Marita Carrejo, after receiving the forensic evidence from the murder scene and the samples taken from Michael Griffith, set out to identify Griffith's DNA and possibly link it to the bodily fluids and stains found on Deborah McCormick's body and clothing and on the large butcher knife recovered from the suspect's motel room.

DNA types are unique to people. That's why DNA typing is sometimes called DNA fingerprints. The only exceptions to this individual uniqueness are identical twins.

Carrejo, a pretty, dark-haired, studious-looking young woman, worked in the third-floor Police Crime Laboratory in the main police building near Houston's downtown area.

Her first objective was to determine Griffith's DNA type by testing the two vials of blood that were drawn in jail.

After that, it was a somewhat complicated process of finding out what portion of the population in a certain area—such as the sprawling Houston area of over four million people—could be excluded from having the same DNA typing as the suspect's.

As Carrejo explains: "What we do, instead of saying that this DNA type belongs to this person uniquely, we exclude people. We say that this DNA type is foreign to 'x' number of people. And the way we know that type is foreign to those other people is that we look at population on a data basis. The FBI has typed large numbers of people to determine the frequencies of these different types within a certain population area.

"Once we have a result of the DNA type from a blood test, we take that result to the population frequency table and determine what percent of that population can be expected to have the same type that I have found to be present on my evidence."

For that purpose, she uses DNA data tables compiled by the FBI on a national basis. The DNA findings are grouped according to race because the frequency of different types of DNA genetic markers vary within different racial groups.

It sounds like going at it backwards, but in DNA procedures the serologists narrow down a particular DNA type by excluding as many other types as possible.

Most commonly used is a DNA testing technique known as RFLP, effective in cases where the technician has a sufficient blood sample from a known suspect and known victim blood samples from a crime scene. Another more refined technique is known as PCR, which is done on much smaller or limited blood samples, or samples that are aged or deteriorated by weather elements or other factors. There also are several PCR techniques. Carrejo used one referred to as D1S80.

She first determined by microscopic comparison if the samples from the suspect and the blood on the victim's body and clothing matched. That established, her next step was to find out what the likelihood was that someone else besides the suspect in the specified population area would have the same DNA type, based on the population tables of the FBI.

The items tested by Carrejo and other lab chemists included the butcher knife; McCormick's pink stirrup pants, panty hose, bra, and gold slippers; the cotton swabs and slide smears made in the victim's mouth, vagina, and rectum; the victim's pubic hair and fingernail scrapings; a vial of her blood obtained from the morgue after the autopsy; foreign hairs found on her right breast and on the pink pants; blood and semen stains on the pants; blood and hair samples from Griffith; and a blood sample from McCormick's boyfriend.

Carrejo confirmed there was human blood where the knife blade and hilt came together. Even if the blade had been wiped off, the blood next to the hilt would have remained.

Her tests disclosed the minute amount of blood stain was a mixture of human blood; the strongest concentration was identified as McCormick's, and an intermixed weaker concentration was identified as that of Griffith.

Carrejo knew that a knife wielder's DNA can get on the knife without him having been cut or actually bleeding. This happens when a strongly thrust knife blade hits something like bone, the jarring impact causing perspiration or other cellular materials to be "fluffed" onto the knife. Perspiration, as well as blood, saliva, and semen contain DNA.

In this case, the DNA was identified as that of Griffith's, apparently from drops of his sweat that were flicked on the knife when he made the powerful jabs into McCormick's body.

Carrejo's other tests revealed:

• The genetic marker in the semen found in the victim's mouth was that of Griffith.

• Three semen stains on the right leg of the pink pants contained DNA consistent with Griffith's; the semen stain in the exterior crotch of the pants also had DNA identified as Griffith's.

• DNA in a semen stain on the inside of her panty hose was consistent with that of her boyfriend, Tom Atwood, who had provided a blood sample for testing at the request of Detective King.

When detectives interviewed Atwood, he confirmed that he and McCormick engaged in sexual intercourse the night before she was murdered, after returning to Houston from the day spent with her parents at the lake.

Based on the FBI population tables, Griffith's DNA type could be expected to occur in only one out of one-half million Caucasians in the three million (all races) population of Harris County.

But the clincher in Carrejo's scientific findings that the investigators believed would put the murder suspect on the Texas death row was this: based on Griffith's DNA genetic markings revealed by one of the more definitive PCR techniques and the FBI population tables, 99.9998 percent of Harris County's total area population of three million residents, including all races, were excluded as having the same type of DNA as Griffith—were excluded from having left the semen DNA in the victim's mouth and in the semen stains on McCormick's pink pants.

And, as the prosecution would later put it, "How many of that minimal percentage left [by the DNA findings] had been to the Always & Forever Flowers? How many had the stolen Ringer credit cards and the murder weapon with them?"

They were questions that Griffith's defense lawyers would not even want to think about—the kind of stuff that is a nightmare for even the most astute defense lawyer.

As if that was not enough, the examination of Griffith's hair samples and the foreign hairs found at the crime scene disclosed that two of the foreign hairs on or around McCormick's body were microscopically consistent with the characteristics of Griffith's sample hairs.

Rideun Hilleman, another chemist in the crime lab, did the hair comparisons.

When she examined the head hairs taken from Griffith, the first thing that Hilleman noticed was that the hair had been dyed "a very dark brown." Other hairs from the suspect that were not dyed ranged from natural gray to dark brown in color.

She looked for the same dyed treatment among the foreign hairs found at the murder scene. Comparing them with Griffith's color-treated sample hair, she saw that the characteristics were consistent, even to the extent of having an undyed portion about the same length on both hairs. Hair grows about one-half inch a month, which could account for the variation of dyed and undyed parts of the hair.

Although it is not possible to state, with reasonable scientific certainty, that a specific hair came from a definite source, Hilleman's opinion was that Griffith's dyed hair sample was consistent in characteristics with the foreign partly dyed hair from the crime scene.

She photographed both the sample and the crime scene hair under a microscope, showing the marked similarities of the two.

In all of her years as a chemist making such tests, she never had seen two samples of hair on two different individuals that had all the same characteristics. That's why the chemist's analytical opinion contains the qualifying words "consistent with."

Boiled down to laymen's understanding, she believed hair found at the murder scene had come from Griffith's head.

The day after Mildred Beech had identified him as the man she saw waiting in the bridal shop before Winn Chen was sexually assaulted, Griffith faced another lineup. Detectives in the robbery unit had noticed that Griffith matched the description of the bank robber given by Sandra Denton, who was shot twice during the holdup of the branch bank on October 14.

Detective Robert Davenport phoned Denton and asked her to come to the police station to view a video lineup of several men.

Denton, with bullet fragments still lodged in her skull, was in a room where she could view the six men in the lineup on a TV monitor. She sat on the edge of a conference table and calmly watched as Davenport started the video and the men paraded before the camera.

Davenport was startled when suddenly, as one man stepped into view, the blonde bank employee began physically shaking and whimpering.

"That's him! That's him!" Denton cried, cringing as if the dark-haired, husky man who was in Position 5 in the lineup would reach out and grab her.

The man she identified was Michael Griffith.

After her initial identification of the suspect, Denton told the detective she wanted to be sure, absolutely sure—although from the extreme fright she showed when she saw Griffith on the screen, there was no doubt in Davenport's mind.

When the lineup was run by again on the monitor, her response was the same. She had no doubt about the man in Position 5.

Although Davenport considered her description given shortly after the bank robbery-shooting as a good one, Denton said she had trouble putting it into words, even though she said she would never forget his facial features and knew she could identify him if she saw the gunman again.

At that time she had described the holdup man as a white male, thirty to forty years old, "looking pretty good for his age," five-ten to six feet tall, weighing 200 pounds, with broad shoulders and "a good build," a tan complexion, dark eyes, dark hair that was combed back and moussed on top. He was wearing tight, fairly new blue jeans, a dark long-sleeved button-down shirt, and possibly cowboy boots.

Not bad at all for a lady who had been terrorized and shot two times, Davenport thought as he glanced over the suspect's description on the original report of the robbery.

Three weeks after his arrest, Michael Griffith, the former deputy sheriff, faced a charge of capital murder in the death of Deborah McCormick, aggravated robbery and aggravated sexual assault in the robbery and sexual attack of Winn Chen, and now attempted capital murder and aggravated robbery in the bank holdup and shooting of Sandra Denton.

He was ordered held without bond on the series of charges—a rampage of violence within 18 days.

Chapter 13

Assistant District Attorney Casey O'Brien was a natural for the prosecution of ex-deputy Michael Griffith. He had become involved in the murder case early on, when homicide detectives started following the paper trail of the brazen knife killer who was living high on the credit cards stolen from his victim's purse.

O'Brien, a bearded, partly bald, good humored Irishman in his early forties, had been for years a member of the Special Crimes Unit of the district attorney's office. It is a unit that works laterally with police investigators in the midst of ongoing investigations, providing legal guidance as needed.

Within the Special Crimes Unit are smaller sections handling white collar crime, consumer fraud, major narcotics violations, and organized crime.

After ten years in the Special Crimes Unit, O'Brien became a division chief of one of the trial divisions, each division composed of several district courts. When he drew the Griffith capital murder trial, O'Brien was chief of Felony Division C, supervising and assisting prosecutors in major cases in six trial courts.

He had been in private practice for a year after getting his law degree but did not like it. He went with the D.A.'s office, where he has been for twenty years.

In capital cases, the division chief works with the district court chief of a trial court. For the Griffith case, O'Brien's partner was Assistant District Attorney Ira Jones, another veteran staff member.

O'Brien and Jones are different in their approach to prosecuting. They have different personalities that, in a sense, complement each other when combined in a trial. O'Brien is outgoing, given to dramatics when necessary in battling a case before a jury. He admits he is an "old-fashioned, hell-raiser Irishman," given to histrionics when he thinks they will make a point. The personable O'Brien has a green-lettered sign posted in his office near his desk computer that reads, "Parking for IRISH ONLY. All others will be towed."

He is a serious-minded prosecutor, but easily erupts into laughter. O'Brien often addresses jury members as "folks," has a homey, easygoing, one-of-the-crowd manner. He relates well to jurors.

He is an avid reader of technical and military intrigue thrillers, and likes such authors as Tom Clancy, M.D. Griffith, and Joe Webber. Or, as he puts it, "If there is a submarine on the cover of a book, I'll read it." He served in Army security from 1967 until 1971, dealing with classified matter.

Jones, a bespectacled, somber-faced man, is textbook rational, methodical, predictable, quiet-spoken and reserved; one acquaintance described Jones as "reminding you of an Army colonel, and I mean that in an admirable way." He is less given to spontaneity than O'Brien.

Jones has a reputation as a tough trial lawyer who can whittle expert witnesses down to layman-size language and opinions. An interrogator who is business-like but direct and to-the-point, Jones can be scathing in the cross-examination of a witness.

He is a stickler for detail, is known for "doing his homework" in whatever special or technical field about which he might be called upon to question expert witnesses.

When they were teamed for the Griffith prosecution, O'Brien and Jones gave careful consideration to the types of witnesses who would testify in the capital murder trial. The trial partners decided who would handle what aspects of the trial work.

Technically, in the team arrangement of division chief and district court chief, neither is in charge. Both attorneys try to divide the work and plan the overall strategy for the best prosecutory results—utilizing the special talents of both prosecutors in areas where they are especially knowledgeable and qualified.

As O'Brien explained the planning for a trial: "You get together and decide what each man's strengths are, and then divide the labor and the trial responsibilities."

Under their plan, O'Brien would examine the witnesses who were expected to give emotional testimony. Following the evidentiary part of the trial, he would bear down on the punishment phase to convince the jury the death penalty was appropriate in the case.

Toward this goal, O'Brien would dig deeply into the personal and professional life of Michael Griffith to show the jury what made Griffith tick.

Jones would take the witnesses dealing with the highly technical forensic work that tied Griffith to the murder of McCormick and the unmerciful attacks on Winn Chen and Sandra Denton.

Jones also would cross-examine the psychologists and the psychiatrists whom the defense attorneys were certain to call in their efforts to keep their client from receiving the death penalty if convicted.

The prosecutors believed the defense already knew from the state's evidence and lineup of witnesses that they had an exceptionally strong case against Griffith. Thus, the defending legal team would make its all-out stand in the punishment phase of the trial to try and save the ex-deputy's life.

The district attorney's office and its huge staff of prosecutors and appellate lawyers occupies its own building at 201 Fannin in downtown Houston, with other buildings such as criminal courts, civil courts, and the courthouse with county offices all clustered in a several-block area among Houston's towering skyscrapers.

The district attorney's building is catercorner to the criminal district courts building, with its several floors of district courtrooms and the district clerk's office—which handles all the court records—located there.

In these days of turbulence and terroristic-type violence aimed at public officials and buildings, the Criminal Courts Building has its own security force on the main floor at the entrance. The security checking point parallels the operations of a major airport security system, complete with electronic alarms and armed attendants.

All visitors, attorneys, witnesses, and the media must go through the alarm-equipped gates to be checked for possible weapons. If the electronic alarm is triggered by a forgotten coin or fountain pen, the visitor is directed to the side and gone over with a special scanner before final clearance to the elevators and the courtrooms above.

Judges and familiar court officials with issued badges are waved through by the attendants.

Courtrooms are locked and under the watchful eye of armed bailiffs up until the time that court is called into session. Judges' offices are behind doors to which the general public is not admitted without clearance through a judge's secretary.

From the beginning, it was obvious to the assistant district attorneys reviewing the investigative and forensic reports that the case against Griffith was a strong one with few, if any cracks, in the array of evidence that tied him to the brutal murder. There was no confession and no eye witnesses, but the circumstantial evidence put together by Detectives King and Kennedy and their fellow homicide officers was overwhelming.

Experienced prosecutors will take a well-investigated and prepared circumstantial case over a so-called eye witness case anytime.

One of O'Brien's major jobs was to track the credit card trail left by the suspect, and even more importantly, locate and interview the long line of ex-wives and girlfriends in Griffith's life.

He would probe Griffith's turbulent relationship with the women; and his contradictory life as a once competent, respected lawman of some twenty years' experience, as compared to the present rebellious renegade who was subject to uncontrolled rage, temper tantrums, and eventually unspeakable murder, sexual assaults, and even bank robbery.

When Griffith had gone bad, he had gone all the way—undoubtedly worse than any of the offenders he had arrested during his law enforcement career. O'Brien had no qualms about going after the death penalty for the former deputy sheriff.

As he viewed the situation, "Whenever I think there is a defendant who is going to kill someone else if he gets the opportunity, I seek the death penalty. I don't lose a lick of sleep over such a case, when I am convinced a person is going to hurt somebody in the future if he has the chance."

Pocketing the four stolen credit cards recovered from Griffith's wallet when he was arrested, an investigator with the district attorney's office started rounding up receipts and sales slips from various department stores, restaurants, motels, small shops, and gasoline stations where the cards had been used.

Donald A. Bernard, the D.A. investigator, was a veteran

officer. He had been on the district attorney's staff for fourteen years. Prior to that, he was a patrolman with the Houston Police Department and also flew police helicopters at one time.

After conferring with Casey O'Brien, Bernard contacted the headquarters of the card companies and obtained a full listing of all charges made on the cards from October 10 through November 3, 1994.

He was beginning to wish he had a chopper to get around the big town as he followed up the card transactions listed on several pages of billing.

He drove to the individual businesses, talked to credit managers and clerks and waitresses and picked up the sales slips signed by the card user. The name on the receipts was Billy R. Ringer, who with his wife, Mary, owned the cards stolen from McCormick's purse. It was Ringer's name but not his signature in his handwriting.

Questioning the salespeople, Bernard was told it was a large, black-haired man who had signed that name on the cards. The investigator now knew who that man was: Michael D. Griffith.

It was a time-consuming job, but when he finished, Bernard had a complete record supported by the actual sales slips and receipts of the transactions put on the cards during that slightly more than three week period.

Most of the purchases charged to the cards had been expensive gifts that Griffith gave to his girlfriends, Erika Rutledge and Amanda Lopez, the investigator discovered later, after the various items were correlated with interviews that the homicide detectives had conducted with the two women.

The first use of any of the cards had been at 8:55 A.M. on October 10, at a service station. The time would have been only about twenty minutes after Deborah McCormick, the pretty floral shop owner was robbed, attacked, and stabbed repeatedly.

In their investigation, Bernard was aware, the homicide detectives had decided that the killer who stole the cards from his victim's purse left the flower shop about 8:35 A.M. at the latest.

Bernard chose a day and the time of morning when weather conditions and the rush-hour traffic were similar to what they would have been on October 10. He drove away from the floral shop on Mangum at 8:35 A.M. to take the most direct route to the service station located at Highway 6 and Westheimer Road, where the card had been used to charge gasoline. Checking the mileage closely, Bernard saw that it was an eighteen and one-half mile trip. It took him slightly over twenty-five minutes to get there just before 9 A.M.

The American Express card of Billy R. Ringer was used to buy the gasoline, and it was that signature on the sales receipt, Bernard noted.

From the company's credit headquarters in Houston, Bernard found that several items had been charged at a large department store, located in the West Oak Mall in the Sugar Land area. This time Ringer's Master Card had been presented. Purchased was a bottle of Ysatis perfume for $68.20; time of the transaction was 7:23 P.M. on October 10, the murder date. Again the name Billy R. Ringer had been signed.

The mall was across the street from the service station where Ringer's Master Card had been used that morning. The mall also was only a few blocks from the residence of the topless dancer, Erika Rutledge, whom Griffith had started dating only the day before his shopping spree.

On this same evening, at 7:32 P.M., the same Master Card was used with the same signature to buy two bottles of quality cologne, Georgio and Draker, at $45 each. Also bought was a Dooney & Bourke purse priced at $297.69. These transactions were at another department store in the mall. The cologne and the expensive purse were bestowed upon Griffith's new girlfriend, Rutledge.

On October 12, at a department store in the Sharpstown Mall, an emerald necklace costing $301 plus tax had been bought, with Ringer's name signed on the sales slip. The time was

7:19 P.M. It was another romance-promoting gift for the topless dancer.

Bernard's roundup of credit card receipts and sales slips also included one at an intimate lingerie shop, others from several expensive motels and restaurants, starting October 28 and going through November 3.

On the round-robin of luxury motels and restaurants and the lingerie shop, the beneficiary this time of Griffith's fraudulent shopping was his former girlfriend, Amanda Lopez.

At one of the restaurants visited by Bernard he picked up a receipt for a meal of shrimp cocktail and a bottle of Sutter Chardonnay adding up to $75.25. Good-time Mike and his old flame were living it up.

The last motel bill receipt retrieved by Bernard had been at the Holiday Inn on Highway 290 on November 3 in the amount of $135.93.

And at that site, Griffith's free-spending and running days were over. Bernard hated to think what the tab on the credit cards would have been if Griffith and Lopez had made it to Glitter City in Nevada, as they had intended.

Milton Ojeman, another district attorney's investigator who is a handwriting expert, examined the credit card transactions and confirmed that the forged signature of Billy R. Ringer on all of them was the handwriting of the same person. And that the person was not Billy Ringer, the cards' owner.

The mug shot of Michael Griffith earlier had been identified by several of the clerks and waitresses as the man who had signed the credit card transactions "Billy R. Ringer."

The prosecutors could have added credit card fraud to the growing list of criminal charges against Griffith, but with what he faced, it would have been a moot gesture, they felt.

They planned to send him to death row.

* * *

Casey O'Brien, as he studied the growing file on the murder suspect, was intrigued. The guy was coming through as a Don Juan who first charmed the women with a deluge of expensive jewelry, perfume, purses, frequent bouquets of red roses, free-flowing compliments, and words of love.

Then he would beat the hell out of them for their failure to live up to his demands of obsessive control and domination of their lives. He seemed to get along with their kids, though.

He always dressed to the nines, was a cleanliness and neatness freak, and apparently was insatiable in his sexual drive, according to reports from the women who were interviewed. One of the girlfriends told detectives that Griffith had five and sometimes more ejaculations a day.

The prosecutor also learned that Griffith in the past had been a good, competent, loyal deputy sheriff, not only in Texas, but in Florida for ten years before he was hired by the Harris County Sheriff's Department in Houston.

His personal records disclosed numerous commendations and excellent work evaluations for duties performed. Before moving to Texas, Griffith once had been named "Lawman of the Year" while he was a deputy with the Bay County Sheriff's Department in Panama City, Florida.

But the brutal crimes for which he would be tried convinced O'Brien that the personable, good-looking ex-lawman had a dark and sinister side that had been there all along, a psychotic bend or perhaps just a damned mean streak that lurked beneath the facade of lawfulness and dedication to his job. O'Brien and the homicide investigators were sure that Michael Griffith had the soul of a killer inside him.

Now—getting ready for a trial during which he hoped to prove to a jury that Griffith's crimes and his wanton, destructive nature had eliminated his right to keep on living—O'Brien needed to know everything he could find out about Griffith's personal relationships, especially with the women who had been his wives and his girlfriends.

To get the death penalty he wanted, O'Brien would have to show that Griffith was a continuing threat to society—most certainly to women—and that he had been that way for a very long time before he committed the recent outrageous murder, attempted murder, and sexual atrocities on three Houston women.

Back through the years of his life, Griffith's dark and dangerous side would be found among the ruins of his domestic involvements and his epidemic bed-hopping practices—O'Brien was sure of that.

To dig up the evidence, O'Brien and his investigators planned to question a bevy of those unfortunate women during the trial preparation. They already knew about four of those abused women from the detectives' interviews and the past incidents of violence that were on record. Two of those women still were employed as deputies of the Harris County Sheriff's Department. One of them was an ex-wife of Griffith, and the other an ex-girlfriend.

But O'Brien would pursue the enigma of Michael D. Griffith all the way back to his first marriage in Los Angeles, California.

Chapter 14

Los Angeles, California was like the rest of America in the late 1960s—living in that turbulent era of post-Kennedy, Johnson-Vietnam years, the sexual revolution that the rebels of youth had won, and the explosive violence of the Watts riots. Man had been on the moon and back, and the Cold War still threatened occasionally to get hot.

But for sixteen-year-old Patricia Manning, she could not have been happier. She was a high school girl, having fun, jubilant about the future.

Her dad, a military man, ran the Air Force Officers Club in Westchester, in the L.A. area. Both of her parents also helped operate a cafeteria in conjunction with the Officers Club.

Manning worked as a part-time waitress at the club. It was there that she met a handsome eighteen-year-old youth named Michael Durwood Griffith. He was employed by Pat's dad as a club steward.

From look one, pretty and lively Pat Manning was bowled over by the rugged good looks and physique and nice manners and charm of Griffith. There was something about the way the broad-shouldered young man carried himself, cool and proud and confident, and how he always was so neatly dressed, clean and well-groomed.

She knew he worked hard on his job, was highly ambitious and wanted to make something of himself besides a club waiter—namely, he wanted more than anything else in the world to be a cop.

They hit it off immediately and started dating. Manning found out that Griffith was attending El Camino College at Torrance, California, and majoring in criminology.

"I have wanted to be a police officer for almost as long as I can remember," he told her.

Griffith had an uncle who was a policeman and, Manning guessed, was sort of a role model. She would be shocked if she knew the reason that he once had given to his step-grandfather, when Griffith was a young boy, for wanting to be a police officer.

Manning later testified she had gotten the impression that Griffith didn't get along too well with his mother, and she had never heard him talk about his father. Later, he told her that his dad had departed from the family years ago, when Mike was three years old.

Over the years of growing up, Griffith never heard from his father, and to hear him talk, his mom was no prize, either, Pat thought.

Manning had met her boyfriend's mother, Sally, who was beautiful and glamorous, but kind of conceited, in Pat's thinking. His mother worked as a restaurant hostess and, Manning heard, as a nurse's aide or something like that at one time—she wasn't sure. She did know that Griffith and his mother never seemed to be close at all.

Manning felt sorry for Griffith. She later testified that at times he had candidly told her about his childhood, how his mother had been an excessive drinker and stayed away from home at night and sometimes days, partying until someone ran her out of the bars to see about her kids.

Griffith had tried to do things for his brother and watch after him. Frequently, he said, he had to call upon his grandparents to feed them and provide what they needed when their mother did not come home. One big plus in the boys' neglected lives had been the benefit of the grandparents' swimming pool, he told her.

In a few years, their mother did manage to mend her ways somewhat, but the emotional chasm between her and especially Mike never smoothed over, Griffith told Manning.

Manning later testified she once witnessed one of the blow-ups between Griffith and his mother. One evening Sally invited them over to have dinner with her. She had been drinking before the couple arrived, Manning thought.

During the visit, Griffith and his mother got into a heated argument before dinner. Sally was about to fry some chicken when the fuss began. At first it was a shouting match, but then Sally struck her son on the head with the frying pan. This shocked Manning and Griffith was embarrassed, as he explained later.

During the few times they were around his mother, it was not unusual for her to get mad and throw things, Manning noticed. She had seen her throw ashtrays at Griffith.

On the other hand, she had observed Mike's grandparents were wonderful people. So nice to him. They seemed to always be the ones that Mike fell back on when he needed help, or who he enjoyed being around from the standpoint of family socializing.

Manning noticed that Sally was more restrained when she was around her mother and stepfather. She did not drink as much, either, in their presence and did not fight with Mike.

Griffith continued to help out his brother, even as they grew older—so Manning heard from her boyfriend.

Pat realized that Mike was working awfully hard. Besides his job with the Officers Club and going to college, the young man also had another job at a gas station. He always showed devotion to his work, whatever it was. He always was talking about becoming a policeman. The career seemed to be his main objective in life, Manning noticed.

Griffith had been born in 1950, the beginning of the so-called Happy Times decade for the country's youth, old-fashioned times when TV was barely born and people still listened a lot to radio and went to movies at theaters and did a lot of things together at home. It was the decade when there were family values and family togetherness in the average U.S. home. Families still went to church together.

But Manning learned from Griffith that he never had enjoyed those innocent fifties much, because he had not been part of a typical all-American family of those days.

Manning and Griffith enjoyed their work together at the Officers Club and the cafeteria. They worked side by side helping with wedding receptions and banquets, doing a little bit of everything at the various functions at the facility that was the social center for the Air Force people assigned or visiting in the L.A. area.

Early on, Griffith and Manning realized they were in love. Their relationship really bloomed when Mike came to live with her and her mother later on, while her dad was temporarily overseas. Both of her folks approved of his moving in.

Griffith did not have any other place to go—his mom had kicked him out of the apartment they shared, one whose rent Mike was helping to pay. She got mad because he would not turn over all of his paycheck to her, so he said.

The Mannings were glad to offer him a place to stay. They were admirers of his hard work and his ambition.

The year that Manning graduated from high school, 1970, her father was re-assigned to duty at Chanute Air Force Base in Illinois. Her mom and her five siblings moved there, too, but Pat, the oldest of the children, opted to remain in Los Angeles—mostly, no doubt, because she was so much in love with Griffith. They already were talking about getting married.

It happened on February 11, 1971.

And almost immediately, the happy, hard-working Griffith she had known underwent a startling change.

His wife's troubles started shortly after they were married. She tried to put their disagreements into perspective, blaming them on several things—such as the financial frustrations that many young couples have. She wanted to believe that their arguments were just the normal spats that come up among most newlyweds.

They hardly had any money in spite of his hard-working efforts, and they were struggling to meet the bills. He was trying too hard to accomplish things he wanted to do, but without any success. She felt that was why he vented his anger on her.

With her family living in Illinois, the couple had no financial help from them. Griffith's family, or rather his mother, never had helped in any way.

After their baby daughter was born, Pat's mother-in-law never came to see the baby or showed any interest in her grandchild. The young wife felt like Sally did not like her or want anything to do with the baby.

Griffith's grandparents did, thankfully. They always were coming over to the small apartment, playing with the baby, buying her things, helping sometimes with the bills.

At first the Griffiths' disagreements were verbal, flare-ups that happened every two months or so. But then Griffith started hitting her and calling her bad names.

One evening, when he came home highly upset about something that happened during the day, he picked up his plate of dinner she served and flung it against the wall with a curse and slammed out the door.

* * *

Before their daughter was a year old, sometime in 1972, Pat decided to take the baby and go to Illinois to be with her family. It was late autumn. She could not have picked a worse time, as far as the weather up north was concerned. It already was cold and deep snow had fallen in Illinois, a drastic change from L.A.'s sunny if smoggy clime.

But her life, and her baby's, were much warmer in the caring company of her folks.

Pretty soon Griffith started phoning, begging her to come back with the baby so they could start over. He promised to mend his ways, repeated over and over how much he loved and needed her and the child. He could always sound so lonely, so sincere, Pat sighed to herself.

She talked it over with her family. She had been raised with the notion that when people get married, they stay together and stick it out no matter what problems occur. That's the way her folks thought that a marriage should be.

She did return, and their life together went smoothly for about a year.

In 1973 the Griffiths moved to Panama City, Florida. They had a second child, another girl. Griffith continued his criminology studies at Gulf Coast Community College, a junior college there. He worked for a while for an armored car bank delivery service and also in a security job with a famous seafood restaurant on the bay, overlooking the Gulf of Mexico. She was employed there as a waitress.

Griffith also had volunteered as a member of the Bay County Sheriff's Department's auxiliary patrol. He made friends among the officers, and eventually he was hired by the sheriff's department as a deputy.

Pat was glad. It was one of her husband's happiest days—finally realizing his long dream of becoming a law enforcement officer.

When he told her, he grabbed her and whirled her around the room; she never had seen him so elated.

The Griffiths' home life underwent changes after he joined the sheriff's department. Pat noticed he spent more time at work or with his buddies on the force than he did at home with her and their children. Four or five days a week, Griffith worked out at a health spa with several of his friends from the department, always coming home late. He would also go off on fishing trips with his lawman pals.

Even when he was home, the atmosphere was tense. Once he had an accident while on duty. He was upset about it and took it out on her. When he was working on an important case, she knew not to press him too closely about anything. He'd blow up suddenly, over nothing.

Griffith had some real funny ways when it concerned his clothing and his appearance. He was a perfectionist—what some people might call a neat freak. He always had to have his shirts starched and ironed, the same with his jeans. He kept his boots shined and gleaming.

Most men were not anywhere near that neat, Pat knew, but she put his habit down to his general attitude of having everything just right and doing everything just right or not doing it.

It was not unusual for Griffith to come home in the middle of his shift to clean some grease or some food or whatever from his uniform or put on clean clothing if he didn't have time to wash or clean what he was wearing.

His patrol car had to be clean all the time, too, inside and out, the same way with their personal vehicle.

* * *

The Griffiths were having arguments regularly now, and he had started hitting her frequently in his anger. Not only did he physically abuse her, she noticed he never apologized, although he got over being mad. He never mentioned any of the incidents.

Patricia Manning also suspected that those times when Griffith was away from home, he wasn't always with his officer friends. She felt sure that he was involved in relationships with other women.

But even with the suspected unfaithfulness of her husband she endured the marriage because of what she had been taught by her parents.

"In our family, you stay with whom you're with, in spite of all the troubles," Pat commented much later, in the murder trial of her former husband. "You make the best of it. That's the way I was raised up. It took me a while to realize I did not have to live like that."

She did it also for the sake of the children. She strongly believed that children growing up should have the benefit of being with both parents.

After a few of these bombastic actions by Griffith, she began to notice some peculiar mannerisms that preceded his angry and violent emotional explosions. She noticed it for the first time when they were sitting on the floor and got into an argument. Griffith began rocking back and forth and his tongue slowly emerged partially and slowly curled up and behind his teeth.

He kept rocking forward and backward, almost as if he were heaving his shoulders against something. He would bite on his tongue and make a sucking sound as he did this, and he was silent, almost deadly quiet. He might keep this up a minute or two before he struck.

If she had time, Pat got out of his way as fast as she could when she saw the storm warnings.

* * *

In sharp contrast with Griffith's conduct as an errant and abusive husband was his professional demeanor and accomplishments with the Bay County Sheriff's Department.

Griffith was proving to be a highly competent officer who learned fast and did his job well. His personnel file was growing with evaluations and commendations that praised his work as a deputy. He was well-liked by his fellow officers and people that he encountered in his tours of duty.

In the fall of 1979 Hurricane Frederick struck parts of Florida. Residents of the areas where the powerful storm was expected to strike had been forewarned and urged by the authorities to evacuate their homes. Most of them did.

The hurricane was blowing in full fury when the dispatcher of the Bay County Sheriff's Department in Panama City received a long-distance phone call from a woman whose voice was filled with worry.

Her name was Beverly A. Rau of Howell, Michigan. Sounding as if she were on the verge of losing control, the concerned woman told the dispatcher that friends had contacted her about her aged father. They said that Roland Nations, 79, had declined their suggestions to leave his home and accompany them to Tallahassee, out of the path of the raging hurricane and the surging tides from the Gulf.

"He told them he was too sick to go," the distraught woman said. "After my friends called, I tried to call Dad at his house and I never received an answer. I let the phone ring and ring, and I know the line was not out of order—I checked on that. I'm worried to death that he is there by himself in that hurricane that hit. I know he has been very ill, and I'm worried that something has happened to him. He was too sick to get out by himself."

She wanted to know if the sheriff's department could go find out about him.

It had taken Mrs. Rau and her husband, both who tried to call the sheriff's office in Panama City, almost two hours to get through because the storm had blown down lines in some areas.

The dispatcher radioed Deputies Michael Griffith and Floyd Moore, giving the location of Nations' home and instructing the officers to check on his welfare.

The deputies drove through the howling 100-mile-per hour winds and deluges of horizontal rain to reach the Pensacola address given by the Michigan caller. With that entire region having been evacuated, they almost were alone in the midst of the destructive storm.

Highways and streets were under water and everywhere was evidence of the deadly storm's wrath—demolished trailer homes, automobiles, boats, tangled high-voltage lines, uprooted large palm trees.

When they finally reached the wind-lashed house, they knocked and knocked and called Roland Nations' name without anyone answering the door. They decided to force their way inside.

When they did, the officers discovered the elderly man sprawled on the kitchen floor, near unconsciousness, too sick to move or to try to phone for help. He had resigned himself to dying.

The lawmen rushed Nations to a hospital. After treatment, he fully recovered.

Within a few days, the sheriff received a letter of thanks from the appreciative Rau.

She wrote:

"I would just like to write a few short lines to thank Deputies Mike Griffith and Floyd Moore for coming to my dad's aid the night that the hurricane went through Pensacola. I since learned from dad that he had been laying there for about three hours.

"There is no doubt in my mind but that your deputies saved my dad's life that night, as I'm sure he would have died without medical attention before his neighbors returned to their home to find him."

* * *

The storm-braving efforts of Deputy Griffith was one of the reasons given by then-Bay County Sheriff Tullis D. Easterlling, when he later nominated Griffith to receive the "Lawman of the Year" award given annually by a Panama City service club.

In his letter of May 20, 1980, to the chairman of the award committee, the sheriff wrote:

"Mike is a twenty-one-year-old native of Huntington Beach, California. He has worked at the Bay County Sheriff's Department for over six years. He was educated in the public schools of Downey in Inglewood, California, and attended El Camino College in Torrance, California, majoring in police science.

"Mike came to Panama City from California in February 1973 and worked as a security guard here before joining our department a year later.

"Since that time, Mike has undergone extensive police training at Gulf Coast Community College. He has completed the basics standards course as required by the State of Florida. He has also completed intermediate and advanced training in the police incentive program at the college.

"Mike is one of the most well-liked officers at the Bay County Sheriff's Department. He is respected by not only fellow employees, but by everyone with whom he comes in contact during the course of his job. His reputation is that of a courteous and efficient law enforcement officer.

"Mike has received several letters of commendation from department supervisors as well as from members of the public. His most recent commendation came as a result of an incident that occurred on February 25, 1980, when Mike while on routine patrol happened upon the scene of a murder at a Springfield bar moments after it occurred.

"Mike was successful in apprehending the suspect and recovering the murder weapon. After effecting the arrest, Mike also was able to secure the crime scene until other officers arrived.

"Mike is married and has two children. I consider him to be a great asset to the Bay County Sheriff's Department and to the people of Bay County.

"I am proud to have him on my force."

Griffith received the award as Lawman of the Year and his photograph receiving the honor from representatives of the club was published in the Panama City newspaper on June 6, 1980.

An incident in Deputy Griffith's home that same year of 1980 would settle the matter of Patricia Griffith's indecision over their trouble-plagued marriage. It brought about a complete attitude change on her part.

She was putting some Christmas presents for the children in a closet when she noticed some other apparent gifts. She asked Griffith about them. He admitted they were presents to him from one of his female friends.

He had brought them home and put them in the closet. It appeared almost as if he wanted his wife to find the presents from his girlfriend.

Their discussion quickly changed into a heated exchange of words that suddenly erupted into physical blows from Griffith.

Patricia was knocked to the floor. As she lay there, crying, Griffith kicked her repeatedly in the side. The pain was excruciating. Later, she would find out that several of her ribs had been broken.

That should have been enough, but still she did not leave.

Another time when they were arguing and Griffith slapped her around, their sobbing little daughter stepped between them to try to shield her mother. Griffith grabbed the girl and shoved her violently across the room, where she struck her back on a doorknob. It inflicted a painful bruise.

Patricia had been willing to take a lot, doing it for the sake of her children, but the injury to her daughter was the last straw.

She filed for divorce, which was granted on April 16, 1981. She was awarded $125 child support for each of the children until they were 18, but Griffith paid it only for a short time, then slacked off.

Later, his ex-wife heard that Griffith had moved to Mississippi and there married one of the women he had been seeing while still married to her.

She would hear from her ex-husband again, years later after he had moved to Texas. He called one night crying about having been fired from the law enforcement job that was his whole life.

She found herself expressing sympathy.

Chapter 15

While living in Mississippi where he had married his second wife, Marlene Trenton, one of the women he had been dating when still married to Patricia Manning, Griffith went to work for a shipbuilder.

O'Brien and his investigators found nothing during their pretrial probe into Griffith's background that indicated he was in any trouble in Mississippi. Griffith did not like the job after a while, and wanted to be back in law enforcement work.

In the summer of 1982 he applied to the Harris County Sheriff's Department in Houston, filled out an application and returned it. When Harris County checked out his references with the Bay County Sheriff's Department, the replies were glowing confirmations that Griffith had been an excellent officer with the Florida department.

The replies included laudatory remarks such as "One of the best officers in the department . . . noticed the efficient and professional manner in which Deputy Griffith conducted himself . . . has initiative and education to enforce his ability in law enforcement . . . dedicated, motivated . . . the type of officer any department would be proud to have on their staff.''

The responses to the queries on Griffith's work with the Bay County Sheriff's Department praised his work in breaking up a burglary ring, handling a murder case, effecting outstanding medical rescues and assistance.

Also mentioned was Griffith's active support of community organizations and drives such as the March of Dimes, Easter Seals, the Retarded Children's Fund, and local civic clubs.

A former supervisor at the Mississippi shipbuilding company where Griffith worked described him as having a ''good work performance and attendance record'' and ''got along well with his fellow employees.''

Ultimately Griffith was hired by the Harris County department. He enrolled and was graduated from the training academy, which is a certification requirement to meet the standards for Texas law enforcement officers, before he could go on active duty. He was assigned soon afterward to patrol duty.

Griffith seemed dedicated to his job as always. After a few weeks, one evaluation described Griffith as ''shows great potential and initiative, very cooperative and conscientious about his career.''

Griffith was promoted to corporal and worked for the Courts Division.

Subsequently, a negative note was made in his work evaluation: ''Needs improvement in the directing and controlling of subordinates and making sound decisions.'' He was rated as average for completing assignments, professional image and good example.

On April 7, 1983: ''Outstanding deputy. Always strives for excellence.''

In June 1983: ''Excellent deputy, very attentive to duties, needs little supervision.''

On June 20, 1984: ''Great concern for quality of his work, has initiative.''

Evaluation in June 1985: ''Griffith with more experience has the potential to become an excellent supervisor.''

June 25, 1986: ''Griffith is very conscientious employee and constantly strives to improve not only himself but his subordinates. His job knowledge is steadily improving.''

He was transferred to the Warrants Division. That suited him fine. He was busy, always had a bunch of warrants to be served, offenders to be located. It could be dangerous, too. He had to keep on his toes, watch for the unexpected from the quietest of suspects who might run or fight.

It wasn't until 1987 that Griffith's evaluations by supervisors took a downward turn.

His romantic meandering continued at a high level. Griffith found a fertile field in which to sow his personal charms among the female employees of the department. He took note of the pretty secretaries and clerks and especially the female deputies.

Within a few weeks, he was dating several of them who were under the impression that he was not married. Griffith himself never mentioned his marital status, and if someone asked, he replied he was divorced.

After he was assigned to the Warrants Division, one pretty deputy who worked in the Inmate Records Unit right across the hall caught his attention and held his interest.

Her name was Laurene Tompkins, a divorcee with three children. Somewhere in her thirties, she still had a figure that drew stares anywhere she went, even in the familiar office surroundings.

Griffith turned on his charm, poured out compliments and his usual fancy gifts, including long-stemmed red roses by the dozen or two, jewelry and perfume, all high-priced stuff, all well-proven to Griffith as romance enhancers.

The red roses always did the job. There wasn't a better aphrodisiac than two dozen long-stemmed red roses that seemed to say it all to a woman.

Tompkins literally was swept off her feet by the handsome deputy's attention.

She liked his manners—so polite and considerate. And the way he dressed and groomed himself. She had never met a guy who was so particular about his personal appearance, his uniforms always starched and pressed and his boots shined, a neat man in every way, Tompkins thought.

He was dark, his face tan, she would have thought he was Hispanic or Italian. Somebody regularly asked him if he was Hispanic, to which he reacted with hostility, she soon found out.

Griffith told her and others that he was an ex-Marine, had fought and been wounded in Vietnam. Although she knew he was dating other women in the department, it was her company he obviously preferred.

Six months after they began going together, Tompkins found out that Griffith still was married to his second wife, Marlene Trenton. When she confronted him with this information, he managed to explain it away, saying they were not living as man and wife and that she was planning to leave. Trenton did depart within a short time after that.

Tompkins had three children—two teenaged girls and an eight-year-old son. She noticed that Griffith related well with the boy, took time to read to him, explain things, almost like a father—which the youngster had not had around for some time. The boy liked him.

With her woman's sensitivity or intuition, Tompkins was aware that Griffith seemed to be more and more under pressure on the job, though he never talked about it with her, except to mention occasionally he was P.O.'d with some of the people in the Warrants Division.

* * *

Around the sheriff's office, they called him "Sergeant Heart Attack."

The nickname reflected Griffith's increasing display of temper tantrums and loud and explosive encounters with his supervisors. Sometimes he paced back and forth like one of the caged lions at the zoo.

Lieutenant Ruben Diaz, commander of the Warrants Division, was trying to explain to Griffith why he had ordered him to have officers on his shift turn over their portable radios for use in a highly sensitive investigation of a dangerous felon.

Members from other law enforcement organizations were present when Diaz gave the instructions to Griffith.

To Diaz's surprise and embarrassment, Griffith blew up, raging loudly against the order and pacing up and down, his face florid, his dark eyes flashing anger.

"Why should my shift be placed in danger by giving up their portables?" Griffith demanded, as Diaz tried to explain the combined agency operation and the need to borrow the portable radios to correlate the inter-agency project.

As Diaz spoke Griffith scowled with disgust, shaking his head negatively.

"Have you secured the serial numbers of your portables?" Diaz asked, wanting to make sure the department could keep track of its loaned-out equipment.

"You bet I did!" Griffith shouted. "That way I know where to come when they mess them up!"

Diaz was getting red in the face now, aware of the other agency officers looking on as Griffith loudly opposed the order given by his supervisor. Diaz had talked with Griffith several times before about these spontaneous eruptions, warning him to keep his feelings in check.

Later, Griffith calmed down, but only after Diaz had given him warning that he was expected to abide by the departmental manual regarding conduct of an officer in relation to his supervisor—to shape up or face serious action.

On the official report that his lieutenant made to higher-ups of the rebellious opposition to an order, Griffith had written in the portion of the form given to "employee's response" to the accusations of policy violations:

"As supervisor of the evening shift it is my responsibility to maintain a high degree of safety of the shift. The order given by Lt. Diaz took the safety factor dangerously low. Lt. Diaz failed in communicating with the undersigned in reference to the above situation and would not listen to any type of reasoning about keeping a portion of the portable radios.

"The one-man units should have kept their portable radios and the two-man units should have been able to keep one of the two radios which they had assigned to them."

Responding to Griffith's response, Diaz wrote on the report:

"This sergeant was advised it was unknown exactly how many radios would be necessary to accommodate this emergency situation. However, he was advised that any radio not being used would be returned immediately.

"Sgt. Griffith's assessment of the danger level placed on his shift is highly inaccurate and is inappropriate.

"This type of oral reaction by him sends him off in tangents. Sgt. Griffith conducted himself in such a manner that he brought discredit to this department as well as to himself while in the presence of another agency."

A year later, to the month, Diaz and Griffith had another run-in that would put Griffith's job in jeopardy. It was the same old story: another of Griffith's out-of-the-blue rampages and belligerent face-offs with his supervisor.

Diaz was sitting in his office, talking on the phone, when he saw Griffith arrive for his evening shift. The sergeant was shift supervisor after higher-ranking supervisors left for the day.

Earlier, Diaz had returned to the sergeant's desk some reports dealing with personnel and a request card for extra-job employment made by Griffith for himself. Diaz attached a note to the papers saying "See me about this."

Suddenly Griffith barged into the lieutenant's office. He was scowling as he slammed his personal belongings on Diaz's desk.

Diaz covered the phone and snapped: "Get that stuff off my desk. Can't you see I'm on the phone?"

Griffith picked up his articles and stormed out. Then Griffith saw the papers left on his desk. He rushed back into the office and started throwing the documents one-by-one on Diaz's desk, loudly commenting on each one.

"I wasn't on duty when this happened, so it's not my problem! And what's the matter with my extra-job request? There's nothing wrong with the way I submitted it!"

He referred to the card on which he sought an okay to work an extra-job assignment while off duty, which the deputies were permitted to do if it did not conflict with their regular hours and duties.

"The information on the hours and days are too vague—I need more information," Diaz tried to explain.

Griffith became louder and more hostile, and as Diaz started detailing what he needed, Griffith picked up the request card and exclaimed, "Oh hell, I'll put something down even if it's a lie!" and went out.

At his desk, he scribbled rapidly on the card and brought it back. He said resentfully, "I filled it out but I made up the date and times of the work because I don't know the true schedule." He stormed out of the office.

Looking at the card, Diaz saw that it was properly filled in, except that Griffith had told him it was false information. Sighing, the lieutenant took the card and walked out to talk to Griffith again.

He found the sergeant in the office of the shift's captain, J.K. Mendenhall, who was talking to Griffith about a payroll item.

Asking Griffith about a personnel matter involving one of his shift detectives that he needed to clarify, Diaz said he needed to know if the problem had been handled.

Griffith again blared, "I told you I won't be held responsible for things that happen on my days off, and I'm tired of it."

Diaz tried to keep his voice level, pointing out he was not holding Griffith responsible for any happenings while he was off duty.

"Did you even read what I left on your desk?" Diaz asked.

"No," Griffith said.

Still talking with Griffith in the captain's office, Diaz asked what the sergeant meant with his remark that he had made up the hours and times on the extra-job request card.

Griffith yelled: "You ordered me to lie, so that's what I did!"

"I never gave you or anybody else an order to lie, sergeant, and I won't condone that tone of voice. I'm going to disapprove your job request until you can fill it out in compliance with the general order." Scooping up the card, Diaz walked out of the captain's office.

Griffith followed and exclaimed, raising his voice: "This is bullshit!"

The boiling-mad Griffith followed Diaz into his office, where the lieutenant immediately marked the card disapproved.

"I am going over your head with this!" Griffith shouted.

"That's your prerogative. Here, take the card back to Captain Mendenhall."

After Griffith returned to Mendenhall's office, the captain called in Diaz to try and resolve the disagreement. Griffith still was loud and insolent and it took a few minutes for the captain to calm him down.

The captain's door was open and deputies at other desks were taking in the confrontation of the red-faced, shouting "Sergeant Heart Attack."

Griffith finally admitted that he was wrong in saying that

Diaz had ordered him to lie. ''He never did that,'' he said quietly.

The raging and shouting was over, but Diaz still had some reservations about Griffith's future as a deputy sheriff.

Diaz spoke of those doubts in a lengthy memo written to the captain about the episode.

Referring to Griffith's eventual denial that Diaz had ''ordered him to lie,'' Diaz wrote:

''He told you that I never did that. Nevertheless, the damage was done. Sgt. Griffith's conduct is inexcusable and cannot be tolerated any longer. His outbursts were loud enough to be heard outside of your office since your door was still standing open and he was screaming.

''This conduct was unbecoming of a supervisor and must not be condoned . . . is not only contrary to all recognized standards of professionalism and propriety, but it strikes at the very foundation of management's authority. To retain a first-line supervisor that thus has demonstrated his contempt for higher rank would breed disrespect for the department's authority and make it difficult indeed for this lieutenant to maintain discipline in the division.

''The problem incurred with Sgt. Griffith is far from isolated. He has been counseled on numerous occasions regarding his behavior. Various management techniques in dealing with this behavior . . . have failed miserably.

''The behavior this sergeant displayed while in your presence has caused me to lose faith in his ability to supervise without supervision himself.''

Still, Lt. Diaz had some complimentary things to say about Griffith.

''The department has invested a lot of time and effort to cultivate this sergeant into an effective part of the Criminal Warrants Division. He's a dedicated and loyal employee to this department, but this alone is not what it takes to be an effective manager.

''It is these positive characteristics that prompted all my efforts toward salvaging this supervisor and attempting to properly motivate him.''

But he added, ''It is my opinion that any further attempts would only be repetitious and even if it had a semblance of accomplishment it would only be temporary.''

For once, Griffith appeared to realize that he had gone too far with his unrestrained outbursts.

A few days later, he phoned Diaz at his home and, as Diaz reported later to the captain, ''appeared to be genuinely concerned over the way he had conducted himself and was very apologetic.''

For Griffith to apologize was clearly out of character to those who knew him best—his ex-wives and girlfriends.

Diaz added: ''He admitted to his vociferous conduct and for the first time made a genuine commitment to work toward improving this behavior.

''He specifically stated he would refrain from shouting out of control and would stop the senseless pacing in the warrant division like a raging maniac.''

Diaz said Griffith had ''always stood firm that this type of behavior was his personality and there was nothing that we or he could do about it. This is the first positive conversation I have had with Sgt. Griffith where he had at least acknowledged having a problem and showed a willingness to correct it.''

Diaz favored giving Griffith another chance ''to regain the respect he has lost among his subordinates and this lieutenant.''

It must have hurt Griffith to grovel, but he had saved his job—for now.

Deborah Jean McCormick, 44, was murdered on October 10, 1994. (*Photo courtesy of Mary Ringer*)

ALWAYS & FOREVER FLORIST
Crestmont Corporation
3500 Mangum Road at Tulsa
HOUSTON, TEXAS 77092-5496
(713) 681-3030

DELIVER TO	PHONE NO.
ADDRESS	DELIVERY DATE
	S M T W T F S ____ A.M ____ P.M.
WIRE ☐ IN ☐ OUT / ASSOCIATION / CODE NO.	CALL TAKEN BY
FLORIST	PHONE NO.
ADDRESS	

☑ ARRANGEMENT ☐ SPRAY ☐ CORSAGE ☐ CUT FLOWERS ☐ PLANT

Doz Red Roses	75 00
TAX	6 19
OCCASION TOTAL	81 19

CARD

pd cash

CHARGE TO	ORDERED BY
ADDRESS	DATE OF ORDER
	PHONE NO.
CREDIT CARD NO.	EXP. DATE

№ 5235 ☐ CASH ☐ CHARGE ☐ C.O.D. ☐ NEW ACCOUNT ***THANK YOU***

Griffith was a frequent customer and a sales slip for the purchase of red roses was found in his car after his arrest.
(*District Court case file photo*)

McCormick always kept the door to the Always and Forever Flowers and Wedding Chapel locked when she was working there alone, leading the police to believe she knew her killer.
(*Photo courtesy of the Houston, Texas Police Department*)

The order of roses Deborah McCormick had wrapped for Griffith was still on the counter when police arrived.
(*District Court case file photo*)

Michael Durwood Griffith after being arrested for assaulting one of his girlfriends in March 1993.
(Photo courtesy of the Houston, Texas Police Department)

When found by her mother, the corner of the curtain in the reception hall was partly covering McCormick's body. (*District Court case file photo*)

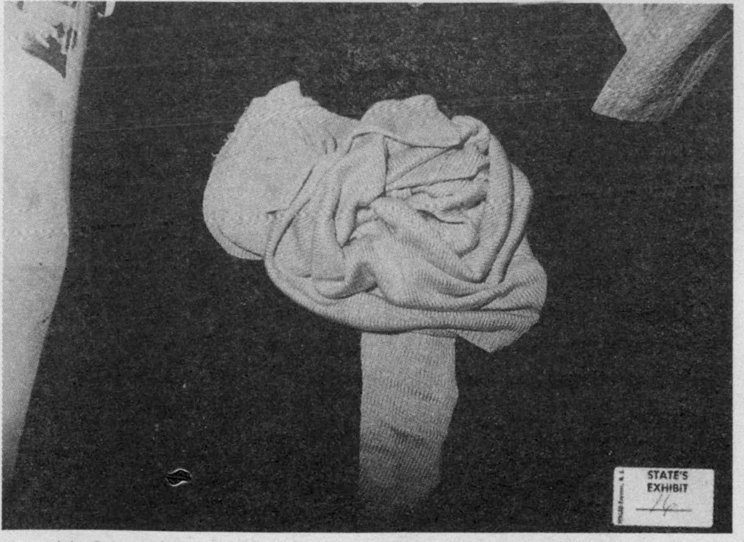

McCormick's sweater was on the floor beside her. The bloody marks where her killer wiped his knife clean can be seen on the leg of her pants. (*District Court case file photo*)

The false thumbnail on Deborah McCormick's right hand broke loose during her struggle with her killer. The nail was found under her body. (*District Court case file photo*)

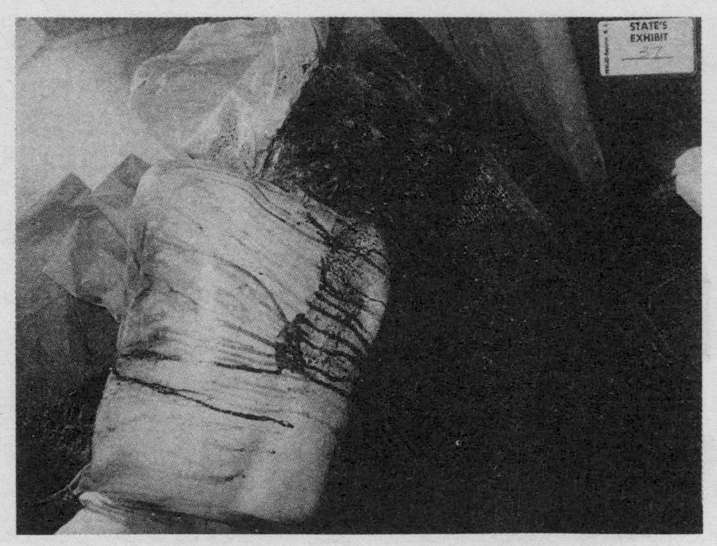

The chemical amino black was applied to McCormick's bloody back wounds in an unsuccessful effort to find fingerprints. (*District Court case file photo*)

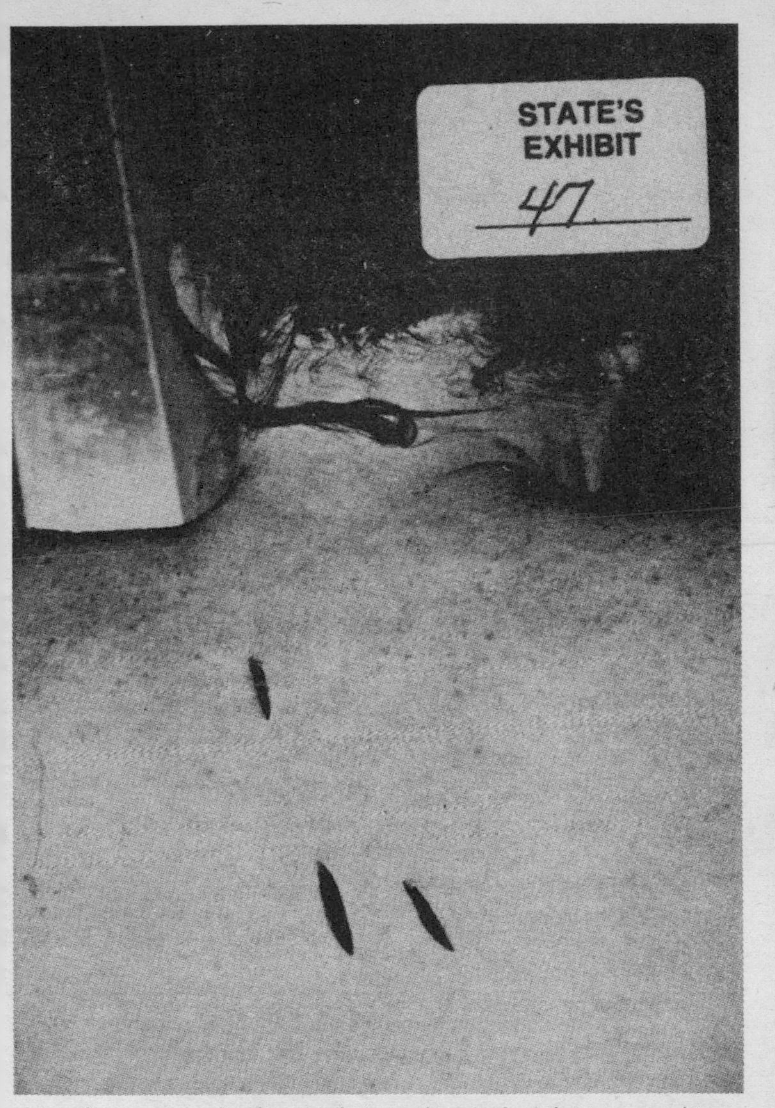

At the morgue, the three stab wounds in Deborah McCormick's back were clearly visible. (*District Court case file photo*)

CRIMESTOPPERS

NEIGHBORHOOD ALERT

REWARD

UP TO 11,000.00
FOR INFORMATION LEADING TO THE ARREST
AND CHARGES FILED ON ANY FELONY SUSPECT

IMPORTANT
Warrants and charges must be verified before arrest.
Never attempt to apprehend any suspects yourself,
as suspects are possibly armed and dangerous.

WHO MURDERED DEBORAH JEAN McCORMICK?

VICTIM:
DEBORAH JEAN McCORMICK

DATE/TIME:MONDAY, OCTOBER 10, 1994 @ 8:45 AM

LOCATION: 3500 BLOCK OF MANGUM ("ALWAYS AND FOREVER" FLOWER SHOP)

The Houston Police Department is requesting your help in solving the following crime.

On Monday, October 10, 1994, the victim was working at the "Always and Forever" Flower Shop located in the 3500 block of Mangum. At approximately 8:45 A.M., the victim's mother returned to the business and found that the victim had been killed. Money was missing from the business and the victim had also been sexually assaulted.

If you have any information about this crime or a possible suspect, please contact Officer R. E. King in the Houston Police Department's Homicide Division at 731-5494 or call the Crimestoppers Hotline at 222-TIPS.

The family of the victim is also offering a substantial reward leading to the arrest and charges filed on a suspect in this case.

CRIMESTOPPERS ANONYMOUS
REWARD HOTLINE AT 222-TIP

Police Crimestoppers Anonymous poster sought information on McCormick's murder.
(Photo courtesy of the Houston, Texas Police Department)

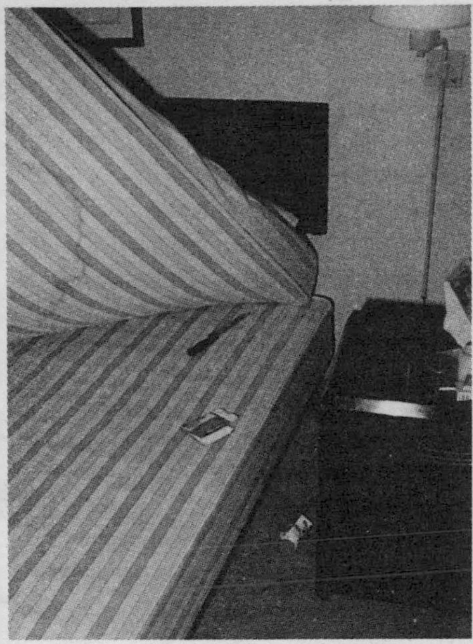

The police found the murder weapon and Griffith's wallet beneath the mattress of the bed in his motel room. (*District Court case file photo*)

Griffith used a butcher knife with a black handle and an 8½" blade. Lab experts found Deborah McCormick's blood where the blade meets the handle. (*District Court case file photo*)

Griffith waited for a customer to leave the bridal and alterations shop before robbing and sexually assaulting 18-year old Winn Chen. (*District Court case file photo*)

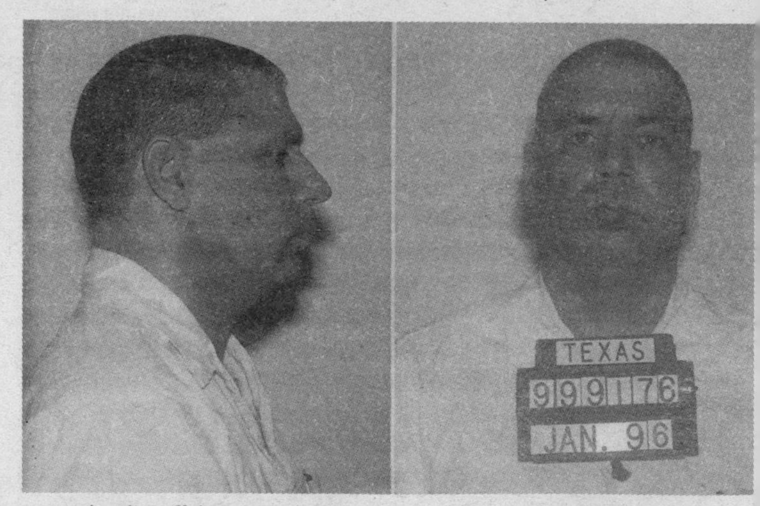

Michael Griffith on Death Row in Texas shortly after pleading guilty to two separate charges of aggravated robbery in the cases of Sandra Denton and Winn Chen. He was sentenced to sixty years. (*Photo courtesy of the Texas Department of Criminal Justice*)

Homicide Detective Robert King of the Houston Police Department was the primary investigator in Deborah McCormick's murder case.

Detective King's partner, Sergeant S.H. "Hal" Kennedy. (*Photo courtesy of the Houston, Texas Police Department*)

Mary Ringer, Deborah McCormick's mother (*right*) and Brandy Ridley, McCormick's daughter.

Assistant District Attorney Casey O'Brien led the prosecution team at Griffith's trial.

Judge Mary Lou Keel of the 232nd State District Court, Harris County, Houston, Texas presided over Griffith's trial for murder.

Chapter 16

Laurene Tompkins and Michael Griffith were married in 1989.

On that very day of their wedding, the groom went bananas. The new bride saw an angry and violent outburst from Griffith that shocked her with its fury.

It happened in her house, where they planned to continue living until they bought a house later. She was not even sure what happened to set him off, but without warning Griffith exploded in a raging fit.

He demolished a triple dresser, ripped off and shattered the mirror, threw and broke everything within reach, cursing loudly all the time.

Laurene stared in stunned disbelief.

Then it was all over—like a tornado gone over the horizon. His rampage ended. The rage was gone. He was strangely quiet, saying nothing to explain the destructive actions, never offering an apology. He hadn't even been drinking.

She could not believe that she stayed with him after that, but she did—much to her later regret.

* * *

From the first day of their marriage, Griffith changed like an actor in a new role, except he was not acting. Gone were his courtly manners and gifts. Once a week, at least, he would unleash a string of verbal abuse at his new wife.

After they had been married for about three months, the bad-mouthing turned to physical abuse. If she did something that made him mad, he would push her, or pull her hair, or hit her, or beat her. He was obsessive over everything she did, everywhere she went, even the clothes she wore.

There was the episode over the dress.

His wife had dressed to go to work; Griffith was not working that day.

"That dress is too tight on you," he said as she started to leave. He told her to change to something else.

"It is not too tight," she snapped. "And I don't have time to change."

When she returned that evening, he was sitting in a chair in the living room. He was quiet and did not acknowledge her greeting. She knew he was really angry, because that was how he acted, not saying or doing anything at all.

Moping, pouting, she would call it, except somehow it went deeper than either of those two emotional reactions. To her, it was as if he had a sickness of his soul.

She went about her usual household chores, getting dinner, talking to the kids, helping with the homework. She and Griffith did not speak. When she went to bed she thought it had all blown over, except Griffith still was not talking.

She was wrong.

She was rudely awakened by him lying on top of her but not to try to make love. He had a gun in his hand, pointed at her head. There was a look on his face she had never seen before, even during his rages.

"I'm going to kill you!" he said, working his mouth funny.

He reached up and ripped her gown down from her shoulders.

"Please, Mike, oh please, put that gun down! Don't hurt me!"

He held his aim with the gun.

"Please stop, Mike! I'm sorry for whatever you're mad about! Please, please don't shoot me!"

It was as if he relished her frantic pleading.

Then he got up, hurled the gun to the floor, and walked off, without a word.

After one tantrum, when he hit her and screamed curses, Laurene told Griffith she thought he needed some help. The department had an insurance program for just such things, which enabled an employee to get counseling and help at no cost.

But Griffith never sought such help. During his rational times, he did not think he needed it.

There were good times, Laurene would be the first to admit that. But even the good times were subject to momentary drastic change. Griffith was a thunderstorm always about to happen.

The year after their marriage, the Griffiths went to Cancun, Mexico, for a vacation. Her three kids went along. So did Deputy C. Ontivaro Olvera, twenty-two, a deputy with the Harris County Sheriff's Department, and his wife and young daughter.

Griffith and Olvera were good friends; their professional relationship was that of supervisor-subordinate. Olvera thought Griffith was one of the fairest bosses he ever had. He was always willing to help out if you got in a bind, on the job or elsewhere. He socialized with his men, too, in sports and workouts at the gym.

* * *

During the Cancun vacation, Olvera and Griffith were hanging out on the beach one day when Griffith suggested they go snorkeling. The young deputy had never done any snorkeling, hardly knew what it meant. Nor was he in good physical shape at the time, but he agreed to do it.

Griffith rented the equipment and showed Olvera how to use it. They practiced for a while in the shallow water close to the beach.

The sun was brassy, the sky and the sparkling water were blue. After a while, Olvera thought he never had had so much fun. It was like something in a dream, swimming through the clear, warm water, following a group of fish farther and farther, unaware of time or space. It was like stories he had read or movies he had seen, this strange, silent, spectacular underwater world.

Both snorkelers were excited over the school of fish they were following farther out into the ocean. They would surface periodically for air, then go under again, feeling almost like fish themselves as they navigated.

When Olvera came up for air, he noticed that the wind now was blowing very hard and the tide was much stronger. He glanced toward shore and could barely make out the tiny figures of their wives. With a surge of panic, he realized how far out in the water they had swum.

Olvera ducked underwater again, swam to Griffith who was nearby, took his arm, and motioned for him to surface.

''Hey, we're too far out, Mike,'' Olvera said worriedly. ''The water's getting bad, and I'm getting real tired.''

Griffith glanced toward shore before he said, ''Yeah, I guess so. Well, let's head back.''

Olvera said breathlessly, ''Mike, I'm really tired. My lungs are hurting.''

He swam along with Mike, growing more fatigued by the

minute, his lungs feeling as though they might burst, surfacing, gasping for air. He knew now that he was not in good enough shape to have ventured out this far.

They were in deep water, fifty to sixty feet Olvera estimated, and he knew as his lungs pained him even more that the only way to safety, to life instead of a drowning death, was that shoreline such a long distance away.

He rose to the surface and was floating there, on his back, realizing with growing panic that he might not have the endurance to reach that shore.

I'm going to die, Olvera thought, *I'm going to drown.*

"I don't think I can make it," he gasped out to Griffith who came up nearby. "I'm done in, got nothing left. Go ahead and save yourself, Mike." He had seen that Griffith too was tiring badly, feeling the grueling effects of the tide's strong surge and the still rising wind.

Griffith urged the faltering Olvera, "Come on, come on, you can do it. You can do it. Just keep moving. Don't think, just swim and float some and keep the shore ahead of you."

Griffith kept coaching him, always nearby, sometimes taking him by the arm, saying "Come on, you can make it, come on . . . we can make it . . . we're not that far out now . . . we're almost there."

Then, Olvera felt the tips of his toes touch the sand beneath the water. A few more yards and they could walk in.

Even doing that was something that took all of Olvera's last reserve of strength. When they staggered ashore, both men collapsed on the sand, blowing hard, but alive.

Later, when Olvera thought about it, he figured if it had been anyone but Mike out there with him, he would have died. Mike had stayed with him, risking his own life, holding on when Olvera felt he was going under.

He was sure that he owed his life to Griffith.

* * *

The next year Olvera and his family accompanied the Griffiths on a trip to South Padre Island. On this trip, the Griffiths were sharing a condominium with them.

Olvera had stepped outside his room when he heard loud voices, the loudest and angriest sounding like that of Griffith. It sounded as if he was mad enough at Laurene to kill her. The yelling and cussing were coming from behind the closed door of the Griffiths' room.

He heard Griffith shout, "What is my personal business is to be kept between us, you understand that?"

Olvera went to the room and knocked hard on the door. "Hey, are you all right in there?"

The loud voices stopped. In a few seconds, Laurene opened the door.

"Are you okay?" Olvera asked.

She did not appear to be hurt.

"Yes, I'm fine. Mike just got upset over a conversation we were having." She smiled, but it was a weak, forced smile, Olvera thought. Griffith never came to the door.

Olvera's own wife and daughter were in a nearby room, and he didn't want this kind of thing happening around them. It had startled him more than he could explain.

He had never seen that side of Griffith. He had the strange feeling that it was a dark side that had verged on something much worse had he not banged on the door.

Back in Houston, with no let-up in Griffith's screaming fits over nothing and her growing fear of his violent temper, Laurene decided the marriage was not going to work.

The tantrums of her husband frightened her children, and she was not sure herself whether he might do physical harm to them as well as her.

They separated, and she filed for a divorce. It was an extremely touchy situation because they saw each other every day at work. But Griffith did not talk to her nor her to him. At the office it was a complete truce in neutral territory. She discussed the situation with her own supervisor, but that's as far as it went.

As for Griffith, he now was openly dating another young female deputy who worked with him in the jail, where he was a sergeant supervisor of the fourth floor.

Her name was Stella Fletcher, a highly attractive brunette.

Laurene supposed that Griffith thought he was free to do what he wanted, since they were separated, and—she had to admit—he was, as far as she was concerned. Not that he hadn't done what he wanted, went out with whoever he wanted, even when she did care, did hope to save the marriage.

Now she wanted nothing more to do with Griffith, except to get rid of him legally in the divorce court as soon as possible.

As for Fletcher, Laurene thought that Griffith probably told her he was divorced.

On October 20, 1992, Laurene Tompkins went to the bank to draw out some money, She spotted Griffith and his girlfriend Fletcher at the bank. They were in Fletcher's car.

After she withdrew $1,400, she drove home and was surprised to see Fletcher sitting in her car parked in front of the house. Almost immediately Laurene saw Griffith. He was striding toward her from the front of her house.

She walked past him toward the door. The front door was not visible from the driveway, located to the side. Now she saw that the front door had been broken down. Griffith had kicked it in.

Griffith followed her inside and demanded her purse, said he wanted the money she had taken out of their joint account at the bank. He had knocked in the door and was looking for her purse when she arrived, apparently thinking she had been home.

Shoving her against a wall, he said loudly, "I want that damn money!"

Thoroughly scared, she said, "It's in the car."

He dashed outside and was getting the purse out when she came up and struggled with him. He hit her a blow to the head with his fist, then kicked her hard. He flung her to the side.

Suddenly he hurled the large flashlight he had been carrying through the driver's window of her car, smashing the windows. She did not know how the flashlight broke all of the windows, but they were broken.

Griffith grabbed the purse, removed the cash, and got back in the car with Fletcher. They drove off.

Griffith's wife went inside and called the police and the sheriff's department. Within minutes a patrol unit arrived, and she reported the manhandling, the car vandalism, and Griffith taking the money from her.

Later, when she cooled off and regained her composure, she decided not to press charges against Griffith. Instead, she reported the incident to the Internal Affairs Division of the department and again talked to her own sympathetic supervisor.

She decided to let the IAD handle it. Maybe they could get Griffith to see a psychiatrist or seek some kind of counseling, or handle it any way they thought best. All she wanted was to make sure that Griffith left her alone.

That's what she told herself anyway, but she knew the main reason she did not file any charges was because she was scared, frightened beyond description, of her weird and sometimes berserk husband. She was afraid he would hurt her.

After hearing Laurene Griffith's story, her supervisor wrote a letter to the captain in charge of the Detention Division, in which Griffith now worked. In part, she said:

> "As we have discussed, Sgt. Griffith of your command recently separated from his wife, Mrs. Laurene Griffith,

who works for me in cross billing and tracking. Last Tuesday, October 20, two deputies answered a domestic disturbance call at the Griffiths' residence.

"According to the report, Sgt. Griffith had already left the residence when the units arrived.

"Also, according to the report, Sgt. Griffith struck Laurene with a closed fist to the head and kicked her while forcefully taking $1,400 from her, which was in her purse, money which apparently was jointly owned due to it having been withdrawn by Laurene from a joint bank account.

"Laurene's daughter witnessed Sgt. Griffith throw a flashlight through the window of the car owned solely by Laurene, by virtue of her having owned the car prior to their marriage three years ago.

"On this date, Laurene called me and requested to come and speak to me. During this conversation she related Sgt. Griffith had been physically abusive throughout their three-year marriage and that she fears his retaliation.

"She stated this was the main reason she filled out a statement for IAD [Internal Affairs Division] in which she stated she does not wish to press charges.

"She also said it is not her intent to cause Sgt. Griffith to lose his job, but she is very much concerned about his mental health and what he might do to her in the future.

"She said his violent outbursts come on so quickly that they are unpredictable . . . I asked Mrs. Griffith if she thought her husband could benefit from psychological counseling. She told me she has attempted to get him to go to counseling when she began having problems with her fourteen-year-old daughter because the counselor wanted to see the whole family.

"She said that she made several appointments for them but that he refused to keep them.

"It occurred to me in speaking to Mrs. Griffith that

maybe Sgt. Griffith would be a good candidate for an administrative referral letter to the Employee Assistance Program. As you recall during our most recent captains meeting this matter was discussed as a possibility for employees who have indicated unstable or violent behavior, mood swings and etc.

"It was generally agreed that this is a matter of utmost importance particularly for peace officers who may demonstrate a tendency towards erratic behavior.

"I believe that this incident, coupled with Sgt. Griffith's accidental shooting of himself in the leg less than one week later [after the incident with his wife] would lead a person of ordinary prudence and caution to believe that psychological counseling would be called for.

"Please note that Mrs. Griffith said she fears retaliation from her husband is not wanting to call her feelings concerning his mental state to his attention. She indicated to me that should he discover that she is speaking to her supervisor of such matters there is no telling what he might do.

"I then asked her if she thought I should write this letter to you, and she said she thought it might be the best approach to have the administrative referral come from his chain of command rather than hers."

Ironically, less than a week after the incident with his wife, it was Griffith who was hurt—shot in the leg by his own gun.

It was a bizarre occurrence.

Griffith, his girlfriend/fellow employee Stella Fletcher, and her two teenaged sons were driving to nearby Baytown. Griffith recently had qualified on the firing range of the sheriff's department, as required periodically of all the deputies.

While Griffith was talking about his shooting scores, one of the boys asked what kind of gun he had. Griffith pulled the car into a small parking lot at the side of the highway, pulled his weapon from its holster, and unloaded it. He handed the gun to the boys to look at.

Griffith mentioned he also had a revolver that he kept beneath the front seat so that their mother would have protection if she were out in the car by herself. He pulled the revolver from under the seat, unloaded it, and handed it to the oldest boy.

After looking at the gun for a few seconds, the boy passed it back to Griffith. The deputy was reloading it when Fletcher heard a "pop." At first she thought it was a firecracker.

With a startled expression she then said, "I think you just shot yourself."

Griffith seemingly had not even realized that he had been wounded. They saw only a small hole in his pants leg, no blood.

But it was much more serious than they realized. Griffith was taken to a hospital, where examination showed the bullet had gone through his right thigh. Fletcher stayed at the hospital with him when he went to surgery and a metal plate was placed in his thigh.

He remained in the hospital for two days and walked on crutches for several days after that before returning to work.

Sergeant J.P. O'Neill made a report about the wounding of Griffith. In it he said:

"On Monday, October 26, 1992, Sgt. M. Griffith was injured by accidental discharge of a firearm.

"According to jailer S. Fletcher, who was with him at the time of the incident, Sgt. Griffith was turning the vehicle around in a parking lot of a credit union office when a .380 caliber handgun slid near his feet from under the car seat.

"Sgt. Griffith stopped the vehicle, picked up the weapon, and as he was inserting the magazine the weapon accidentally discharged. Sgt. Griffith was transported to the hospital via ambulance. Officer R.E. McDonald conducted the investigation. Sgt. Griffith's condition is stable at this time."

Chapter 17

In July 1992, Stella Fletcher was classified as a ''black-shirt'' with the Harris County Sheriff's Department. This designation meant that she had not completed the academy training and thus was not fully certified as a deputy sheriff for service in the field.

As a ''black-shirt,'' Fletcher was assigned as a jailer. She did not carry a gun.

The supervisor on her floor was a big, good-looking, black-haired guy named Mike Griffith. Everybody called him Sergeant Heart Attack, but not to his face unless it was a good friend doing it. They said he got the nickname because of his emotional blow-ups and hot temper.

Fletcher had never seen him act any way but really nice to her. He was helpful and patient as she learned the jail routine.

Sgt. Griffith always went out of his way to make her very much aware of him—not from a professional aspect of being her supervisor, either. He was sort of Hispanic-looking, Fletcher thought—was well-tanned, had rugged features that made him attractive to women.

The sergeant made Fletcher feel like she must be the prettiest, smartest woman trainee who ever came along.

He was so nice, she thought, a top-flight guy to be working for. He gave her encouragement and was free with compliments about her work.

Griffith started sending her roses, beautiful long-stemmed red roses, two dozen at a time. She knew this was not for the job she was doing as a jailer.

By September, they were dating regularly. The roses now came once or twice a month. He had the rose bouquets delivered to her at work sometimes; occasionally, they would be pink roses or some kind of exotic flower that grew in Hawaii—but usually his favorite, red roses. There were other lavish gifts—dazzling jewelry and exclusive-line perfumes and sexy lingerie. They became intimately involved, but were careful on the job to downplay their closeness.

When they first began going together, Fletcher did not know that Griffith was married. Much later, when they were deeply involved, she found out that another deputy in the department, Laurene Griffith, was married to him.

But Griffith told Fletcher that he and Laurene were just waiting for the divorce that she had filed to become final, and his marital relationship already had ended when he had started seeing Fletcher regularly.

Fletcher noticed Laurene and Mike did not speak unless the circumstances required and generally ignored each other at work.

Griffith was extra-nice to her two boys, which thrilled Fletcher, and they enjoyed being around him.

Late in 1992, Fletcher saw and experienced another side of her personable boss. He had become possessive of her, extremely jealous, and wanted her to account for all of her time when she was not with him.

Griffith demanded to know where she was going and when

she would be back, and in between, he insisted that she stay in touch with him by phone or call his pager. If she was not back at the time she said she would be, or did not call and give a good reason, he blew up. She noticed he was getting angry over nothing these days.

She had to keep in touch with him at regular intervals, or face his bad temper. He always wanted his way in everything and would not tolerate any interference in his rigid expectations and demands.

One time Griffith arrived at work already mad. He didn't go into detail but mentioned it was a phone call he had received earlier. He took his feelings out on Fletcher and they had words.

Toward the end of the shift, Griffith said he was leaving, and if she wanted to ride with him she had to leave now. They had ridden to work together that morning.

Fletcher still had a few minutes left before her shift would end, and planned to stay past her regular hours to do some things she needed to do.

"I can't leave right now, Mike," she said.

Scowling, he whirled and left.

Minutes later, a deputy told her that the sergeant wanted to speak to her on the phone. He must be calling from his car, she thought, but she was busy and could not answer his call.

Later, the deputy told her that Griffith said he was not waiting and she would have to get a ride home. She knew he would be fuming at her for not answering the phone when he called.

Griffith's jealousy flared one night in December when they were at his apartment. He apparently had the idea she was seeing somebody besides him.

Going into a rage, he started choking her. Then he picked up a gun that was on a table. Leveling the gun at her, he exclaimed, "I ought to shoot you. If I can't have you, no one will!"

Suddenly cold all over and trembling, Fletcher pleaded,

"Please put that down! Please don't shoot me, Mike! You know I love you!" She began crying, certain he was going to pull the trigger.

Then, as if nothing had happened, Griffith put the gun back on the table. He spoke calmly. "I'm sorry. I don't know what's wrong with me."

The way she felt at the moment, Fletcher was going to file charges against him. He talked her out of it, promising nothing like that would ever happen again.

He called her in January, about three weeks after the choking and gun-threatening incident. He sounded contrite. He was thinking about getting some counseling, he said, because he knew he had a problem. As he talked, Fletcher had the feeling he was his old self again, the Mike Griffith she had fallen for back in September.

He asked Fletcher if she would come over to his apartment so they could talk.

She said she had to go to work, but she would stop by his place when she finished the shift. He still was living in the apartment on Watonga Street. It was a nice apartment complex, where the residents had to use a key to get inside the always-locked security gate. An iron fence completely surrounded the apartments.

When she arrived Griffith was belligerent. Fletcher was regretting her decision to give him another chance. He sat with his head in his hands, raving about his messed-up life.

"Everything is falling apart," he said, his voice breaking. "My whole life is falling apart. If I lose my job, if they kick me out of law enforcement, I don't know what I will do, Stella. The job is everything to me—it's the only thing I ever wanted to do. I wanted to be a police officer since I was a kid. Now it's all crashing."

She knew he had been under investigation by the department's IAD for the incident in which he hit and kicked his wife, took her purse, and broke her car windows. It had been a nasty episode, one she unwittingly had witnessed. She had been required to give a statement to the IAD investigators.

Griffith, she knew, had had problems before—mostly with his supervisors, the result of his bombastic, instant reaction to opposition of any kind. It seemed almost imminent that he was going to lose his job.

''I don't know what I will do if I can't be in law enforcement,'' Griffith repeated.

''Mike, it will work out. Things usually work themselves out if you just leave them alone. But I've got to go, I'm on early duty tomorrow,'' Fletcher said, standing up, an inner feeling telling her that she had to get out of there as quickly as possible.

''Sit down. You're not going anywhere,'' Griffith said coldly. His pleading demeanor was gone.

He had that look in his eyes that she dreaded. He was working his mouth that funny way she had noticed before, rocking back and forth.

He walked over to a table and picked up her car keys and put them in his pocket.

Whatever took over inside him was happening, Fletcher knew. In seconds the transformation had come. She thought about the Dr. Jekyll and Mr. Hyde movie she had seen years ago.

It was the beginning of twelve hours of terror, during which she believed she would never leave the apartment alive.

Griffith was not drinking. Alcohol never had been his problem. He was an average drinker, got intoxicated once in a while if he was at a nightclub. But he was not a compulsive, binge drinker.

Griffith became destructive. The bedroom and bathroom were on the second floor of his apartment. There was a balcony overlooking the downstairs living room. As his raving increased, he started dropping and throwing things from the balcony, candles in glass holders and other breakable items that shattered on the floor below. He raved incessantly about his life falling apart.

They were in the bedroom. Fletcher watched transfixed as Griffith's upheavals went on and on to the sound of crashing noises and glass breaking.

Suddenly, he grabbed a pair of scissors and holding them by the closed handles like a knife, moved toward her threateningly, the scissors raised.

"I'm going to stab you, damn you!"

Fletcher jumped on the water bed, screaming.

"I'll stab the water bed and you, too!" His screamed threats left her cowering on the bed, sobbing and pleading with him to stop.

"I ought to kill you! I should have killed you a long time ago!" He was bent over her as she lay on the water bed. Then he turned, put down the scissors and walked into the bathroom.

When he shut the door, Fletcher quickly grabbed the scissors and concealed them under the cushion of a loveseat across the room.

He looked for the scissors when he came out.

"Where are the scissors?" he asked curtly.

She tried to be nonchalant. "I guess they are around somewhere." Humor him. Act like nothing was wrong, nothing had happened, just some misplaced scissors.

It was now past 5 A.M. In an hour, Fletcher was supposed to be at work. Griffith had been silent for the last fifteen minutes. He sat in a chair and stared at her but said nothing.

"Mike, they are expecting me at work. If I'm not there, they are going to wonder where I am. They will call my apartment, and if they don't get an answer, they may start looking for me."

He stood up. For a few seconds, it hung in the balance: he

might become violent again, or he might concede to her need to report to the job.

"You love law enforcement, Mike. You know how important it is to be there when you are expected, and they are depending on you."

He reached in his pocket and pulled out her car keys.

"I won't let you drive, but I'll take you in your car and come get you later. Promise to keep your mouth shut at work. If I find out you have said anything . . ."

Griffith drove. It was a bizarre trip. First light was streaking the eastern sky. It would be awhile before the freeways were jammed with rush-hour traffic. Motorists who were out had their headlights on in the pre-dawn.

Griffith rolled down the window on his side. He started throwing out anything of Fletcher's that was loose in the car.

He stared out the window. He slowly turned his head toward her. "It's a good day for you to die today. But I will let you tell your kids good-bye before I kill you."

They were on the freeway headed downtown, toward Houston's skyline, the heart of the city where the courthouse and jail were located.

Fletcher's mind was whirling in panic. Should she try to signal the other traffic humming along the expressway? In her fright she even thought about jumping from the car, but she knew it was moving far too fast for her to survive.

Where are all the cop cars? She had not seen one.

Her heart was pounding. He might do something crazy any time, crash into the traffic, push her out of the car.

He made a sudden exit from the expressway and turned onto Smith Street, in the vicinity of a spaghetti warehouse.

He turned around in the middle of the road. "Don't worry, I'm going to let you go to work."

Was he going to kill her in this dark and deserted area? The terrifying thought almost caused her to be sick.

He was not headed toward downtown anymore. They had been only three blocks from the courthouse when he turned off. She realized he was going back to the apartment. He was toying with her like a cat does a mouse before killing it.

She was too exhausted from the long night to think, did not want to think what might be ahead for her if he got her back into the apartment.

He pulled up before the locked iron gate. He would have to get out to unlock it with his key.

She would bolt from the car if he took his eyes off her for just seconds.

Then even this last chance was wiped out. He began unfastening a pair of handcuffs that Fletcher carried on her uniform belt. To keep her from getting away while he unlocked the gate, he was going to handcuff her. She knew she would never leave the apartment alive. He started to lock the cuffs into place on one wrist.

"I'll go in, Mike. Don't put the cuffs on me, please."

He hesitated. "Okay, but I promise if you run I'll chase you down and catch you and you will wish you never had run, do you hear what I'm saying?"

"Yes, yes. I won't run."

But she knew that she would. It would be her last opportunity, regardless of the poor odds, of escaping with her life.

Griffith stepped from the car and walked toward the gate. Immediately she bolted through the car door.

She ran as fast as she could down Watonga Street toward a service station, the bright lights of which loomed ahead like a paradise of safety. So close but so far.

She could hear him running after her. She did not look back. Then she did not hear him anymore. He's gone to get the car to come after me, she thought.

Breathless and fearing that he might even shoot her down, she made it to the service station. She ran inside and tried to hide behind a display.

The startled young woman in the bulletproof, locked booth called out, "What's the matter? Are you okay?"

"A man's after me and is going to kill me!" Fletcher shrieked.

The clerk hurried to unlock the door to the booth, and told Fletcher, "Get in here, quick!"

Fletcher ran in and still tried to conceal herself. The clerk picked up the phone and called the 911 number of the Houston Police Department.

Within a few minutes a patrol car officer braked to a stop on the station drive. He came inside and asked, "What's going on?"

When Fletcher gasped out her story, the officer returned to his car and radioed for a back-up.

Outside, Michael Griffith drove by the service station in Fletcher's car, turned around and drove by again.

Officers who converged at the patrolman's request for assistance were given the description of Griffith and the car he was driving as provided by Fletcher. They spotted the vehicle when it pulled to the curb and parked.

The black-haired man at the wheel sat calmly watching the station, as if nothing was happening.

It was daylight now, and morning traffic was increasing, some of the drivers slowing to look as they saw the police cars in the area. Several officers surrounded the car and took him into custody.

As he was being transferred from one police car to another, Griffith broke and ran. It was a short chase. He was returned to the car in handcuffs and taken to the police station.

He was arrested in the assault on Fletcher, but later she declined to prosecute, hoping that he would seek the help that he needed.

He never did.

* * *

On January 21, 1993, Griffith's worst fears became a reality: he was fired from the Harris County Sheriff's Department.

Major D.V. McKaskle, commander of the Criminal Justice Detention Command of the sheriff's department, wrote the termination letter to Griffith. The letter said:

> "You are hereby advised that effective on the date of this letter, your employment with the Harris County Sheriff's Department is terminated.
>
> "The reasons for your termination are set out below.
>
> "An investigation conducted by the Internal Affairs Division has disclosed on October 20, 1992, you were involved in an incident in which you were alleged to have intentionally and normally threatened imminent bodily injury to Laurene Griffith and demonstrated violent behavior by throwing your flashlight through Laurene Griffith's car window. However, no criminal charge was ever filed regarding this incident because Laurene Griffith refused to file.
>
> "On January 8, 1993, you were involved in another incident in which you are alleged to have assaulted Stella Fletcher. This resulted in your being charged with the offense of assault Case No. 9301080 currently pending in county Criminal Court at Law No. 9 of Harris County, Texas.
>
> "The conduct demonstrated by you in the above stated incidents was unprofessional and constitutes behavior which is unacceptable to this department.
>
> "It has thus been concluded on account of your actions as described above you should be terminated for demonstrated violation of the following sections of the Department Manual: Policy and ethics, violations of laws, general behavior, disciplinary action defined, improper conduct defined, willful violation of any of the rules set forth in the Department Manual or any special or general order.

"You may refer to the Harris County Sheriff's Department Civil Service Regulations Rule 12, Section 12.04, regarding your right to appeal this action to the sheriff within 10 days. You are further notified that this document will be placed in your personnel file effective immediately. If you so desire, you have 15 days in which to file a written response.

"The response also will be placed in your permanent personnel file."

Deputy Olvera was worried. Griffith had been fired on January 21, 1993. Olvera saw him briefly that day and could see he was taking it hard.

Olvera had an apartment in the same complex where Griffith lived, and the next day after the firing, the deputy went to visit with Griffith.

Griffith seemed to be in deep depression. He told Olvera he did not know what he would do now. Law enforcement had been his life. His termination as a deputy left Griffith adrift in depression and frustration, uncertain about his future, Olvera observed.

He already was in a hell of a mess with all of his women.

He told Olvera he wasn't sure what he would do or where or when he would try to go to work.

The next time Olvera tried to contact Griffith he could not find him. The ex-deputy did not answer his apartment door and did not answer the phone. He did not return the calls Olvera made to his pager. Olvera decided his former boss needed space right now, and he would leave him alone.

Griffith finally did go to work again, forming a partnership with Stephen Glassgow in an office janitorial and cleaning service. It was a far cry from the career that Griffith had destroyed.

The first week in October 1994, somebody was pounding on Olvera's front door. He angrily opened the door, expecting to see a door-to-door salesman.

It was Michael Griffith.

He had never seen Griffith look or act as he did standing in the doorway. His face drawn, his hair not neatly combed as usual—dishevelled, distressed, seemingly bewildered.

Even his voice didn't sound like Griffith. He appeared at this moment helpless, something Olvera never thought he would have been. Gone was all the confidence and arrogance that Griffith had exuded. The former deputy was a shell of his old self, Olvera thought.

''What do you want, Mike?'' Olvera asked. In light of what he knew about Griffith's recent hell-raising, especially the savage beating of Amanda Lopez the previous month, Olvera did not feel the old friendliness that once was there between the two men.

''I need help . . . I don't know what to do or where to go . . . I need help.'' Griffith appeared to be close to crying.

''Do you know there is a warrant out for you for assault?'' Olvera asked, referring to the warrant issued in the assault on Lopez.

Griffith registered surprise.

''There's a warrant on me?''

Was it possible he did not know that his ex-girlfriend Lopez had filed the assault charge? That was unlikely, Olvera conjectured, because Griffith had been too hard to find by his friends or anyone else in recent weeks including officers searching for him on the warrant.

Olvera knew he should arrest his friend, but his gun and handcuffs were in the upstairs bedroom of his apartment. He also had known Griffith long enough to believe he might not go so gently into custody.

Griffith turned and started for the gate.

Olvera whirled and dashed up the stairs, grabbing up his gun and handcuffs and a cordless telephone. When he ran out the door he heard Griffith's car starting.

''Mike, wait a minute, this won't work! Hold on!''

Griffith ignored his shouts and roared away.

He could tell that the fleeing ex-deputy was talking to himself as he drove off. He must be completely spaced out, Olvera thought. Flipped, decidedly out of it.

Olvera tried to phone Lieutenant Diaz, the head of the Warrants Division, but he was out. He left a message that he had seen Michael Griffith and was going in his car to try to find and arrest him.

Olvera made several swings through the surrounding area in the northwest part of the city. But he did not spot the fugitive or his black Camaro.

Since it was Amanda Lopez who had filed the assault complaint against Griffith, Olvera drove to the beauty salon on 34th where she worked. It was only a few blocks away. He warned her that Griffith was in the area and to be careful. Then he resumed his personal search, but Griffith had vanished from the area.

Griffith would remain on the run until almost a month later, November 3, when he was nabbed at the Holiday Inn.

Not that he was suffering that much as Olvera thought when he saw him that day. Griffith already was involved in a hot affair with a new girlfriend, Erika Rutledge, the topless dancer, whom he had met at the club where she worked.

Later remembering it was October 9, 1994, when Griffith had come to his door and fled before Olvera could arrest him, the deputy would be haunted by his failure to capture Griffith when he had the chance.

Griffith's unexpected visit was on Sunday, the day before Deborah McCormick was butchered in the Always & Forever Flowers, only a few blocks from the apartment complex where Olvera lived and Griffith had resided until shortly after he was fired by the sheriff's department.

As Olvera put it: "I know there would not have been a victim that next morning if I had caught him."

Chapter 18

Early fall in Houston in 1995 was like any other year. It still was hot and humid most of the time and sometimes foggy as the Gulf moisture lowered the ceiling.

Both the district attorney's prosecutors and the defense team for Michael D. Griffith were preparing for the capital murder trial of the former deputy sheriff.

Griffith still was lodged in jail, the facility he once helped supervise.

A writ for *habeas corpus* to obtain Griffith's release on bail had failed, having been denied by the court after a short hearing that included testimony by Mary Ringer, the murder victim's mother; Detective Bob King, the lead homicide investigator in the case; and Winn Chen, the teenage Vietnamese victim of the perverted sexual assault in the bridal shop; the Chen assault had occurred only four days after McCormick apparently had been forced to kneel and commit a similar sexual act on her killer before being stabbed to death with a large butcher knife.

During the writ hearing, the prosecutors were able to bring out the fact that McCormick undoubtedly had recognized her killer and willingly admitted him to the flower shop, trusting him completely for obvious reasons.

To establish those reasons, Assistant D.A. Casey O'Brien asked Ringer: "Do you remember the first time that Michael Griffith ever was in the Always & Forever Flowers?"

A. Yes, it was on Valentine's Day 1993. We were very busy, and I remember the gentleman coming in, and how he was dressed in a black suit, tie and shirt, nice shoes and all. He was just a nice-looking gentleman coming in to buy flowers.

Q. Nothing unusual about that experience with that customer, correct?

A. No, sir. Except he did come back two other times, I definitely remember.

Q. The thing that sticks out in your mind was that he was in a business suit and seemed to be a nice guy?

A. He was dressed very nice.

Q. Was there anything unusual about the flowers that were ordered by this stranger?

A. No, sir. They were roses, long-stemmed red roses.

Q. Do you remember what time this stranger entered your shop on Valentine's Day?

A. I want to say morning. I believe it was A.M. We were there by 7 A.M. that day, it being such a busy day for us.

Q. When did you see him again?

A. I believe it was about three weeks before my daughter was murdered. When he came in he always had a dark suit on, dark shirt and tie, and dark shoes.

Q. The clothing seems to be the thing that sticks in your mind?

A. Yes, sir. That's the thing that does. Other than the hair. I know he had black hair, and an olive complexion.

Q. You started to describe a third encounter with him?

A. It was sometime in September 1994. I haven't been able to put an exact date on it. It was a weekday.

Q. Who was working at the store that day?

A. My daughter and myself were.

Q. What happened that day?

A. When he came into the shop, I was on the telephone. I was taking a phone order. I know that I usually was on the phone when he came in and bought something and left.

Q. I assume your daughter was the one waiting on the stranger?

A. Yes, sir.

Later, outside of the courtroom and talking to news reporters, Mary Ringer elaborated on why Griffith would have been trusted and admitted to the shop by her daughter.

Ringer said, "We were always nice to him. He always bought red roses. He was very presentable, not the type person you would think that would come in and kill you."

Ringer said that she was sure that Griffith had mentioned to her and McCormick during his earlier visits that he was a law enforcement officer, which added to their trust of the customer.

If there was anyone that McCormick or she would let through a locked door it was a law enforcement officer.

Casey O'Brien did not question Ringer about it, but he wondered in his own mind what might have happened if Ringer had been in the shop with her daughter when Griffith came calling that fateful October 10 while Ringer was on an errand.

Would there have been two violated, brutally murdered women found in the floral shop? O'Brien wondered.

Representing Griffith were two experienced criminal defense lawyers, David Cunningham and Michael Charlton.

Early after their entry into the case, the defense attorneys had agreed that the State of Texas had an extremely strong case against their client. The evidence, both the forensic and the witness testimony, was overwhelming.

The defense lawyers were convinced that the best defense for Griffith was to try to save his life during the punishment phase of the trial, to try to convince the jury that Griffith should receive life imprisonment and not the death penalty because of what they considered to be mitigating circumstances of his childhood that left their scars on Griffith the adult.

They shied away from an insanity defense for the ex-deputy sheriff. As they say in Texas, that old dog would not hunt at all in a situation such as they faced.

It was a situation where Griffith, a veteran law enforcement officer himself of almost twenty years' experience, had been on the run and trying to avoid arrest since beating up a girlfriend before the murder and the crimes that followed. Crazy people who can't tell right from wrong don't hide out.

Griffith certainly knew the difference between right and wrong from the legal standpoint, knew it so well that he had done his best to keep from being caught or identified.

Thus an out-and-out insanity defense would fall flat, would crash before it ever got off the ground.

But there were other forms of mental incapacity that might, if presented skillfully to the jurors, deter their returning the verdict that would put Griffith on a gurney in death row's execution chamber at Huntsville, waiting for the Big Needle.

There could be little doubt, in the defense lawyers' viewpoint, that Griffith had not been operating on all cylinders when he went around doing all the bad things that he was supposed to catch people for doing.

Psychiatrists and psychologists would have to tell the jury what they thought made Griffith do the things he had done.

There was another legal front on which to wage the fight for Griffith's life, too.

If they could attack the legality of the evidence against Griffith—a large share of it obtained when officers entered his motel room with an arrest warrant, not a search warrant—

maybe they could keep that damning evidence from being admitted by the judge.

Toward that end, Griffith's defense attorneys asked for and were granted a preliminary hearing on October 10, 1995, in 232nd State District Court, to present a defense motion to suppress evidence secured during the search of the motel room where Griffith was nabbed and the later search of his automobile at a separate location.

To attack the state evidence that the detectives recovered from the motel room, the defense called to the witness chair Michael Griffith himself. It would be his only appearance as a witness in behalf of himself.

He would not testify during the murder trial two months later in the same courtroom.

Referring to Griffith's arrest at the Holiday Inn in Room 262 on November 3, 1994, Cunningham asked his soft-spoken client, who seemed calm and unaffected by the proceedings:

Q. Did something attract your attention to the door [of the motel]?

A. Yes, sir. A knock.

Q. What did you find when you answered and looked outside?

A. It appeared to be five or six police officers.

Q. Did the officers have a warrant for your arrest or a search warrant?

A. No, I did not visibly see one. [This would prove to be a circumventing answer.]

Q. What did you do?

A. I responded to their demands to turn and go to the floor.

Q. How long were you on the floor?

A. Possibly three to four minutes.

Q. Did the officers enter the room?

A. Yes.

Q. Did they enter your room without your permission?

A. No, sir.

Q. What happened?

A. They started checking and randomly searching around for unknown items.

Q. Did they ask you while you were laying on the ground your consent to search [the room]?

A. No, sir.

Q. After three or four minutes on the ground, then what happened?

A. They lifted me up and put me into a chair.

Q. Were you handcuffed while on the ground?

A. Yes, sir.

Griffith testified that his handcuffed hands were changed from behind his back to in front of him to facilitate his signing a form.

Q. Were you given a consent-to-search form?

A. King dropped the document in front of me and told me to sign it.

Griffith testified that prior to signing the form, he had not been "Mirandized," or given the required legal warning by anyone.

Q. Did you sign it freely and voluntarily?

A. Yes.

Q. What was Detective King's demeanor, his appearance? How did he treat you while you were in the motel room?

A. He was overbearing. He appeared to be antagonized by something. I tried to alleviate the situation because I knew it was volatile at the time.

Q. How did you try to alleviate it?

A. Just to do what I had to do to get it over with.

Q. Did you make any statements about the case under investigation?

A. No, sir.

Under further questioning by his attorney, Griffith testified that after about twenty minutes, he was escorted handcuffed to a patrol car by Patrolman McDonald. On the way to the police station Griffith volunteered to show the officer where Griffith's black Camaro was parked at another apartment complex on the northwest side of the city.

When they arrived, said Griffith, he saw two Houston detectives standing beside his car, both doors open and the vehicle's alarm system activated. They asked for and he gave them the code to deactivate the alarm, Griffith claimed.

At that point, Detective Yanchek asked Griffith if he would sign voluntarily a consent form to search the automobile, which he did sign before he was returned handcuffed to the patrol car, Griffith testified.

Griffith testified that the next morning he was questioned by detectives without being given the required legal warning. He also claimed "their demeanor was overbearing and nonprofessional . . . they spoke in a rough, harsh voice . . . wanted some answers."

After the questioning during which Griffith said he did not want to make any statement, the defendant testified, he was taken downstairs to the jail and was not segregated from other prisoners even though a television set in the cell block area was carrying coverage of the arrest of Griffith, a former cop.

Ex-cops are outcasts and natural targets among the general run of jail inmates, a fact that obviously concerned Griffith.

He said he asked to be transferred from the general population "two or three times" but this was not done.

In the cross-examination of Griffith, prosecutor O'Brien lashed into the claims by the defendant of not being properly warned of his legal rights and not seeing a search warrant.

Griffith admitted he signed a consent form for the motel and automobile searches. He said he was not surprised to be asked to sign such a form—he had seen hundreds of them—but added he did not bother to read the one presented to him. He admitted that he knew he was not obligated to sign anything.

When O'Brien displayed a state exhibit to him, Griffith identified it as the search and seizure consent form for the motel room that he signed voluntarily.

Detective King, after first being quizzed by the defense, said under cross-examination that he asked Griffith how far he went in school and if he could read and write the English language. He read the Miranda rights card to Griffith and after the suspect waived his rights to have an attorney present, gave him the consent-to-search form.

Griffith read and signed it, King testified. It was witnessed by two other detectives whose signatures were on the card.

Given legal permission for the search, King found a large butcher knife and Griffith's wallet that contained the credit cards stolen from the flower shop at the time of the murder, King testified. He said the stolen cards were among other credit cards belonging to Griffith.

After completion of witness testimony, defense attorney Charlton argued that the officers entered the room with an arrest warrant, not a search warrant, and asked Griffith to sign the consent-to-search form several minutes after they already had gone over the premises.

"So I think that all the evidence from the search of the motel room has to be suppressed, your honor."

In response, O'Brien told the judge, "This is, perhaps, not the most usual defendant. This is a defendant of some twenty years of law enforcement experience. This is a defendant who conceded that he knew he was wanted by police as the result of a warrant. This is a defendant who apparently was hiding out. This is a defendant who testified on cross-examination that, in fact, the consent to search the motel room was voluntary, that the police followed the book.

"Perhaps he did not like the fact that the lead detective was rude to him, as he claimed. I don't believe that the detective was rude, but rude doesn't constitute coercion in any respect.

"The defense has not shown any coercion, have not shown that evidence secured in both the motel room and later in the car should be suppressed."

The judge ruled: "It is my opinion that the arrest was legal, that the consent was voluntary, both forms signed for the search of the motel room and the car."

The defense's hopes of throwing out the evidence was down the drain.

Michael Griffith was scheduled to go on trial on a capital murder indictment in the first week of December 1995, in the same state district court.

Chapter 19

Prosecutor O'Brien had a case conference with the lead homicide detective, Robert King, as the Griffith trial date neared. They met in O'Brien's office on the sixth floor of the Criminal District Attorney's Building.

O'Brien and King were about the same age. The assistant district attorney remembered King as a witness in another case that O'Brien had handled.

The case was that of a rapist who had attacked two women in an apartment. Both women happened to be lawyers, and O'Brien knew them well. At that time, Detective King was a member of the police tactical team, SWAT. And it was King who had captured the rape suspect after a chase.

The fleeing suspect jumped a fence and King, an ex-Marine who kept himself in good physical shape, followed him over the hurdle. Somehow as King engaged the suspect in a tussle, the officer suffered a broken arm—but he had held on to the prisoner.

The detective was methodical and painstaking and had a

sharp investigative mind, O'Brien knew from past courtroom experience when King had been a state witness.

Now he was highly appreciative of the work that King and his partner Kennedy, and the other homicide men and police forensic technicians, had done in tracking Deborah McCormick's brutal killer.

From the beginning, O'Brien and his co-prosecutor, Ira Jones, intended to get a death sentence for the ex-deputy turned woman killer and sex attacker. They believed they had all the weapons to do it.

The jury members, when questioned earlier by the lawyers seeking to qualify them for jury service, heard the defense attorneys say something not frequently heard at this stage of a major trial.

In the voir dire, the legal term for the examining of prospective jurors, the defense attorneys made it clear that the defense would not be contesting the state's evidence against their client.

However, the defendant entered a plea of "not guilty," after the reading of the capital murder indictment alleging that Griffith "did then and there unlawfully while in the course of committing and attempting to commit the robbery of Deborah Jean McCormick, intentionally cause the death of Deborah Jean McCormick by stabbing her with a deadly weapon, namely, a knife."

A murder committed in conjunction with another major crime such as robbery or rape is classed as capital murder under Texas law and is punishable by either life in prison or death by lethal injection. The latter was somewhat of a technological refinement over the electric chair, known as "Old Sparky," that had been used for decades at the Huntsville walled prison where the death row cells and green-interior execution chamber were housed.

If nothing else, the state's electrical bill was down after the introduction of the so-called more humane method of dispatching the condemned prisoners.

Christmas was less than three weeks away when the capital murder trial of Michael D. Griffith began in the Criminal District Courts Building in downtown Houston.

The Yule season in coastal Houston doesn't look anything like traditional snow-covered scenes on Christmas cards. Snow is the rarest of rarities in Houston.

But all of the other signs of Christmas were there: the Salvation Army Santa Claus bell ringers, Christmas decorations and lights and Christmas music blaring in the department stores thronged by shoppers.

On this Monday, December 5, 1995, the opening day of testimony, the previously selected jury was seated. Judge Mary Lee Keel was presiding in the 232nd State District Courtroom on the fifth floor. Judge Keel was a youngish and pretty former assistant district attorney who only recently had been elected to the court bench.

Until seeking the judicial office, she had been in the appellate division of the district attorney's office, handling criminal cases in the appeals courts.

This was her first time to preside over a capital murder case, but both the state and defense attorneys had a high respect for her abilities as already proven in her budding judicial career.

Defense Attorney Michael Charlton, in the briefest of opening statements to the jury, declared candidly:

"As most of you gathered throughout our voir dire discussion, this case is not about guilt or innocence. You will not hear much from us over the next several days.

"This case is about punishment. It will lead—the evidence you will hear for the next several days—will lead to the conclusion that the state seeks. That's not an issue."

Prosecutor O'Brien smiled slightly to himself at that remark. Proving to the jury that Griffith was guilty was a hell of an issue, in the prosecutor's mind.

Charlton continued, "We are not contesting that, and you

are not going to hear much from us. This case is solely about punishment. We simply ask you to keep an open mind until you hear our evidence.

"Thank you very much."

It had to be one of the shortest opening statements in legal history. Not often, either, did a jury hear of the defense admitting in so many words that the accused did it, but still entering a plea of "not guilty"—except in outright self-defense cases or cases in which the defense would be a claim of insanity.

Taking his turn at opening remarks before the jury, Assistant District Attorney Casey O'Brien said, "Let me start by telling you the purpose of the opening statement.

"Sometimes cases are rather convoluted. Sometimes they are long, and sometimes the anticipated order of witnesses is intermingled. So the purpose of any opening statement is to permit us to give you some indication of what the crime is about, how we anticipate we will present the case to you."

Explaining that he and the co-prosecutor, Ira Jones, had broken the state's presentation into "definitive stages, or parts of the evidence," O'Brien displayed a blackboard on which he had written the order in which witnesses would be called to prove the case facts.

He detailed the stages of presenting the state case: the crime discovery, the investigation by homicide detectives and forensic technicians, the tedious back-tracking that went into the gathering of evidence and the eventual arrest of the defendant, all of which would be shown to the jury in crime scene photographs and videos and the testimony of witnesses.

The able prosecutor first set the scene where the heinous murder of pretty forty-four-year-old Deborah McCormick took place on the Columbus Day Monday of October 10, 1994.

Always & Forever Flowers was a family business operation started about twenty years ago in the northwest part of Houston. McCormick and Ringer worked together taking telephone floral orders, making the floral arrangements and sending them out on the delivery truck. The shop also had its share of walk-in customers.

On that black day in October 1994, Always & Forever Flowers was to become a shop of horrors.

For security reasons, the two women made a practice of always keeping the front door that was protected by security bars locked if only one of them was inside.

After telling the jury that Mary Ringer left the floral shop early that morning to go to the grocery store, O'Brien said:

"Mary was gone until approximately 8:45 A.M. She came back, used the key in the front door, walked in, and Debbie—that's what her family called her—was not in the customer or the flower shop portion of the business.

"She then took a right just inside the work area portion of the business and down a small hallway. Some twenty feet down the hallway is the reception hall. Much to her horror she found in a far corner of the reception room the dead body of Debbie McCormick.

"She will describe to you how Debbie McCormick was lying in a pool of blood. She had no clothing from her waist up.

"She was wearing pink stretch pants. The knit sweater she had been wearing was now off to her side. Her bra, still clipped in the back, was down at her waist.

"And she went over to the body, didn't hear any breathing, couldn't get a pulse, attempted CPR, then called 911. She said, 'My daughter has been murdered! My daughter has been cut!'

"And they suggested she do CPR. She tried, again got blood all over her, but Debbie was already dead."

O'Brien wrapped up his opening statement by promising the jury that testimony from a police expert in DNA science—the identification of genetic markers in the blood—would positively link Michael Griffith to the gruesome murder, along with other damning evidence run down by homicide detectives.

He said the DNA testimony, based on carefully conducted laboratory tests, would prove that Griffith's DNA type was found on the body and clothing of the murdered Deborah McCormick. The accused's DNA also was found on the murder knife that was recovered from Griffith's motel room when he was arrested; also on the same knife were bloodstains that contained Deborah McCormick's DNA, O'Brien pointed out.

In the same room, in Griffith's wallet, were four credit cards stolen from the victim's purse when she was slain.

O'Brien called his first witness, Mary Ringer, the blondish, attractive mother of the slaying victim. She testified about leaving her daughter alone at the floral shop, locking the door behind her—as was their habit—when she left for a brief time to buy some needed items at a grocery store.

Her drawn face now reflecting the stress of the terrible memories, Ringer said she returned to the shocking sight of her daughter's bloody, half-naked body on the floor. She spoke rapidly, tears rolling down her face, as she described the scene.

O'Brien said in a sympathetic tone, "Slow down, please. Would you describe the manner in which she was clothed at that time?"

Ringer brushed at her face. "She had pink stirrup pants on, little flats, her foot was bent back, and then her top was—she did not have her top on."

The courtroom was silent, the jurors and the spectators holding their breath, feeling for the mother having to relive the horrible details.

O'Brien displayed a pink sweater already entered as a state exhibit. "Can you identify this?"

Ringer took it gingerly, turned it over, the tears were flowing again. "Yes, it's the [sweater] that Debbie had been wearing."

O'Brien said, "I observe there is tearing on the left side and the right side. Was her [sweater] torn like this when you left?"

"No, sir." The answer was barely audible.

O'Brien, noting the strained expression of the witness, asked,

"Are you okay, Mary? Would you like a little break for a little while?"

She shook her head. "No."

"Are you sure?" the prosecutor persisted.

Ringer raised her chin and her voice. "Yeah, just get it over with."

O'Brien asked, "When you returned and found Debbie, can you describe the manner in which her clothing was arranged?"

The witness had regained her composure and spoke more firmly and louder now. "She had on her pink stirrup pants. She did not have her top on at all. [The sweater was on the floor beside her] and her bra was pulled down to here, where she had been stabbed and cut."

After Ringer testified that knives with a blade of about ten inches were kept in the work area of the shop to pare flowers, O'Brien picked up a large knife with a black handle that was marked as a state exhibit.

He extended it to the witness. "All right, ma'am. I want to show you what's marked State's Exhibit 20, and ask you to look at this and tell the jury whether, prior to the death of Debbie McCormick, this knife was ever in your business?"

Mary glanced at the knife held by O'Brien. She was pale, and gulped and said softly, "No, sir."

Ringer related that her daughter's purse had been rifled and was open on the counter. She said that $400 cash she had left before going to the store to be given to one of McCormick's daughters to pay for car insurance was missing.

In her emotional trauma of the moment, the mother said she had not missed the credit cards that were stolen from the purse, did not realize they were gone until she received a monthly billing containing fraudulent charges on the cards.

During her testimony, Ringer recalled that she later recognized Griffith, after his arrest, as a nice-looking customer who had visited the floral shop three times previously before McCormick's murder.

Now, in a tense moment, O'Brien asked:

"Do you see the man here in the courtroom who used to come into your flower shop?"

Ringer did not look toward the defendant when she replied with a simple, "Yes."

"For the record, would you point to him?" O'Brien said.

Pointing to Griffith, she said: "Yes, sir. The gentleman sitting there in the striped shirt."

She said it quietly, without any defiance in her voice or face.

Griffith did not look at her.

O'Brien said, "May the record reflect the witness has identified Michael Durwood Griffith."

The defense had no questions for Mary Ringer.

Chapter 20

To the jury it must have been more fascinating than any TV crime drama featuring the modern wizardry of crime scene analysis. Or might have been, if the film had not been so full of real horror.

DaLynda S. Wilker was a twenty-year veteran of the Houston Police Department. For three-fourths of that service she had been one of the Crime Scene Unit's specialized techs in the homicide division. The crime scene experts turn murder scenes upside down and inside and out in their meticulous collection of evidence and clues.

Wilker worked the scene at the Always & Forever Flowers, a tough job because she had known the victim personally and had bought flowers at the shop for years.

The crime scene specialist took the jury on a video tour of the floral shop. She supplemented the video views with dozens of still photographs she had snapped to capture the evidence before it was retrieved and sent to the crime lab for examination.

Wilker's narration filled in details of the flower shop's physical layout and afforded the jury some close-up looks of the murder victim as she was found.

As the video unwound on a screen before the transfixed jury, Wilker explained: "That is the exterior of the scene . . . [from] the common parking lot of the floral shop and the wedding chapel . . . This is a fence gateway and pathway to the rear of the wedding chapel, and it had a padlock and the gate was secured. It didn't show any sign of tampering.

"The floral shop is to the right. This is the front door to the floral shop. This is the wedding chapel that is to the left as you face the floral shop."

The video panned the inside of the shop, showing the partly wrapped roses in place on the counter.

Wilker continued the description of the video.

"This is a connecting hallway between the floral shop and what is a banquet-reception room where tables and chairs are set up. This is the reception-banquet room that they had adjoining the floral shop. That is the body of the victim as she was found."

The jurors could see the half-clad body of McCormick was faceup and partially on her side, one arm extended upward, one foot bent back, the white frilly bra down around her hips. Her eyes were closed.

"Those are cut crystal candy dishes [on the tables]. One had candy in it and the other was overturned as you see it. There was a balloon hanging there over the victim. [Apparently one that Mary Ringer had brought from the store.]

"Those are close-ups of what appear to be blood smears on the corner of the tablecloth."

After a close-up view of the bra that was still hooked came on the screen, O'Brien asked the evidence tech:

"What is significant to you to show that the bra is not unsnapped?"

Wilker replied, "To show that it was forcibly pulled down over her hips and it was not disconnected. It appears to have been ripped. That is a pullover sweater that was laying on the floor by the victim. The [front door] was locked, and there were exterior burglar bars across the front of it.''

O'Brien interrupted the narration of the film. ''Did you find any evidence of disarray or a scuffle in that room?''

Wilker replied, ''[Nothing] other than the one tablecloth corner being pushed up and the corner of the curtain of the window over the victim.''

Wilker identified the color 35 mm photographs she had taken, various shots of the victim's body, the sweater beside her, her stained pant legs and crotch area—one stain appeared to be a blood swath left when the killer wiped off the blade of the murder knife on the pants leg.

The technician testified she had seen at least six stab wounds on the body—at least three in front and three in back.

Speaking of the blood stains on the leg, Wilker said: ''The objects that are visible in the smears are body tissues that have been pulled out and wiped on the pants leg. In the center of the apparent blood stain on the leg you see a glob that is fatted tissue.''

She testified that she found numerous foreign, loose hairs on the body and around it, which she placed in plastic envelopes for later examination in the crime lab. She said the fake nail that came off the thumb of the victim's right hand was found beneath her body when it was turned over.

Scanning his notes, O'Brien inquired: ''Based on experience, do you have an opinion of what left the mark on the left leg of the victim's pants?''

The witness answered immediately. ''Based on my experience, it appeared to have been three swipes taken with a knife blade [being wiped off].'' She said the stain was the natural width of the murder knife later recovered in Griffith's motel room.

Everyone in the silent courtroom had to agree that the sharp evidence tech had done well in developing the evidence that would nail her friend's killer.

* * *

Deborah McCormick had been subjected to a degrading sexual attack by her killer before she died a painful, savagely inflicted death.

The graphic details were given to the jury by Dr. Tommy J. Brown, an assistant medical examiner with the Harris County Medical Examiner's Office, who did the autopsy.

He was questioned by co-prosecutor Ira Jones.

McCormick had five stab wounds in the front of her body, including four in her mid and lower chest around her left breast and one in the left upper abdomen below the left breast, the medical witness explained. The pathologist found a sixth wound in the victim's left side. Two of the blade thrusts had plunged through her heart.

The path of the knife wounds to the chest were from right to left and slightly upward, the doctor said. The gaping wound to the abdomen indicated the knife had been shoved in from right to left at a slightly downward angle.

Jones asked, "Were you able to determine when those wounds were inflicted in relation to the other wounds on her body?"

"My opinion is the three were delivered toward the end of the stabbings and after the frontal stabs occurred, and she probably was lying face down when they were delivered . . . before her demise."

The prosecutor wanted to know if the back wounds were inflicted before or after McCormick died.

"I think they were delivered right before she died," said Brown.

He explained his reason. "Around the wound margins it is not as red as on the anterior part of the body, which would indicate she had a strong blood pressure at the time the frontal wounds were delivered. The stab wounds in the back would indicate, because the margins are less red, that her blood pressure was either diminishing at the time or had stopped completely."

Jones asked, "So when the three were inflicted to the back, she was either dead or almost dead?"

"That's what I believe, yes, sir."

"So we have nine stab wounds in all, besides the two small cuts on her right hand you mentioned [described as defensive wounds and indicating McCormick struggled and grabbed at the knife]?"

"Yes, that's correct."

"Are these painful injuries, or do you know, doctor?"

"Stab wounds are painful, yes, sir."

Brown confirmed that the swab tests in the mouth, vagina, and rectum of the victim showed the presence of sperm in her mouth and vagina.

The prosecutor next asked, "Doctor, let me offer you a hypothetical situation and you tell me whether or not the wounds of the victim are consistent with this, all right?"

Jones continued, "Assume that a person such as Deborah McCormick had been forced to remove her [sweater] and her bra was pulled down—you see no stabs or cuts in her bra, do you?"

"No, sir."

"And you see just one small hole in the sweater, correct?"

"That's correct."

Jones further described the hypothetical situation. "Now, the woman is forced to get on her knees and perform oral sex on the man?"

"Yes, sir."

"Could that, then, account for the semen in her mouth?"

"Yes."

"And then he stabs her in the chest, as I am now indicating, with an upward angle, is that consistent with what you found?"

"Yes, it would be."

"And she fell on the floor on her face, and he stabbed her in the back, is that a consistent scenario with what you found?"

"Yes."

"Assuming that as he ejaculated, causing the semen to go into her mouth, she pulled away, he stabbed her and ejaculated on the body. Would that be consistent with your findings?"

"It could be, yes."

What the prosecutor was trying to show the jury was that as the victim was performing the oral sex, something happened that may have caused her to jerk away. Probably Griffith started stabbing her at that time, and his ejaculation at the time she pulled away left the string of semen stains on the left leg of her stretch pants.

Jones was through with the sordid reconstruction of the murder.

He had one more question: "Simply for the record, doctor, in your opinion what caused the death of Deborah McCormick?"

"She had two stab wounds of the chest [both into the heart] and one of the abdomen that caused death, and we term that as a homicide."

Another scientific expert, Pamela McGinnis, forensic chemist in the crime lab of the medical examiner's office, gave testimony positively linking Griffith to the murder knife and the body of slain Deborah McCormick.

McGinnis testified to being present for the autopsy on the victim early the next day at the county morgue.

Before the pink stretch pants and other clothing had been removed for the autopsy, she noticed the stains on the victim's left pants leg that the pathologist had also observed. Dr. Brown mentioned the stain and asked her to do a Poly Light test of the spots. They both thought the spots were semen stains.

"In the field I work in, serology, we are trained to look for certain kinds of stains, and one of them is a semen stain or seminal fluid."

Their suspicions were confirmed when she used the special alternate light source called a Poly Light to scan the victim's clothing. Under the light, the stains on the left leg and the crotch of the pink pants glowed or "fluoresced," as it was technically described, revealing the stains were semen, the chemist said.

Later, an acid phosphate test on the stains further verified the semen, McGinnis told the jury.

Now the state introduced the pavement-pounding results attained by the hard-working police homicide detectives and the investigators from the D.A.'s office—the paper trail that the killer had left behind him like a well-signed road pointing to Griffith.

Detectives Bob King and Hal Kennedy had done the early spade-work in the murder probe, tracing the stolen credit cards used during the high-living spree by the accused killer and his various and assorted girlfriends.

There's no spender like a spender flashing stolen plastic, the detectives had found out.

Waitresses, waiters, restaurant managers, and motel clerks had put the finger on Griffith as the black-haired man who presented the four stolen credit cards. Usually he had been accompanied by a beautiful woman, and he always signed the transaction tickets and sales slips with the name of Billy R. Ringer, the name on the cards.

Donald A. Bernard, a former Houston cop and now an investigator for the district attorney's office, ran out Griffith's hot plastic trail on a hot August day before the murder trial started, following up the previous work of King and Kennedy.

On the stand now, he reconstructed the tracking job, starting with his driving from Always & Forever Flowers to a service station eighteen and one-half miles away, through visiting a slew of department stores, first-class restaurants, and motels where he gathered up receipts and sales slips signed by the user of the stolen cards. The records showed Griffith and his unsuspecting girlfriends had lived it up.

After the fraudulent receipts were rounded up by Bernard, another D.A.'s investigator, Milton Ojeman, who was a trained handwriting analyst, compared all of the receipt signatures and concluded they had been signed by the same person with the name Billy R. Ringer.

A handwriting specimen was obtained from Griffith and compared by Ojeman to the writing on the forged receipts. Blown-up photographs of the signature on the credit card transactions and the same name that Griffith had been asked to write showed the writing matched.

The signer was identified by the various employees of the visited establishments as Griffith. Some of them remembered him as a big tipper.

Said one waitress of the well-dressed couple using the credit card: "They left me a twenty percent tip, and I remember people that leave me twenty percent."

Chapter 21

Erika Rutledge was black-haired, beautiful, and obviously sharp. One investigator had said she had the body of a topless dancer, and the brain of a first-class executive secretary. She knew a lot about law enforcement officers, too: she once had been married to one.

On the witness stand, she related her three-week fling with the handsome, black-haired man whose name was Michael Griffith. She said she met him October 4, 1994, at the topless club where she worked. She knew him as the owner of a janitorial business, although he once said he was a retired Houston cop.

She testified he deluged her with expensive gifts, red roses by the dozens, high-priced perfumes, an expensive purse, and a valuable emerald necklace, among other things.

He had moved in with her and her small daughter in their house at Sugar Land, Texas. He was irresistible, had well-groomed black hair, starched shirt and jeans, and highly polished black cowboy boots, she recalled.

As she identified Griffith in the courtroom, O'Brien asked if she noticed any difference now in his appearance.

"He's got gray hair now," she said, coolly glancing again at the defendant. She described it as "coal black," when they were going together.

Rutledge testified she was staying with him in a motel on Monday, October 10, 1994. He had called her at the motel between 9 and 11 A.M. that day, saying he was getting his black Camaro washed and waxed and suggested that she pick up her daughter at the baby-sitter's and the three of them have lunch together.

That would have been only a short time after Deborah McCormick had been savagely murdered in the floral shop. At lunch, Griffith had been as debonair and charming as ever, she recalled.

She remembered an incident a day or so later when she came out of the shower to find Griffith coming from the garage where her washing machine was running and angrily wadding up a pretty purple shirt.

He had told her, "A crazy girlfriend tore up one of my shirts."

He tossed it in a wastebasket. Rutledge said she liked the shirt and retrieved it. She saw that one shoulder in the shirt had been torn badly.

Investigators believed that was the day Griffith may have washed and thrown out the shirt he wore when he killed McCormick, that was ripped by her clawing nails as she resisted or as she fell.

"Did you ever have occasion to ride in his car and see a knife?" O'Brien asked.

"Yes, it slid out from under the seat, about three-fourths of the blade."

When shown the butcher knife found in Griffith's possession, she identified it as the knife she had seen in his car in October 1994.

She said that Griffith became frantically possessive as the

days passed, insisted she phone him regularly from the topless club. Sometimes she could not call him back when he called her at work, and he "got very upset about that," she said. She said she got upset back.

"If I can't call, I can't call you," she had snapped at him.

Rutledge said she came home one day, around October 19, and Griffith was gone. On her bathroom mirror was written in lipstick the words, "I love you."

She never heard from him again. Rutledge did not realize it then, but she was lucky to get off as lightly as she did in her relationship with Griffith.

When Amanda Lopez sat down in the witness chair, the jury saw another very shapely and pretty brunette, a hairdresser by trade. She was the one who had dyed Griffith's hair dark brown, almost black, a color job that later would help identify his hair at the murder scene.

She recalled it well. "I dyed his hair three or four times, anyway about once a month. Dyed it dark brown, but it was almost black. He didn't like the gray in his hair."

Lopez said she broke up with Griffith in September 1994. She did not tell why—she would relate that terrifying experience later on in the trial when she returned to the stand.

Yet, in early October, she tried to page Griffith. "I just wanted to see how he was doing—if he was doing okay." Casey O'Brien did not understand why she ever would have been sympathetic enough to care, after what Griffith did to her. The prosecutor said much later, "A woman who has that personality—you know, the personality of liking men that do that, then I guess they don't get over the guy."

In late October Lopez and Griffith were back together, setting out on a week-long spree of doing the better restaurants, staying at the upper-class motels, and Griffith—as he had done when they first met months before—showering her with high-cost gifts. He used credit cards to pay for them, she recalled.

That first steak and wine dinner they shared in the glow of their reconciliation was at a popular restaurant about lunchtime. The date was October 28, 1994—the day that sometime after that lunch Griffith went to the savings and loan branch bank and robbed and shot down Sandra Denton.

Griffith and Lopez went out to dinner that night. She had no knowledge of his afternoon foray that culminated with the woman teller being shot twice in the head.

The pretty hairdresser and her smooth-talking lover made plans to go to Las Vegas, Nevada, and get married. But first she wanted to visit her two daughters one more time, to tell them she would send for them later. It was the beginning of the end of Griffith's freedom.

She testified about how the police closed in when she arrived at her mother's house to pick up the girls to take them to breakfast.

"As I pulled up in the driveway, all of a sudden I saw a bunch of cars gathered around me and detectives. It scared me because I didn't expect it."

She told the officers where Griffith was staying.

The party was over.

Detective Bob King took the jury through the day that began with intercepting Lopez at her mother's home and the arrest of Griffith about mid-morning at the Holiday Inn that capped an intense investigation by King and his partner Kennedy. He described the finding of the butcher knife under the mattress and the stolen credit cards in Griffith's wallet after the suspect had been fully warned of his rights and had signed a consent-to-search form.

Five days after the arrest, King related, he went to the Harris County Jail with a search warrant obtained that morning from a judge and obtained samples of Griffith's blood, saliva, and hairs that the suspect pulled from his head and pubic region.

It had taken King and his cohorts less than a month to

nab the ex-deputy murder suspect, a grim-faced, somber, non-talkative type who knew all the questions before they were asked and knew all the routine legal warnings by heart from giving them himself to countless offenders.

King kept his professional cool from start to finish of the murder investigation, had made what prosecutor O'Brien described as "a highly professional, excellent witness." But the capable detective kept something well-concealed: he despised this one-time law enforcement officer who had tarnished his badge in the darkest of all evil ways.

Taking the stand was Rideun Hilleman, a chemist with the Houston Police Crime Lab who worked in the trace evidence section.

She had made the tests on the foreign hair strands found at the murder scene on the body and on the floor near the victim and had compared those hairs with the hair samples obtained from Griffith by King.

Hilleman told the jury that when she made a comparative analysis of hairs she looked for such similarities as basic color and thickness, and internal characteristics such as the size of the pigment granule as in the medulla, which is the central core running down the center of the hair.

In the case of the loose hairs recovered at the scene and the hair samples from Griffith, the chemist had an even more blatant identifying aid.

The first thing she saw was that one of the crime scene hairs and Griffith's sample hairs had been dyed. In his mind O'Brien said a silent thanks for the color job by Lopez.

Hilleman said, referring to her notes: "In examining the head hairs [from Griffith's sample] I discovered that the hairs were color-treated—that was the first obvious, somewhat unusual feature of the hair. It was dyed very dark brown.

"Hairs that were not dyed ranged from natural gray to dark brown color. Dyed hair goes from one color to another completely different color very quickly,'' the hair expert said. ''The color change is very, very distinct.''

The prosecutor asked: ''Did you look for the same features in the unknown hair sample from the crime scene?''

''Yes, I did.''

''Did you discover any that appeared to have the same feature?''

Looking at her notes, Hilleman said, ''There was one that had the same features. It was a dyed hair, and the dye color was the same dye color from the known portion of Griffith's hair. All characteristics of the hair were consistent with the known sample [the hair found on the victim's body].''

Hilleman said she concluded that the hairs at the scene were consistent with the known samples and could have come from the same person.

During his cross-examination of Hilleman, defense attorney Cunningham asked, ''It is impossible, is it not, to state with reasonable scientific certainty that a particular hair came from a definite source, and the most that can be said is that it is *consistent* with hair from a known source?''

''Yes, that it is consistent.''

''When you say it is consistent with a known source, [that] could very easily mean that it is consistent with a number of known sources?''

''The possibility exists because of the biological variation of hair that another person could have some of the same characteristics, yes.''

Cunningham pursued the ''most you can say'' issue: ''As a matter of fact, the standard comparison vehicle is that the most that we can determine is the race and the gender and the portion of the body from where the hair came?''

''Those are characteristics that can be determined, as well as the comparison.''

Casey O'Brien asked on re-direct examination: ''In the fourteen years that you have been doing this, how many instances have you actually seen when you have hair from one known source and hair from another known source that have all the same characteristics?''

''I have never seen two samples of hair on two different people that have all the same characteristics. I have seen two people who have *some* characteristics that overlap, but I have never seen two samples that are *exactly* the same.''

O'Brien pressed on to make his point for the jury. ''Were there any dissimilar characteristics you found in regard to the hair from State Exhibits 76 and 77 [crime scene hair and Griffith's hair]?''

''No, there were not.''

''So when you say that your opinion is that they came from the same person, it is a very strong opinion, is it not?''

''Yes, it is.''

It might be said that the prosecution had Griffith by the short hairs.

The expert witness who would tie the hangman's knot, so to speak, in the state's case against Michael Griffith was Marita Carrejo, a scholarly-appearing serologist in the police crime lab. She was an expert in DNA testing, a baffling science at best to the average person, but one that is accepted in the medical field as a reliable and valid theory of science.

To question this witness, Assistant District Attorney Ira Jones again took over.

DNA is a field that requires thorough technical knowledge by anyone attempting to translate the scientific jargon by asking questions that produce witness answers that a jury of lay people can understand. He should almost know enough to run a DNA test himself.

Jones had made a study of DNA—talked with experts and read textbooks about the procedures—for the purpose of examining this witness, and other similar witnesses in past trials.

Even with a good understanding of DNA, it was a subject that had to be reviewed, or "boned up" on, before any trial involving the complicated DNA techniques with names such as RFLP and PCR, sounding like something from a Washington, D.C., bureaucrat's phone book.

During the direct examination by the prosecutor, Carrejo said that her job was to test body fluids, including blood, sweat, and semen, using highly refined DNA procedures.

Linking a DNA type found in stains at a crime scene to a suspect is done by excluding the largest number of people in a certain area of population who would not have that specific DNA type, the witness testified.

"DNA is unique to individuals," Carrejo carefully explained. "The only two people that would have identical DNA would be identical twins.

"So we can type the DNA in an unknown sample of bodily fluid [such as found at a crime scene] and determine whether it matches a known sample that we have from some individual in a case."

Once she identifies a DNA type from blood or some other fluid sample, she compares her DNA test result with a population frequency table compiled by the FBI. The agency has typed large numbers of people to determine the frequency of different DNA types within large population areas of the United States.

The area she compared her DNA finding with was the huge Harris County area of some three-and-one-half million residents. For comparison purposes, that figure was reduced further by comparing the DNA type within its particular racial group in the same area.

Carrejo gave what she called a simplified example: "Say I determine this blood sample is type AB, the least common type. I can look at the FBI table and see that it has been determined that the frequency of type AB in the specific population area is only about four percent. Thus, I have eliminated the other 96 percent of the population from whom this particular type of blood could not have come."

The prosecutors hoped the jurors were listening carefully and not of a mind-set that this DNA stuff was something that nobody could understand if it was explained all day long.

The nitty gritty of Carrejo's testimony concerned DNA tests she had made on the black-handled butcher knife found in Griffith's motel room; the stains on McCormick's pink stirrup pants; stains on the panty hose the victim was wearing; the cotton swabs that were inserted in the slain woman's mouth, vagina, and rectum to test for the presence of semen; and blood samples taken from McCormick, Griffith, and Tom Atwood, the murder victim's boyfriend.

A truly delicate piece of work by Carrejo had positively linked Griffith to the murder of McCormick with test results that revealed the DNA types of both Griffith and McCormick were on the butcher knife. The results showed conclusively that the knife found in the suspect's motel room between the box spring and mattress was the murder weapon that ripped out the life of the pretty florist.

The chemist had used a DNA testing technique known as D1S80 on the knife. It is the most effective PCR procedure when the blood sample to be tested is extremely limited, the witness pointed out.

"I saw what appeared to be blood where the blade meets the handle, a tiny area on both the front and back of the knife," Carrejo said. "Even though the knife had been wiped free of blood, this would not have affected the area where this minute amount was found, right up against the hilt."

The delicate test confirmed it was human blood, a mixture of two different blood types. The largest concentration in the blood was consistent with the murder victim's DNA type. There was a much weaker concentration that was consistent with Griffith's DNA.

Prosecutor Jones posed a question that had to be made clear to the jury members. For effectiveness, Jones asked the question in a skeptical manner.

"Explain to me, if you can, how a person's DNA can get

on a knife when stabbing someone even though they themselves were not cut?''

He picked up the knife, stabbing the air with it and asked, ''If I was repeatedly stabbing her in the heart and chest and back, and hitting bone, how could my blood get on here without ever cutting myself?''

The blood scientist had a ready explanation. ''If you are familiar with swords and other cutting weapons, there is usually some kind of protection for the hand of a swordsman because what happens—if the knife hits some kind of hard object—the hand would tend to slide on to the blade, which might cause bleeding, or perspiration or other cellular materials to be fluffed onto the knife.''

Jones pushed the point further. ''Is it possible that just the violence of the thrust and the blade stopping suddenly against a hard object such as bone, could that cause bodily fluid transmitting DNA onto the knife hilt?''

Carrejo nodded. ''The body fluid would be perspiration that carries cellular material.''

''So it's possible to get your DNA on a knife handle without actually bleeding?''

''It is possible.''

In fact, she was certain that was what happened. Griffith's sweat had tabbed him as the killer of Deborah McCormick.

The DNA expert continued to hammer the evidentiary nails into Michael Griffith, definitely identifying him as the merciless knifer and sex assailant who ravaged and butchered McCormick.

She had compared the DNA on the oral swabs to the DNA in Griffith's blood sample obtained from him by Detective Bob King. The DNA in sperm cells found in McCormick's mouth matched the genetic markers in Griffith's blood sample, Carrejo testified. DNA markers are found in blood, saliva, sweat, or semen, the witness explained.

His DNA also was matched to that in the semen stains on

the victim's pants leg. She said another stain on the leg was consistent with the DNA types of both McCormick and Griffith.

A convoluted test result reported by Carrejo was the stain in the crotch of the pink stretch pants: it contained DNA that was consistent with the DNA of Griffith but also with the DNA of McCormick's boyfriend, Atwood.

The presence of the boyfriend's DNA in the stain gave rise to an unexplained mystery for the jury, since it had been established that neither the panty hose nor the stretch pants had been removed from the victim, or even disturbed, according to the crime scene investigation. This meant that her killer did not have vaginal intercourse with her.

The DNA type of Atwood was found inside the panty hose, said Carrejo. Griffith's DNA was not found on the panty hose. Carrejo testified she had taken a blood sample from Atwood at the crime lab on December 13, 1994, to use in the comparisons made with the crime scene stains.

Under further questioning by Jones, Carrejo testified that when the less-common DNA type of Griffith was compared to the FBI population tables it showed that his DNA classification could be expected to be present in one out of one-half million Caucasians in the three-and-one-half million population figure of Harris County. The three-and-one-half million people included all races in the county.

Which meant, said the DNA expert, that 99.998 percent of the entire population of Harris County would not have the same DNA type as Griffith's and the type found on the victim's body and clothing. As prosecutors would point out to the jury, that startling percentage figure was about as "beyond a reasonable doubt" as could be found.

Chapter 22

On the day that Tom Atwood was to be called as a witness to give urgently needed testimony, he did not show up. O'Brien kept checking with the court bailiff as the DNA testimony by Carrejo neared its conclusion. Casey O'Brien was worried.

O'Brien liked Atwood. The prosecutor had seen how the shocking murder of Deborah McCormick had left Atwood devastated—torn apart physically and emotionally.

The boyfriend could not eat, sleep, or do his job well. The tragedy seemed to have destroyed everything Atwood had. In all of his years as a prosecutor, O'Brien could not recall seeing anybody as wiped out by the death of a loved one as was Atwood.

The assistant district attorney offered to get professional counseling for him, but this idea was turned down. All that Atwood wanted now was to be left alone by the outside world.

He was a difficult man to know. He was a private individual who mostly kept his thoughts and emotions to himself, O'Brien observed as he came to know him.

When he was getting ready for trial, O'Brien had told Atwood that he wanted him to testify. Atwood's testimony was crucial now that the DNA findings left a puzzling question about the intimate panty hose stains.

It was also important to show the jury the kind of relationship that McCormick and Atwood had enjoyed for nearly six years. When first questioned during the pre-trial preparation, Atwood said they considered their romance far more than a casual relationship. They thought of themselves as married; he described their love affair as that of "life mates," though no formal marriage ceremony had been conducted.

When O'Brien first asked him to be a witness, the boyfriend refused. His face full of anguish, Atwood explained that he "couldn't keep it together" to testify about their intimate love that had been everything. He said Deborah McCormick was the woman he had been seeking all his life and never found.

"I can't even stand to think about how she died like that—so unexpectedly and so terribly horrible—without breaking down completely," he candidly told O'Brien.

"We have to have your testimony, Tom, or we are in trouble," O'Brien said.

O'Brien enlisted the help of Atwood's private secretary. She was close to her boss in strictly a professional and platonic way. They were good friends who made a good work team, and O'Brien knew that Atwood listened to her concerning all the important things that came up at the office.

O'Brien, in stating his problem, told the secretary: "I need him to testify. He definitely has got to let the jury know about that time of his life, the kind of relationship that two respectable middle-aged people had together. Please try to change his mind about not testifying."

Finally, Atwood agreed to take the witness stand. It probably was the hardest thing he ever faced.

* * *

But on this day when he was next on the witness schedule Atwood still had not shown up. O'Brien phoned Atwood's secretary.

"Don't worry," the secretary said. "I think I know where he is, and I'll get him there."

She said that Atwood, when he wanted to get away from everything, had a habit of simply going to the racetrack and losing himself in the frenetic atmosphere of the races.

True to her word, the loyal secretary arrived soon with Atwood in tow. She had gotten in her car, found him at the racetrack where she thought he would be, and almost had to lead him by the ear to the courtroom.

After Carrejo finished up, O'Brien called Atwood to the witness chair.

Speaking slowly and quietly, he identified himself on the stand as assistant vice president of an international trade company that operated ships between the United States and South America.

"How long had you known Deborah McCormick?" prosecutor O'Brien asked.

"Five to six years."

"You remember going to the police station on December 13, 1994 [about two months after the murder]?"

"Yes."

"What did they do there [in the crime laboratory]?"

"They took a sample of my blood."

"Will you tell the jury the kind of relationship you and Deborah had over the six years?"

Now Atwood showed the strain. Tears came to his eyes. "It was the best there could be. I mean, all your life you look for somebody, and you find somebody you think you are going to spend the rest of your life with . . ."

At this point defense attorney Cunningham objected to the witness's answer, claiming it fell into the category of victim impact testimony.

"I respectively object to his testimony about his relationship with McCormick. I submit to the court it is victim impact evidence and it is not appropriate."

Judge Keel sustained the objection.

O'Brien responded, "If I might, judge, may I explain to you what the relevancy is?"

"Okay."

"The relevancy is that I anticipate he is going to testify that he had a sexual relationship with the victim the night before. I don't believe that it is fair to the victim to place that circumstance in a vacuum, to characterize that person, the victim, as an individual who had a fanciful affair the night before she was murdered, and we are entitled to put it into its proper perspective. I'm not trying to elicit emotion out of this man, but I think [the jurors] need to know that."

"Okay, and I agree," said the judge. "But let's not go into the victim impact, which is what it was sounding like."

The judge instructed the witness, "Okay, Mr. Atwood. You need to listen to the question and answer just the question that is asked."

"Okay."

O'Brien, his voice tinged with sympathetic understanding of Atwood's personal ordeal, told the witness: "If you will, just listen to the questions that I ask. I'm not trying to make this emotional for you. The relationship that you had, you described that—I'll lead you a little bit—would you describe that as a very close relationship, a warm relationship?"

"Very warm, very close, yes."

"Did Deborah McCormick live with you?"

"No, we maintained separate residences."

O'Brien said, "After work, would you spend your evenings together at one of your residences?"

"Yes."

O'Brien wanted to clearly emphasize to the jury that the couple's love affair had not been a one-night stand sort of relationship. "Was that every day?"

"Pretty much every day, yes."

"When you were not working, you and Debbie McCormick were together?"

"Yes."

"Now, again, I'm going to lead a little bit."

"Okay."

"Did that relationship include a sexual relationship?"

"Yes."

"Over the course of the many years that you were together?" Again, the stress by the prosecutor on the permanency of the couple's intimate relationship.

"Yes."

"I want to ask you specifically about the evening and night you were together on October 9, 1994. On that evening before her death, were you with her?"

"Yes."

"When were you with her? During the whole day, or just that night? The night would have been on a Sunday."

Atwood swallowed and cleared his throat. His eyes were teary again. "We went up to the lake that day and then we came back to my house."

O'Brien paused for emphasis before he asked his next question. "Sometime during the course of the evening of October 9, did you have sexual relations with Debbie McCormick?"

"Yes."

Why Atwood's DNA had been found in the sperm stain on the panty hose of the murder victim was cleared. Also, O'Brien believed the jurors had sensed the depth of Atwood's and McCormick's life together these past years.

"Pass the witness," O'Brien said.

The defense had no questions.

O'Brien and Jones felt it was time to wrap up. The chemist-cops had done their jobs. They had tied the murder weapon, the sperm in the victim's mouth and on her pants leg, and the loose hairs left at the crime scene to Michael Griffith. The distressed boyfriend had kept his word and had been a highly effective witness.

Also, the state had shown through Mary Ringer's heartbreaking testimony that Griffith was familiar with the daily routine at the floral shop, was known by the victim and her mother, and undoubtedly would have been admitted by McCormick through the locked door.

At this point in the guilt or innocence stage of the trial, the state had removed any doubt beyond a reasonable degree that Michael Griffith was Deborah McCormick's murderer, in the opinion of the co-prosecutors.

Considering the strong DNA testimony, and the undisputed facts that Griffith had the butcher knife that was identified as the murder weapon and also the four credit cards stolen from the victim's purse at the time of the slaying, it can be understood why the defense did not contest the conclusions from the state's evidence.

After O'Brien announced the state was resting its case, Judge Keel asked: "What sayeth the defense?"

Cunningham said, "We have a matter to bring to the court's attention."

Judge Keel turned to the jury: "Members of the jury, I am going to excuse you for the evening. I request that you return tomorrow . . . You are under the same instructions you have been under throughout the trial. Don't discuss this trial with friends. Don't watch or listen to news reports about the case. The jury is excused."

After the jury had left the courtroom, Cunningham told the judge that he was going to ask for an instructed verdict of not guilty because the state had not proven its case.

After listening to him briefly, Keel said she would deny the motion.

With the court officially in session again, and on record, Cunningham said:

"On behalf of Mr. Griffith, your honor, at this time we move for an instructed verdict of acquittal and urge to the court that the state has failed to prove each of the elements of capital murder. The court has heard the evidence and you know what they are asking for, and I don't think any arguments are necessary."

Judge Keel replied: "Denied."

The first part of the trial was over. Tomorrow, both sides would present their closing arguments to the jury, which then would decide if Griffith was guilty or not guilty of capital murder in the killing of Deborah McCormick.

After consulting the attorneys, Judge Keel declared each side would have one hour to present their closing arguments.

Then the punishment phase would begin—depending, of course, on the jury's verdict. But not even the defense had much doubt what that verdict would be.

Chapter 23

The next day, the state waived its right to give the first summation argument.

Defense Attorney Charlton stepped before the jury box.

"I will be extremely brief. As you no doubt inferred from the voir dire and as we told you in the opening statement, this case solely turns on punishment issues.

"The evidence you heard leads to one conclusion. You took an oath to base your verdict on the evidence, and if, as I assume, all of you do that, you took that oath seriously, you must base your verdict on the evidence and it is the only issue that you have."

The attorney paused to let his remarks sink in. As much as he hated it, he knew himself that the evidence was stacked solidly against his client. There was only one way that a reasonable juror could go. But he wanted to get the jury to thinking seriously about what the defense battle plan was from the start: to save Griffith's life.

If they could do that, they had won a legal victory.

"I stand up here only to reiterate again, as I told you during voir dire, and again as I told you in the opening statement, that you keep an open mind because this case revolves around issues and they are to be generated during the punishment phase.

"I want to thank you for your attention, and you will not hear from us until after you have finished your deliberation as to the guilt or innocence phase."

He walked to the counsel table and sat down.

Casey O'Brien, as he rose and took his place before the jury, was preparing himself for a performance. He knew in his own mind that even though he was arguing whether the defendant was guilty or innocent, there was a manner for doing that.

It was a manner that, not even subtly, could start the jurors thinking even before the punishment phase about what a horribly cruel, depraved, cold-blooded murder this had been. Establish that convincingly to a jury—the horror of the crime—and the state would have taken its first big step toward affecting how the jurors were going to vote when it came to the choice of either life in prison or death for Michael Griffith.

There could not have been a better qualified prosecutor for the act on which O'Brien was about to raise the curtain. As O'Brien had explained to a writer, "I'm a good, old-fashioned Irishman and hell-raiser. I'm the one who screams and hollers, jumps up and down, gets on the floor on my knees, points the weapon at my ear, stabs at the jury box with the knife."

The first thing that O'Brien did, however, was to answer the question he knew was uppermost in the minds of the jurors: the defense had all but admitted outright that Griffith did it, in spite of the not guilty plea to the charge. So why the hell does the state have to take up our time to go over the case again, and why can't we just go out of here and take a vote?

O'Brien began, "You perhaps wonder why I'm up here, why Mr. Jones will be up here speaking to you for another thirty minutes after me, why we spent two days putting on some twenty witnesses, considering the opening you heard and the kind of closing you heard [from the defense]. Why not let you go back there and sign on the dotted line and get it over with?

"Well, the reason we put on the evidence is because we have to. They are entitled to a fair trial."

With that explained, O'Brien raised the curtain on his performance. He warned that he was going to give a graphic and upsetting description of the events that took place in the usually pleasant flower shop that became a shop of horrors.

"I am going to tell you, based on the evidence, what I think happened."

In the few seconds that O'Brien paused, the courtroom was silent with anticipation.

He started out quietly enough, recounting how Deborah McCormick and Mary Ringer arrived for work early that morning of Monday, October 10, 1994, and went about their usual chores until Ringer left to pick up some supplies. The prosecutor said he wanted to tell the jury exactly what took place during that half hour before Ringer returned.

He warned again it would be graphic.

"Perhaps ten minutes after Mary Ringer left, a man arrived, a man Debbie McCormick knew, a man to whom Debbie McCormick had sold flowers on numerous occasions, roses they were. He went up to the secured door of the flower shop, and he rapped on the door, and do you see this in your mind, folks: Debbie McCormick smiled and approached the door seeing a person she knew, a person she conversed with before, probably chatted with, standing at the door wanting to come in, and, as she probably surmised, to buy flowers.

"She let him in.

"And you can imagine for a few minutes or so there was cordial conversation and that he indicated he wanted a half dozen of red roses—red, long-stemmed roses depicted in this photograph." O'Brien picked it up and walked to the jury box with it.

"And she probably went to the cooler and extracted the roses and put them on the counter. Probably there were a couple of minutes of friendly, cordial conversation, a valued customer. Someone she knew.''

Walking over to the exhibit table, O'Brien picked up the butcher knife identified as the murder weapon. ''Now, I don't know where this was hidden. I don't know where it was tucked in back there. I don't know whether it was in his pocket, but it was concealed and he brought it with him. And he pulled it, and he threatened her, demanding money.

''First, robbery. And I tell you why I know that happened first. Because there wasn't any blood on the purses.

''There wasn't any blood behind the counter, and that's why he went through the purses first and got the money, $400 and some dollars and put it in his pocket. And he rifled through Debbie McCormick's purse, and got the credit cards of Billy and Mary Ringer and stuck them in his pocket while he had the knife on Debbie McCormick.

''Premeditation, deliberateness. Could have left then, he could have left. Goal accomplished. No, no! [O'Brien's voice was rising; he flourished the knife] And then the thought . . . knife in back, this knife held at her back. I don't know what he said to her. I don't know what he told her he was going to do to her.

''I don't know whether she knew at that moment and time she was going to die. She didn't go willingly that twenty paces [down the hall to the reception room]. A sharp left and turn, as you get into the room where people celebrate their wedding . . . knife at her back, pushing her to the left, pushing her to the left through that hall.

''You know she had a sweater on. He got her to the point where they faced each other. I don't know how that happened. I don't know whether he demanded that she turn or whether she turned on her own. But at that point, in the middle of this, he was going to rape her and perhaps demanded she take this off.'' He held up the pink sweater.

''She didn't comply and he jabbed her once, right there, [indicating small hole in the sweater]. And with this other hand he grabbed the sweater with sufficient force, folks, to do this, to tear it, tear it like that, grabbing her bra at the same time, tearing it in the center, not unhooking it in the back, forcing it down to her waist.

"She fell to the floor, folks. She fell to the floor with the force of the heave that caused her to have that sweater pulled up from the shoulders, and there she is on the floor and she has that knife pointed at her." O'Brien dropped to his knees and held the knife pointing at himself.

"The assailant pulls his turgid penis from his pants and at knife-point, folks, insist that she comply. Surely she had to, she had no choice.

"That sweater has now been pulled completely off her body, over her breasts, her bra is now around her mid-section, and he forces that evil, deviant intercourse upon her. As he ejaculates, folks, she is stabbed." O'Brien stabbed with the long-blade knife as he spoke.

"She pulls away, and I tell you why I know that." Picking up a photograph of the stains on the pants leg, he turned back to the jury displaying it and saying, "this is not perhaps the best photograph, but she pulls away." He dropped to his knees again. "Semen is scattered along her leg as she is on her knees like this. She pulls away. Semen is left in her mouth. Semen is now on her trousers as she pulls away from him, and he begins to stab her with force [thrusting over and over with the knife].

"Dr. Brown tells you that one of the stab wounds penetrated two inches through skin, through organs and through her heart, and she is on her knees. Her hands are in front of her. She received wounds on her right hand trying to defend herself.

"She has a minute to live, and I know that, folks. I know that from the blood. I know that she was on her knees as she was stabbed because it dripped down from the wounds, folks—it dripped right on to the front of her pants. You know that she was on her knees. She grabbed him, grabbed him and managed to latch onto the shirt with her right hand with enough force so that it tears that shirt, with enough force so that fingernail comes off, and folks, with enough force because he utilized his weapon so that blood is all over it.'' Again, stabbing with the knife, O'Brien exclaimed, ''As you thrust the knife six times in somebody with enough force to penetrate the heart, you have blood on it. It will backlash.''

The prosecutor's rising voice now was pitched with the tone of incredulity as he thundered: ''Is he through? No! She's dying, she's dying! She's on her knees dying and perhaps still grasping his shirt, and she falls from her knees forward.

''What did he do? Three more jabs to the back insures that this lady dies a brutal, horrible, violent death!

''I'm angry! I guess that's apparent! But then the assailant, he's not through! He's not through! Then he has the very wherewithall—perhaps that's the polite way to say it—the wherewithall as this knife now has blood and tissue and whatever kind of material on it. He has the wherewithall to take the knife three times, wipes it across the pants leg of his victim!

''Debbie McCormick has died! She's dead! He's cleaning up his murder weapon!

''It's now pretty close to 8:30 in the morning. Debbie McCormick is lying dead in the pool of her own blood in the corner of the reception room. Mary Ringer comes back. The assailant was gone. He beat it ten minutes earlier perhaps, got in his car and left.

''Debbie, where are you Debbie? Down that twenty paces in the hall. My God! My God! That's her forty-four-year-old daughter lying in a pool of blood dead! The assailant is already ten miles away, on his way up to the highway west to a small service station. She goes and checks her daughter.

''She knows she's been murdered! She gets on the telephone to call the police, 911. She runs back to her daughter. Does CPR. Her daughter is dead, folks! Her daughter is dead! The CPR is useless! She's dead! She tries to breathe life back into her daughter who has been dead for fifteen minutes already, She is all bloody from trying to help her daughter.

"The SOB who did this is already using the credit cards ten miles or so away. He is using the booty already.

"There was a robbery! There was a rape! There was murder! They were all intentional. They were all premeditated.

"That makes the crime, folks, capital murder. Mr. Jones is going to tell you who did it. Thank you. That's all I have, judge."

O'Brien slowly sat down, obviously emotionally drained as were the jurors and courtroom spectators who had sat transfixed by his dramatic portrayal of the vicious murder.

Pointing out the importance of making reasonable inferences from evidence, Jones reminded the jury that the judge had instructed the jurors they must determine the accused specifically intended to cause the death in order to find him guilty of capital murder.

"What reasonable inference can you draw from this evidence?" Jones asked. "The dying, the nine wounds, count them . . . two piercing the heart after she was dead. She was already dead, and he wanted to make sure she was very, very dead.

"That is very specific intent—to stab people after you killed them, to make sure they are dead. This wasn't an accident. Why did he have to make sure that she's dead? Because she knew him; think about that. Not leave a witness behind to testify against him. She wouldn't have let him in the shop unless she knew him, you know that.

"He came in, obviously buys the flowers. He's been there before, you know that. Not only did Mary Ringer tell you that: remember, we showed you a receipt that came out of his car's console with the name Always & Forever Flowers on it. Proof that he had been there before."

Jones said that Griffith robbed her, and "then that wasn't enough. He had other plans. She had to die, folks."

The prosecutor talked about the "horrible things that went on in that banquet room."

"He marched her in there. He said, 'Take off your [sweater].' You know one thing—she wouldn't do it. Mr. O'Brien showed you the ripping. There's one more hole in there. He said take off your [sweater] and it's reasonable to tell you she told him no.

"He just stabbed her instead. 'I told you to take off the [sweater]!' He forced her to take that [sweater] off. This is probably when the fight started, we don't know. Yes, she fought him through . . . broke a fingernail, tore her [sweater] . . . torn bra . . . torn shirt. Her children and family, they are entitled to know that: she fought him all the way."

Jones reminded the jury of Erika Rutledge's testimony about retrieving Griffith's favorite, brand new, torn shirt after he washed and discarded it.

"We suspect from the evidence that this is when it happened, the ripping of the shirt. He forced her to perform that awful sex act upon him. And I submit from the evidence to show you that she fought him over that. He had her get down on her knees. It's reasonable that he forced her by grabbing her. How else could his sperm get in the mouth? He forced her to do this terrible thing.

"I suspect from the evidence that as he began to ejaculate she pulled away. If you look at Pat McGinnis's photograph of the pants leg, the circled streaks of the ejaculation on the clothes area.

"Look at the angle. If you look very closely—a glob and a streak. It hit the leg, that's what happened. Then he begins to stab her, repeatedly, very viciously. She falls. He's not going to leave any witnesses."

But he did, Jones said.

"What happened is he left a hair by her body. He left the DNA in her mouth and his DNA on the pants. Think about the inferences of the premeditation of killing, murdering. He had to bring that knife. Mary Ringer told you it didn't come out of the shop. So he had to bring that."

Why did he have to bring a knife just to buy flowers, asked Jones.

Answering his own question, Jones said, "Because he thought about using that knife a long time ago, thought about it even before he got there. He knew what he was going to do before he ever came there. Clearly and calculatingly, he knew what he was going to do.

"She fought. He wiped the blood off from his knife on her pants. But he forgot the DNA around the hilt. There was a part of Debbie's DNA with his on that knife.

"And afterwards, Griffith had his car 'detailed,' washed inside and outside, and he covered up the evidence. See, he knew what he was doing."

Then came the reminder of the state's big hammer. "We have to prove his guilt beyond a reasonable doubt. What the lady told us is that we have proved [through the DNA results and FBI tables] to the point of 99.9998 percent that it was Griffith's DNA found in the victim's mouth and on her clothing. We have excluded most of the people in the United States except him.

"How many of those had the murder weapon? Had the stolen credit cards with them? Had been to the Always & Forever Flowers shop?

"You probably will never be so sure of anything in your life as this man's guilt," Jones declared.

Lastly, Jones told the jury that the war against crime is not won in the streets by the police. "Rather, it's won in juries, just like this one. You see, if you don't do it, then nothing gets done. . . . If you don't do anything about this, then the brutality and the horror just go on and on. Only you can stop crimes like this with your verdict. Later you can say, I found that man guilty because he was guilty, and I'm proud of it.

"Thank you."

The jury left the courtroom and began deliberations on the fate of Griffith.

It wasn't long before the jury returned to the courtroom. The jury foreman read the verdict:

"We, the jury, find the defendant, Michael Durwood Griffith, guilty of capital murder as charged in the indictment."

Judge Keel thanked the jury for its verdict. Then she said, "The punishment phase of this case will start as soon as you have a cup of coffee and take a little break."

Chapter 24

The prosecution was ready to open Griffith's mental can of worms—his bizarre, brutally violent, mentally and physically abusive relationship with his wives and his harem of girlfriends—all exes now who had nothing but stories of terror to tell the jury.

Deborah McCormick, who knew him least of all, never had a chance to personally tell her story of horror. Pathologists, forensic and laboratory experts, and terribly ghoulish and bloody photographs had had to do her talking, and they had done them well.

Almost from the beginning of all of his relationships with women, beginning with his own mother, Griffith had an underlying, seething hatred for women (a polite investigator described it as "a basic disregard for women"), a burning desire to dominate them and control them and hurt them and eventually to kill one of them.

There lurked inside Griffith some dark and strange evil that all of the psychologists and psychiatrists would never satisfactorily diagnose or explain. Inside the once competent and award-winning lawman was a killer waiting to come out.

His defense team would argue that Griffith's beloved law enforcement career kept that lurking and murderous nature on a leash. When his career was shattered, the killer inside him burst forth like a demonic force—at least, so said the defense.

Over the next few days, the state would take serious issue with that contention.

Much later, when the trial fireworks were over, Casey O'Brien would philosophize about the effectiveness of psychiatric testimony in the defense of the accused, not only in this case but any other murder case where it so often was used.

Speaking softly as he does when not arguing in ingenious arguments before a jury, O'Brien said, "I don't think psychiatrists are all that significant. I think they play a big role in capital cases, and I think that is a defensive ploy that hardly ever works.

"Typically, in a capital case, the first time a guy sees a psychiatrist is because a defense attorney sends him over. Then they develop some kind of malady as a result of a couple of tests and an interview. And that's just going to backfire on them most of the time.

"You can't tell what's going on in somebody's head as the result of a few subjective tests."

The state opened its punishment phase testimony by recalling Amanda Lopez, a slam-bam witness in every respect, as the jury would soon realize. In direct examination by O'Brien, Lopez related her life with Michael Griffith during those months before she had left him and then came back to him in late October 1994.

After meeting him as a customer who came into the beauty salon where she worked, she and her young daughters had lived with him for several months after Griffith moved into their home about March 1994.

At first came the usual barrage of gifts and compliments, followed not long afterward by fanatic possessiveness, domination, and physical abuse.

It was the morning of September 19, 1994, that something terrible happened that broke up the love affair until Lopez went back a little over a month later.

She testified, her words gripping the jury in attentiveness:

"I had been going to some special color classes I was taking, and that morning I was in a hurry to get to class. And I had not finished my notes, kind of like homework, so I was cooking breakfast and trying to get my kids off to school.

"And Michael said, 'Well, I'll help you write your notes down,' and I said okay. I cooked breakfast and my kids left for school and then I served him a plate of breakfast.

" 'Here go ahead and eat, and let me take over my notes,' I said. I felt like I needed to write them down so I would know what I was going to look at anyway. But he went ahead and finished the notes. He got mad, got up from the table, grabbed the plate of food and threw it into the floor.

"I looked at him and I said, 'What did I do?'

"And he said, 'I try to do things for you. I try to help you and you don't appreciate anything I do for you.' And he was just raving. He had given me a TV set in August, and he went into my room and he lifted it up over his head, threw it on the kitchen floor and it just shattered into pieces.

"And I said, 'You know what? You need to just leave! You need to get out! I want you out of my house now! I've already been through this with my ex, and I do not need this again in my life!' So I just said, 'Get the hell out of here! Find a place to go! You're not staying with me anymore!'

"I don't know how it happened because we were in the kitchen. But I ended up in my daughters' bedroom. I guess he was so enraged, he grabbed me. Let me back up a little bit. He had given me some flowers. They were there on my table.

And I picked the flowers out of the vase and just threw them at his face. I was so mad. I just said, 'Get the hell out of here!'

"And he said, 'Well, you don't satisfy me anyway!' And I said . . . something that upset him and he came after me. All I remember was I was in my daughters' bedroom and I was on the floor and he was beating me. He was on top of me, hitting me with his fist."

O'Brien interrupted her monologue. "Where was he hitting you?"

"He hit me on my breast, and I just remember him on top of me and hitting me on my breast. He had my arm twisted. He wouldn't stop. I didn't think he was going to stop. I didn't think I was going to be there for my daughters when they got home. I thought they were going to see me there on the floor. And I said, 'Stop, Michael! Please stop!' " Lopez was sobbing loudly as she tried to speak.

"Just a moment, you want to take a break, ma'am?"

"Yeah."

Judge Keel said, "Let's have a five-minute break, ladies and gentlemen."

After the brief recess, O'Brien resumed his questioning. "Amanda, what caused him to stop beating you that morning, do you know?"

"I just kept saying, 'Please, Michael, stop! Please! You're hurting me!' He did finally stop."

"What happened when he stopped?"

"He sat down on the floor and grabbed his head. Just sat, grabbed his head and just sat. He sat on the floor and I sat on the bed. I was scared. I told him, 'I can't believe you! You need to go! You need to get out!'

"He said, 'Come here and sit down by me and let's talk.'

"And I said, 'No, I don't want to get near you!' We just sat there. I wanted to just run, to get out of there, but I couldn't."

"Why couldn't you leave?" O'Brien asked.

"Because I was afraid he would grab me if I even tried to leave the room. He was sitting on the floor by the dresser, where the door was. He was closer to the door than me. I was on the bed and I just felt like if I even tried to leave, he would grab me. I was afraid, so I stayed. I don't even remember how I left the room."

"Do you recall saying, 'I want to go and get a Coke?' "

"Yes, I do. I guess I said I better go to class or something, and he said, 'You're still going to go to class?'

"I guess he went into the kitchen and I felt kind of out of it. I guess we were in the kitchen, and before I went to get the Coke he said, 'You look tired.' And I said, 'Yeah, I'm tired because I was hurt.'

"I hurt in the back of my head. He had hit me really hard. And so he said, 'Why don't you go and lay down for a while?' And all this time I didn't know what to do. I just felt like I was afraid to leave. So I laid down, and he said, 'Come and lay down beside me. I'm sorry.'

"We laid down on my bed, and I was trying not to fall asleep because I wanted to get out. But I did. Kind of dozed off because I was hurt. He made me put my arm around him, but I didn't caress him. I guess he wanted to be caressed or something. I just put my arm around him and I just laid it there and kind of fell asleep.

"I woke up and I kept thinking, I need to get out of here. I need to go to get my girls because they were going to come home from school. It was just about one o'clock. Like when he hit me, it happened around eight in the morning, right after they left. I just knew I had to get out.

"So I said, 'Well, I'm going to change out of my clothes. I guess I'm not going to class after all.' So I went and changed into some shorts and a shirt. And I sat on the table and we talked.

"And I said, 'Look, Michael, you need to find a place to stay, because you're not going to stay with me.' He was using my phone and said, 'Let me call somebody.' And I said, 'No, go to the store and use the phone. But find somebody to stay with. You can leave and go use the public telephone,' and so he went ahead and used the phone anyway. I didn't fight him or anything. I just let him use the phone.

"And I said, 'I'm kind of thirsty. I think I'm going to get some Cokes.' And he was on the other side of the table, and he just looked at me and said, 'Okay.' And I just grabbed my purse and left. I went to a friend's house because I was afraid to go to my family."

"Why were you afraid to go to your family?"

"I guess because they would be upset that I let myself go through all this."

She later had filed assault charges against Griffith. But in mid-October, she had decided to page him to see how he was. She returned to Griffith, something that O'Brien never could figure out.

Amanda Lopez was back with him on that Friday, October 28, 1994, the day that teenage Winn Chen was sexually assaulted in almost a carbon copy of the perverted attack on Deborah McCormick, except that the pretty Vietnamese girl had escaped with her life.

Lopez said she worked that day at the beauty salon. When she finished about 5:30 P.M., she paged Griffith to come pick her up as he had told her to do. He arrived about 6 o'clock. That would have been about two hours after Chen was assaulted and left with her hands and feet tied behind her back.

Griffith picked up Lopez in her car, which he was driving that day.

"From there, where did you go?" O'Brien asked.

"We did go to a movie on 34th and Highway 290. After the movie we went to a motel and checked in."

Griffith had been neat and clean as usual, she recalled. "He was always very, very clean. His apartment was spotless. Every time that he got in and out of the car, he would pull out the mat and shake it. He was just a clean freak. But he had a weak stomach. There were certain things that would make him sickish. He just had a weak stomach. He was picky on everything.''

O'Brien thought to himself, yeah, weak stomach and picky. He sighed and passed the witness.

Cunningham of the defense questioned Lopez about a tranquil incident in her relationship with Griffith. ''Was there ever a time that you took Michael to your mom's house and you and he and the family had dinner?''

''Yes.''

''Was that the time that during the meal, or afterwards, that Michael started to cry?''

''Yes.''

''Because he felt good or was happy that he had been accepted, or that the family had had him over, he felt grateful for that?''

''Yes.''

The defense cross-examination homed in on the fact that Lopez had not been so scared of Griffith that she didn't go back to him and even consent to marriage. ''After filing charges, you thought you had the man out of your life?''

''No.''

''After September 19, or the day you filed charges, he didn't call you in the weeks after that until you paged him, right?''

Lopez answered affirmatively and admitted that she paged him in early October because she was anxious about him.

''You decided that the man who had whipped you, you wanted to see him, and you started seeing him again, correct?''

''Correct.''

''The week before November 4 you all spent the week hanging out, going to lunch and bowling and shopping and things like that, and you even considered going to Las Vegas with him to get married, correct?''

''Uh huh.''

''And you were allowed to go see your kids before you left, correct?''

''Correct.''

None of Lopez's testimony helped O'Brien or the jury understand why she decided to return to Griffith.

Chapter 25

For the state to show that Michael Griffith would be a dangerous and continuing threat to society—one of the two issues it had to prove to get the death penalty—what could be more effective than history? History repeats itself, especially the turbulent history of Michael Griffith.

Before the trial, the prosecutors had dug deep into history to bring to the witness stand Griffith's Girls.

Having shared Griffith's history of violent rages, in addition to Lopez, were Patricia Manning, his childhood sweetheart, wife, and mother of his two children, now living in Florida. Two other pretty ladies, once his co-workers, had known his raging upheavals: Laurene Tompkins, who was married to him for several years, and Stella Fletcher, his girlfriend while the former Tompkins still was his wife. They were easy to locate, as both of them still worked as deputies for the Harris County Sheriff's Department.

Manning testified that her romantic visions of Griffith as a hard-working, ambitious boyfriend and then loving husband began to fade soon after marriage. After they moved from Los

Angeles to Panama City, Florida, and he joined the Bay County Sheriff's Department, home life got even more bumpy, she testified.

"He wasn't at home very much, spent a lot of his time at the sheriff's department or the health spa or taking a trip with his officer buddies."

She learned he was unfaithful to her, but she still tried to make the marriage work; that's how she had been raised, to make the best of bad things. By now they had two little girls.

Near the end of their marriage the worst episode occurred, said Manning. Over the years she had endured physical and verbal abuse and violent temper fits when Griffith smashed and broke everything in sight. But the worst happened just before one Christmas.

"There were presents from a lady that he brought into my home. I found them in a closet I was putting the kids' Christmas presents in. When I asked about it, we got into a fight and several of my ribs were broken. He kicked me. I was on the floor and he kicked me."

She stayed with him after that. But when he hurt one of their girls, that was the clincher, she related to the jury.

"There was an incident where one of my daughters tried to come between us and Mike picked her up and shoved her across the room. She hit her back on a doorknob. She was in pain for a while."

"You were willing to take it as long as it was you and not your children?" the prosecutor asked.

"Yes. I always felt the children needed both parents, that they needed their dad. But I decided they would be better off if I took care of them and not let him go about his business."

Manning asked for child support which Griffith paid irregularly. Finally, after he had gone to Texas, she went to a Florida agency to make him pay up from Texas. Even that worked only for a while.

The defense tried to make points with Manning, who still showed detectable signs of compassion toward her ex-husband. She admitted under cross-examination that they talked on the phone after Griffith moved to Texas.

"After he was fired from the sheriff's department here in Houston did you speak to him on the phone?"

"Yes. We probably talked an hour at one time."

"When you talked to him, was he real happy and go-lucky?"

"He was upset. He was crying. He sounded like he was depressed over the loss of his job. That's all he ever worked for. That's all he ever wanted—to be a law enforcement officer."

Deputy Laurene Tompkins, a divorcee with three children, first met Griffith in 1985, a year or so after he came to work for the sheriff's department. They started dating and were married four years later.

While they were going together, Griffith still was married to his second wife, but Tompkins did not know that until later, she told the jury. By the time she found out, that Griffith marriage was on the rocks.

On the very day that Griffith and Tompkins tied the knot, Griffith gave a sample of why she should not have wed him. Up until then, he had been charming, polite, complimentary, and lavished gifts upon her.

On their wedding day, he went bananas, smashed a triple dresser of his wife's, ripped off the mirror and shattered it. He threw things around the house, smashed everything in sight, and cussed loudly. Then he stopped, like nothing had happened. He never apologized, of course.

Four or five months after their wedding, Griffith beat her up for the first time. Thereafter, he frequently pushed her, pulled her hair, and once threatened to kill her with a gun in the middle of the night because of a tight dress she wore to work.

"Late in the night or early in the morning, I woke up and he was on top of me," Tompkins testified. "He had a gun pointed at my head. He took the mattress off the bed, threw it across the room. He tore my gown.

" 'I'm going to kill you,' he raged, his face full of fury.

"I pleaded with him, and he finally just put the gun down and walked off."

After they had separated, Tompkins ran into Griffith and Stella Fletcher, another deputy he was dating, at the bank. They were in Fletcher's car, she said. She ignored them, withdrew about $1,400 from their joint account and drove home.

"I went home and they were sitting in my driveway, in her car. I got out of the car. Michael was already at the door, and he broke my front door down. I guess he kicked it. My driveway is over a little bit, and I didn't see the front door immediately.

"I don't know whether he kicked it in or what. He went inside. . . . He wanted the money I had withdrawn. He pushed me against the wall, and he was looking for my purse. I told him my purse was in the car, and he went out to the car. He got my purse and we struggled a little bit over that. He was getting into [Fletcher's] car then, but he walked back and threw his flashlight into my car and broke all the windows."

She called the police and the sheriff's department. They came out and made a report. But she did not follow up with any formal charges against Griffith.

"After the incident, he called and asked me not to file charges and threatened me if I did. I was scared. I gave a statement to the Internal Affairs Division, but I didn't file charges. I was scared he would hurt me."

Under cross-examination by the defense, she said she had hoped Griffith would seek professional help, get some counseling. But he never did, she said.

Tompkins testified that Griffith had developed a close relationship with her eight-year-old son. He had assumed the role of a father and her boy responded, she said.

Cunningham again was looking for points. ''You saw enough positive character traits in him, first of all, to go out with him?''

''At that time I must have.''

''Then you found enough positive things about his personality to want to be married?''

It was hard for her to remember ''positive things'' now, but she replied, ''Yes, evidently.''

The defense lawyer turned to the bank episode. ''Was the dispute over the money whether it belonged to you all as a couple or whether it belonged to you or to him?''

''Right.''

''The money you withdrew and the money he actually took came from a joint account?''

''That's correct.''

Although Tompkins did not file a criminal complaint in the assault on her and the vandalism to her car, she had pushed through a divorce as quickly as possible.

She had endured all she could stand of Griffith.

Griffith seemed to make a habit of getting a new girlfriend while still married to another woman, even though the marriage was in the last crumbling stage.

Laurene Tompkins, when she began dating Griffith, had not known he was married. Stella Fletcher was unaware that Tompkins was still Griffith's wife when Fletcher began dating him.

Fletcher testified she had been a trainee in the Detention Division when she met Griffith, who was the sergeant supervisor of the jail floor where she was assigned.

It had been the same old routine: flowery words and beautiful flowers, especially long-stemmed red roses that he sent to Fletcher two dozen at a time. Sometimes the extravagant bouquets were delivered while she was on duty.

As the pretty deputy told her story to the jury, she was asked by Prosecutor O'Brien: ''Did he change?''

''Yes, sir. By the end of 1992, he became obsessed. He

didn't want me out of his sight, wanted to know everywhere I was and when I was going to be back if I went somewhere.

''He became awfully possessive, extremely jealous. I had to let him know at all times of the day where I was by calling on the pager or phone. He was upset if I wasn't someplace at the time he thought I should be.''

The sergeant's good nature that Fletcher had known abruptly vanished. She knew then why they had nicknamed him Sgt. Heart Attack.

One time during a fit of rage he had choked her, threatened her with a gun, said he should kill her, Fletcher testified. Crying almost hysterically, she pleaded with him and he finally tossed the gun away.

After one such occurrence, Griffith phoned her and said he had decided to seek counseling because ''he realized he had a problem,'' Fletcher recounted.

''He asked me to come over to his apartment so we could talk.'' She dropped by that night after work. The visit turned into a nightmare straight out of a horror novel.

''He became upset and said everything in his life was falling apart,'' said the witness, who held the jury's rapt attention. ''He said he didn't know what he was going to do if he couldn't be in law enforcement, that all he had ever known was law enforcement.'' [This was during the period that Griffith was on the carpet for growing reports of misconduct.]

The deputy testified that her plight became worse as the long night dragged on. She was exhausted, and he made it plain he would not let her go to work at the jail when morning came.

''Every time I tried to go, he told me, 'You're not going to leave!' He wouldn't let me have my car keys.''

It was a night of terror. Any minute she expected to be killed whenever the whim hit him. Meanwhile, he seemed to enjoy toying with her. It became apparent she was a prisoner in his apartment.

Besides raging around the apartment, throwing breakable items from the second floor balcony to the floor of the rooms below, Griffith started playing a game of cat and mouse with her.

Fully clothed, she was lying on the water bed in the upstairs bedroom when it started. As she testified she showed the strain of remembering that horrible ordeal.

"He had a pair of scissors, holding them like a knife or dagger. I was laying back on the bed and he would come at me like he was going to stab me with the scissors. He threatened to stab the water bed and bust it. He was raving. He would lean over me with the scissors and say he ought to kill me."

Fletcher said it went on for two hours; she was certain she was going to be slain with the scissors as he played his sadistic game.

"At one point he went into the bathroom. I got the scissors and hid them under a cushion of the loveseat. He came back and asked about them, where they were, and I said they were around someplace, or something like that."

As night edged into morning, Fletcher said, she told Griffith, "Mike, I need to go to work. They're expecting me. If I'm not there, they're going to wonder where I am."

Griffith eventually agreed to drive her to work in her car, but would not let her have the keys. On the drive downtown to the jail, Griffith started throwing anything that belonged to her out the window.

She said, "He would look out the window and say, 'It's a good day for you to die today, but I will let you tell your kids good-bye before I kill you.' "

They were within three blocks of the county jail building when Griffith changed his mind, turned around, and headed back toward his apartment, Fletcher testified.

When they pulled up to the locked iron security gate surrounding the large apartment complex, she knew he had to get out to unlock it. When he did, Fletcher decided, she would make a desperate try to escape.

"He was going to take the handcuffs I had on my belt and

handcuff me so I couldn't get away. I knew that I would not come out of that apartment alive.

"He got the handcuffs on one of my wrists, and I talked him out of it. I told him I would go in with him if he wouldn't put the handcuffs on. He had to get out of the car to go unlock the gate, and he told me not to run because if I did he would chase me and catch me. I assured him I would not run, but I knew I would.

"Soon as he got out of the car, I jumped out the door and ran down Watonga Street toward the flower shop and a service station."

The flower shop was Always & Forever Flowers.

Fletcher told the jury, "He chased me for a ways, then I didn't hear him anymore behind me. I ran into the service station and the girl on duty let me in the locked security booth with her and called the police."

Not long afterward, Griffith came back and parked across the street. Police officers spotted him and took him into custody. While being transferred to another police unit, he broke and ran but was caught after a short chase.

It was obvious the prosecution had made its point to the jury: that Michael Griffith was a continuing threat to society, particularly women. But the most harrowing testimony of women in peril from the man with the black hair was yet to come from two witnesses.

One was Sandra Denton, the young bank teller who had been ruthlessly gunned down during a robbery of a branch bank.

And all of the humiliating and degrading details of a savage and deviant sexual assault almost exactly like the one that had ended in the butcher murder of Deborah McCormick would be told by petite Winn Chen.

The difference was that Chen had lived to tell about it.

* * *

The State of Texas had brought before the jury highly effective witnesses—the ex-wives and the ex-girlfriends who had been the brunt of Griffith's temper rampages. Next, the prosecutors turned to Griffith's career as a deputy sheriff.

Taking the stand was Lt. Ruben Diaz of the Harris County Sheriff's Department, who had worked with Griffith for a few years even before he became Griffith's supervisor in the Warrants Division.

"I knew him, directly, as his supervisor, for about five years," Diaz said.

The prosecutor asked, "Based upon those years of knowledge and supervision have you come to know his reputation for being a peaceful and law-abiding person?"

"That's not the reputation that I knew," Diaz replied firmly.

"Was that reputation good or bad?"

"Bad."

Taking the witness, the defense had its first opportunity to enter into the records as exhibits a mass of letters, police standards certificates, memorandums, work evaluations, reports, and other material that backed up its allegation that Michael Griffith had been a highly competent, loyal, and dedicated law enforcement officer.

All of the exhibits had been taken from Griffith's personnel file from the Harris County Sheriff's Department, Defense Attorney Cunningham explained as he introduced the exhibits one by one and went over them with Diaz.

Former sheriffs for whom Griffith worked in Bay County, Florida, commended him highly as a "conscientious, dedicated officer anyone would be proud to have on their staff."

There also was a copy of a story from the Panama City, Florida, newspaper with a photograph of a much younger

Michael Griffith receiving an award from a Panama City, Florida, service club. The club honored him as "Law Enforcement Officer of the Year."

The story said Griffith had saved the life of an elderly man who had collapsed on the floor of his home during a hurricane and was unable to move or summon help. It said Griffith and his partner had braved the storm's raging winds, torrential rain, and roiling flood waters to reach the stricken victim after being notified by out-of-state relatives that he did not answer their phone calls.

The defense also entered as exhibits numerous reference letters from Bay County written to the Harris County Sheriff's Department when Griffith applied for a job in 1983.

"Honest . . . trustworthy . . . loyal . . . dedicated . . . one of the best officers in the department." They went on and on.

There were job evaluations from Diaz praising the work of Griffith as a deputy in the Warrants Division.

At the same time, Cunningham could not avoid various complaints Diaz had made in some evaluations concerning Griffith's insubordinate conduct at times.

Cunningham asked: "Mr. Diaz, there is a qualifier in one of your evaluations that says, 'He tends to become overbearing at times and his zealousness causes him to act before things are understood.' Was that a concern or complaint you had about Mr. Griffith during the time you were his supervisor?"

"A continuing complaint, yes."

There was no way around it. Cunningham had to face it and ask about the bad, along with the good. The exhibit was in evidence.

But at the same time, the lawyer stressed a favorable point. He asked, "But on this initial evaluation you recognized his loyalty and his genuine concern for doing a good job?"

"Yes."

"You felt he had to have things his way, correct?"

"Yes."

"You also expressed a concern about him practicing self-control. Mr. Griffith had a habit, did he not, of being a little overwrought, a little wound up, a little over-zealous, is that a fair statement?''

''Absolutely.'' Diaz would have liked to mention Griffith was nicknamed Sgt. Heart Attack, but restrained himself.

Cunningham asked about another memo in which Diaz said he had talked to Griffith about ''spontaneous eruptions in the past.''

''Numerous times,'' the official replied.

''Sometimes he just gets very upset?''

''He was a volcano. You never knew when he was going to erupt at any moment,'' Diaz said.

''Is it fair to say, though, Mr. Diaz, that throughout the time you supervised Mr. Griffith you never had a question about his dedication or loyalty to the Harris County Sheriff's Department?''

''Yes.''

Chapter 26

Anticipating that Griffith's attorneys would contend that he was suffering from a form of mental illness and at times could not control his behavior, Prosecutor Ira Jones bore down on this point in his requestioning of Diaz.

''The exhibits the defense attorney showed you, particularly those from Bay County, involved a period of times and letters from former sheriffs there, is that correct?''

''Yes.''

''Saying all sorts of nice things. Would you form the opinion that they are talking about a person who is capable of doing the right thing and making right decisions any time he wanted to?''

''Yes.''

''From the records they showed you, do you see any evidence there is anything emotionally or mentally wrong with the defendant to the extent he can't control his behavior [if he wants to]?''

''Yes, he should be able to control his behavior. There is no evidence of trauma where he would not be able to do his job as a policeman. None.''

''In refrence to his volcanic temperament, can he control that if he desires?''

''Yes, he can turn it off or on.''

''From what you knew in the beginning, you took the word of Bay County, correct? After hiring him, what did you later find out about those recommendations?''

''We found out that they were not consistent with what we were forced to evaluate him by.''

''Is it fair to say you made a mistake [in hiring Griffith]?''

''Yes.''

''As a supervisor, how do you tell, on the one hand that he appears to be doing a good job as a policeman, then you find out he's doing something else in his private life. What do you do?''

''Well, you try to evaluate how he's doing on the job, but you realize there is a problem. There is a dark side, and that has been brought to his attention many times. During the course of duty when we see that bad temper, it appears it goes off in a moment's notice—well, with no notice actually.''

''What do you do after you see there's a dark side that he can control and turn off at his whim?''

''If it can't be corrected, we start taking disciplinary action.''

In such cases, Diaz said, he would recommend that appropriate action be taken against Griffith, which he had done.

Diaz said that Griffith could have received psychiatric help paid for by the county under the Employee Assistance Program, which is available to an employee showing unstable or violent behavior.

But Griffith never had sought the free help—in fact, he rejected it.

* * *

When she spoke, Sandra Denton, the pretty, demure, blonde bank teller, seemed to be living that afternoon of terror and pain all over again.

There was a tremor in her speech and a shadow of fear remembered in her eyes. Now, more than a year later, as she settled into the witness chair, there still were bullet fragments in her skull that the doctors had chosen not to remove.

She told the jury that on October 14, 1994, about 2:30 P.M., she had been getting ready to balance her ledger but also was waiting on customers. She was alone in the front part of the bank.

That's when the man with the black hair pulled at the locked front door.

She stood up so that he could see her through the glass and asked on the intercom if she could help him. He nodded, and Denton punched the button to open the door.

O'Brien asked, "For the purpose of the record, do you see the man here in the courtroom who came to the door at the bank on October 14, 1994?"

Almost painfully, the witness turned and looked toward the counsel table. She raised her hand and pointed to Griffith. "Yes. He's right there, with the blue-gray striped shirt."

After relating how Griffith approached her desk and brandished a gray handgun and demanded money which she gave him, Denton testified:

"He asked me if there was somewhere he could lock me up. I told him that he could lock me up in the restroom. He told me, 'Go back that way,' waving his gun slightly in the direction. I turned around and walked back toward the restroom.

"As I entered the doorway going to the back, I simultaneously heard a noise. It sounded like gunshots. I realized I was hit in the back of the head by a gunshot.

"I was propelled forward and I was slumped on the wall that was next to the restroom. Just kind of slumped down and fell to the floor."

"Would you turn your head, please, and show the jury where you were shot by this defendant," O'Brien said.

Turning and pointing with her hand, Denton said, "I was shot here, at the base of my head, with the first shot. But there was another shot, and I didn't realize then I was shot twice. It was toward the top of my head. I learned later the bullet shattered, and I still have the fragments trapped in my skull."

"Then what happened?"

"I'm slumped on the floor, and I'm screaming. After I stop screaming, I hear a voice that says, 'Lay down and be still.' And I open my eyes and I see him standing there. He's still in the building. I believe he is shooting at the security cameras in front. I closed my eyes immediately and waited, probably not even a minute. And I decided to get up and go try to find help.

"I couldn't hear anything but a loud, ringing noise."

It wasn't the bank alarm going off. It was a ringing in her head from the impact of the bullets.

Bleeding, she had wrapped her jacket around her head, approached the front area in a crouched position looking to see if the gunman had left, and then set off the robbery alarm connected to the police station. A few minutes later she saw a patrol car turn into the bank parking lot and ran outside toward the police unit, Denton told the jury.

She was rushed to the hospital where she stayed twelve hours before being released. Miraculously, the shots had not gone through to the brain or done serious damage.

"I presume because of the hair on my head and everything the doctors didn't realize I had been shot a second time. I didn't find out I had another wound until I went to my personal doctor two days later."

"Did you get a good look at this man during that robbery?" O'Brien asked.

"Yes."

"Any doubt in your mind that this is the man who shot you?"

"No."

She noticeably shuddered.

The witness sounded like she would be good at memorizing somebody's license tag number—and with good reason. Mildred Beech had a bachelor of science degree in police science and law enforcement and currently was pursuing a master's degree in criminal science.

It was fortunate, prosecutors would agree, that a witness of keen observation abilities had been in the combination bridal shop-alteration and dry cleaning firm that afternoon of October 28, 1994, shortly before the teenage girl working there became the victim of a sexual atrocity.

Testifying now, Beech told the jury why she noticed the black-haired man in a chair in the waiting area of the shop where she had gone to pick up some dry cleaning. She answered the questions precisely, with the attitude of one who knows her business.

She related that she was talking to the clerk, Winn Chen, when she heard a cough behind her. "I turned around and I saw a man."

She identified Michael Griffith as the man she had seen sitting in a chair behind her. "He seemed to be very nervous. It was the way he was sitting in the chair, slumped and kind of scrunching down. He was very nervous. His eyes were kind of wandering around. I was suspicious of him."

Beech said she continued watching the man in the large mirror behind the counter. His image was implanted in her mind. Part of her studies included training to be a careful observer and to mentally record details.

She didn't do that with everyone, of course, but she had an intuitive feeling about the tan-faced man with the coal-black hair and eyebrows. Something was wrong or something was going to be wrong; she was overwhelmed with that feeling.

Beech testified that when she returned to her car parked in

front of the large, front plate-glass window, she sat there without starting the car. As she kept her eyes on the man, he turned slowly in his chair and looked directly at her—almost as if he were willing her to leave.

Beech thought about calling the police. She hated to drive away and leave Winn there alone. She was fearful for the girl, of her being robbed or perhaps worse.

"I just knew something was wrong," Beech related. "I was very uncomfortable."

But she told the jury she thought the police would think she was crazy, "if I said something was going to be happening but I had no proof, you know, just this feeling—so I left."

Shortly thereafter, Winn Chen's afternoon of hell on earth took place.

Winn Chen had the petite, smiling beauty of Asian young women. The dark-haired twenty-year-old, came to the United States from her native Vietnam in 1978 and attended American schools. She always was a top student. She was ambitious and studied hard.

Of all things, this tiny wisp of a girl—who stood four feet, eleven inches tall and weighed ninety-five pounds—was planning a career as a chiropractor. She was in her second year at the University of Houston. After graduation, she planned to enroll in the Texas Chiropractic College at Pasadena, Texas, near Houston. It was hard to imagine this elfin girl snapping the vertebrae back in place for some mountain of a patient.

On October 28 Chen had been dismissed from classes at the university about 2:30 P.M., earlier than usual, and she had come to help out a distant relative at the bridal-alteration shop, she testified.

She told the jury that the big man with black hair, tanned face [she thought he was Hispanic], and neatly dressed entered the shop while her relative, who was the manager, was out on an errand.

Ira Jones asked if she could identify anyone in the courtroom as the man who came to the bridal shop.

"The gentleman right there—" She gestured toward Griffith. "—and he's wearing a blue-and-white striped shirt."

"Did you notice anything unusual about his mouth?"

She paused before answering. "I mean it was really—I don't recall. I know it was different."

As the details unfolded, it was ironic how they matched the events at the Always & Forever Flowers on that Monday, October 10 when Deborah McCormick was alone, her mother also away on an errand.

Speaking so softly that prosecutor Ira Jones had to ask her to speak up for the jury's benefit, she testified the man asked about renting a white, silk tuxedo, which was not immediately available in stock. Chen said she suggested he might talk to the manager, so he sat down to wait.

While he was there, Mildred Beech came in.

"After she left the store, what happened next?" Jones asked.

"He stood up and asked me how much longer it would take. I told him it already had been a while, but the manager told me it was going to take like ten minutes. And I said, 'It's been ten minutes, so she might be running a little late.'

"He became all fidgety, and I said, 'If there's something you need to do you might go ahead and do it. I'm sure the manager will be here by then.'

"He said, 'No, I'll stay here and wait a little longer.' "

Sitting stiff in the witness chair, Chen was becoming tense as she dipped into her memory about that afternoon.

"He waited for, oh, maybe three minutes. And then he stood up, and I noticed when he got to the counter his right hand was behind his back, and I looked up and saw him pulling out a gun. The gun was small and gray, a revolver I believe.

"He put it beside his hip, I guess to hide the view of it from the front window. He had it real down low, just enough that I could see it. He said, 'Give me all the money in the register.'

"I gave him the money, about $60, and then he told me to go to the back room."

The girl's eyes were wider now, as if she was again seeing the scene. "I started walking toward the back room. He stayed behind me with the gun. We went into the back room, which is an alteration area. Just as I was approaching the back room, he asked me, 'How old are you?' "

"What did you tell him?" Jones asked.

"I mean, I was afraid of what he was going to do to me back there. So I told him I was fourteen at the time."

Chen had been eighteen then.

"What were you afraid was going to happen?" Jones continued.

"I thought he was going to rape me."

"Then what happened?"

"He mumbled something like, 'You're too young to die.' I can't really remember, but I remember him saying something to that effect. So I went to the back room and just as I turned around to face him, he had already unzipped his pants."

"Did he still have his gun out?"

"At that time I wasn't focused as to whether he had his gun or not. I knew he had one, but I noticed I was more scared than when I saw the gun."

"All right, you turned around. What's the next thing he did?"

"He turned around. He already had his penis out of his pants. He said something like, 'You know what to do!' I told him, 'Please don't hurt me! Just take the money and leave!' He ordered me to remove the top portion of my clothes."

"What were you wearing?"

"That day I was wearing a jean shirt and jeans."

"He told you to take off your shirt?"

"Yes, he did."

"Did you take off your shirt?"

"Yes." Chen was speaking low again. "I didn't take it off right away because I was scared, and he said, 'If you don't, you know what's going to happen to you.' So I have to take off my shirt.

"Then he told me to remove my bra. I hesitated, and he said again, 'You know what's going to happen to you if you don't.' So I took off my bra."

"Then what happened?"

"The phone rang."

"So you're standing there, nude to the waist, he's got a gun and his penis out, and the phone rings?"

"Yes . . . I mean, I looked at him wondering if I should answer that. I mean, he was basically telling me what to do then, and I just said, 'Should I answer that?' And he said, 'Answer it, but don't let anyone know that I'm here!' "

When she answered the phone, Chen said, it was the manager calling.

"You try to say anything to her?"

"Yes, I did."

"You speak in English or Vietnamese?"

"Initially it was English. She asked me are there customers waiting for her there, and I said, yes, yes, there are lots of customers here. I was trying, like, to get help."

"What did the defendant do while you're talking on the phone?" Jones asked. Then noticing Chen's increasingly disturbed emotional state, he quickly added: "Do you need a little break, Winn?"

She nodded, and the judge ordered a five-minute recess.

When the girl resumed her place on the witness stand, Jones asked, "Okay, Winn? If you need a little break, would you tell us?"

"Yes." Her voice was barely audible.

Jones said, "When we finished, the phone had rung. You're talking on the phone to the manager. Okay, what happened next?"

"I started to say something, maybe a word, you know, that wasn't English, and then I noticed he had a knife out, and it was near my face, so I could feel it."

Jones interrupted his questioning and walked to the exhibit table. Picking up the black-handled butcher knife, he held it before Chen. "This is Exhibit 20. Does this look like the knife that he had to your face?"

It was the same knife that ripped and tore through Deborah McCormick's body, the blade now pressed against her young face, cold and sharp!

Winn Chen never would forget that terrible-looking, murderous-looking knife. It had made her blood run cold.

"He was swinging it around, swinging it, reminding me not to say anything to give him away, that he was there. After a while, he started saying, 'That's enough! That's enough! Get off the phone!' "

It sounded so bizarre, she recalled. He was speaking quietly so he would not be heard by the person on the phone, but speaking urgently and viciously. She felt at any second he would lash the knife across her face and or jab it into her body. Help was so close, in her ear her aunt was speaking, yet help was so far, far away.

"Did you finish the conversation?"

"Yes. I asked her how long it would be before she got back, and she said she's got to make one more stop, and then she'd be back. And I just said, 'Okay.' There was nothing I could say."

She said she hung up the phone, left it sitting on the sewing desk.

"What happened next, Winn?"

She was silent, head bowed, then looking up and blurting: "He told me to get down on my knees!"

She had obeyed, fear surging through her half-nude body. "He said, 'You know what to do!'

"I didn't want to!" Chen exclaimed. There were tears in her eyes. Her face was growing darker, flushing. "But he kept saying, 'You better do it! You know what's going to happen to you!' "

"What happened next?"

Head lowered, her words hardly audible, she said, "I did what he told me—perform oral sex—so I had to." Chen began crying quietly.

Jones said with sympathy in his voice, speaking softly. "While that terrible thing was happening did he say anything to you, do anything to you?"

"Yeah, he said, 'You've done this before,' and he said, he goes something like, 'You've done this before.' "

"What did you do?"

"After that I just kind of started to pretend to vomit on the floor and spitting out."

"Did he react to that?"

"Yeah, he said, 'Okay! Okay! Hold on! Hold on! Settle down! Settle down!' "

"Then what did he do?"

"I just stared at the floor because I didn't want to look back up at him."

"Did you notice he did anything while you were looking down?"

"Yeah, I looked up once, and I saw him masturbating."

"And did he ejaculate on to you?"

"Yes, he did." It had splashed into her hair and on her jeans.

"You're still on your knees on the floor?"

"Yes. Then he told me to lie flat down on the floor, facing downward. I did as I was told. He started looking around for something to tie my hands up with. I can't remember . . . I guess he tied my hands with my bra, and he went out of the room. And he got the vacuum cleaner cord and he wrapped that up around my wrists, and he bound that with my ankles in the back."

"He tied your hands and your feet together? In Texas they call that being hog-tied. You've heard that expression?"

"No."

"So you're bound hand and foot. What did he do next?"

"He said, 'Don't call the cops and don't do anything because I know where you're at, and I'll come back for you,' and I laid there. I honestly thought he was going to shoot me in the back of the head before he left.

"I laid there quiet for a minute or two. I heard the front door chime again, and that's when I knew he left, but I was still scared to move. I stayed there about five or ten minutes."

After she felt sure that he was gone, the horrible man with the black hair, Chen was not sure whether he might come back and kill her even yet.

The nightmarish thought spurred her into action. She told the jury, "I wanted someone there with me, and I needed help, so somehow, I don't know how I did this, but somehow I got on my knees and I scooted all the way toward the sewing table, and I stared at the phone on top of the table for about five minutes.

"I didn't know how to get it off the hook or how to call, but I finally knocked it off with my head by using my mouth and head. And I dialed my friend's number."

The prosecutor asked, "How were you able to do that?"

She had a better grasp on things now, the worst of the awful testimony was behind her and it showed in her voice. "I have no idea. I turned around with my back to the phone and I stretched my hands real high, and I had to, like, lift my legs up real high. I have no idea, but I did it."

"At this time, you're still tied up, and all you have on are your jeans?"

"That's right."

She managed to dial the home of her friend, a young man. "I guess I was crying on the telephone. He didn't understand what I was saying, but I told him I needed him to be here, and he said, 'Okay,' then hung up the phone."

Then Chen managed to dial the 911 emergency number. She had spoken only a few words when the line was disconnected.

She was shaking with fright and desperation now, not sure whether any minute the man might come back with the gun or the knife.

Then the phone rang, and she was able to twist her body

into position to speak into the receiver. It was the 911 operater, the police, calling back the number registered on the dispatcher's display screen when she first called.

The voice said they were on the way.

Knowing that someone was coming and she was one-half naked, the spunky girl placed herself in a face down position on a chair, "covering my front body down so when they got there all they did was untied my hands in the back and both legs. And just when they were untying my legs the manager came back in the store."

Pausing now, turning slightly and indicating Griffith, who had remained silent and unemotional, displaying no reaction during Chen's testimony, Jones asked quietly:

"Are you sure this is the man that did this to you?"

The girt almost snapped the words. "Absolutely! Positively!"

"Pass the witness," Jones said, leaning back in his chair. The girl's pitiful testimony obviously impacted the jury, he could tell that.

The defense attorneys had no questions.

"The State of Texas rests, your honor," Jones said.

The defense lawyers advised the judge that they would have their witnesses present to testify in the morning to begin the defense part of the punishment phase. It was here the defense had promised the jury they would make their stand.

The jury would, as promised, hear from them in earnest the next morning.

Judge Mary Lou Keel always arrived at her office reasonably early, in plenty of time before the 9 A.M. opening of court. The courtroom doors were locked, with armed bailiffs inside, to be opened only when court commenced and the day's crowd was allowed inside. On this day, the crowd was larger than usual.

Keel's 232nd District Court had been a big drawing card the past few days. Besides the usual courthouse hangers-on and the trial freaks, there were off-duty cops and sheriff's officers and attorneys who were interested in watching this bizarre story of a once-good cop gone wrong.

The news media contingent was larger than usual, both print and electronic reporters.

If Judge Keel looked slightly weary, which hardly was detectable on her attractive features, it was understandable.

The judge, who had been a prosecutor in the district attorney's office before winning the judge's bench in last year's election, knew her way around the tough world of defendants of all kinds and looks and temperaments and crimes. But in spite of this long and familiar association with the creepier elements of the criminal justice world, Judge Keel had been having nightmares.

She dreamed that Michael Griffith, the quiet, politely speaking defendant who always said "Yes, ma'am," and "Yes, sir," while in court, was trying to break into her home to do her harm. Such a dream was highly unusual for the level-headed jurist.

But it happened, and would so again before the trial was over.

It was the worst of nightmares.

Strangely enough, during his trial, the defendant accused of a murder that could well cost him his life, seemed more interested in what he was going to eat. He asked if he could get hot meals instead of the usual jail fare while the trial was going on. He appeared to be worried more about food and its temperature than his hide and its future.

"Griffith is a whiner," one court worker said.

Chapter 27

Patricia Manning, Griffith's ex-wife, was recalled to the stand by the defense as it opened its efforts to save the ex-deputy's life. David Cunningham asked her about Griffith's family life when she first knew him in Los Angeles, California.

Manning said his mother had a bad drinking problem, sometimes threw ashtrays at Griffith, once hit him with a skillet, stayed away from home to the extent that Griffith and his younger brother had to fend for themselves.

Or they would call their grandparents when they ran out of food. The grandparents would take them under their care.

Speaking of their mother, Manning said, ''She was a conceited person. She felt like she was a very beautiful and glamorous type person. She was good to the younger brother, but I think she slighted Michael because he was more independent. He worked hard. He tried to help her. His brother kind of had things handed to him. I know Mike was giving him money for the extra things he needed.''

The boy's mother became hateful when she drank, said Manning. ''The more she drank the more hateful she got.''

During their heated arguments, "Mike would never hit his mother," said Manning. "He did talk back to her, though. He would yell at her."

Manning said when Griffith came to live with her and her mother it was because his mother had kicked him out.

Cunningham asked, "Do you feel that Michael became a policeman just so he could one day arrest his mother?"

The ex-wife seemed to flare at the idea. "No, sir. I didn't believe that at all. He had an uncle who was a role model as a policeman, and he always wanted to be a policeman."

Cunningham's question about "wanting to arrest his mother" was prompted by statements that Griffith's grandfather had made when questioned.

The grandfather, Robert Riley, was unable to come to Houston to testify in person. Attorneys had made arrangements to have a court reporter go to Riley's Los Angeles home. The lawyers then interviewed the grandfather by telephone. The interview was recorded and replayed in the Texas courtroom.

Riley testified that Michael Griffith did have problems with his mother, that she did neglect her two sons, leaving them at home alone for long periods of time when she was partying. According to Riley, Griffith had often remarked that he wanted to be a policeman so that he could arrest his mother and throw her in jail.

On the other hand, said the grandfather, Griffith had liked the man who his mother later married. His own father had left when Michael was three years old.

The stepfather had been good to the boys and tried to be a good substitute father, to the point that he won the approval of the grandparents, according to Riley's recorded testimony.

In a few years, their mother seemingly had overcome her problem, but by that time, Griffith was long gone from home and his brother had joined the Marines.

Riley said the boys never suffered from lack of food. Michael would call the grandparents and they would come get them. Not only that, the grandparents had a swimming pool at their home the boys enjoyed.

Griffith had done well in school, had been an honor student, according to Riley's testimony. He worked hard in school and later at various jobs.

Overall, it was the opinion of state's attorneys that the defense did not make much headway with the testimony from Manning or Riley, certainly not enough to persuade a jury that Griffith had committed a murder thirty years later because of his early abusive home life.

The big guns in Griffith's defense would be three professionals in the mental illness field, including a psychiatrist and two psychologists. The three had generally agreed on the diagnosis of Michael Griffith's mental state.

When he took the stand, Dr. Oliver Zigler, a psychiatrist, gave an in-depth report about the conclusions that he and the psychologists reached on what ailed the mind of the defendant. As such testimony goes, it was necessary for the jury to listen carefully to absorb the lengthy explanations and the technical terms.

After the psychiatrist gave a detailed summary of his testing and diagnosis of Griffith, defense attorney Michael Charlton asked, "What is the part of this diagnosis as applies to Michael Griffith as an explanation of why this murder occurred?"

That was laying it on the line, one of the reporters covering the trial observed to a colleague.

Zigler replied, "Based upon the psychological test results he does have disassociative states. When he becomes intensely angry it was more than the kind of anger that most people experience. It was an anger which he was unable to control once it had begun and which was really almost a separate part of his personality that took over. As if he were a completely different person acting the opposite way he usually acted as the police officer, Michael Griffith.''

Charlton pursued the point: ''Is it your suggestion, then, to the jury, that he essentially in very simple terms, that the loss of his job could cause, in effect, the murder of Deborah McCormick and those other two offenses?''

The doctor replied he believed that was what held Griffith together ''psychologically and emotionally'' for most of his adult life: the fact that he was a police officer.

''That was his central reason for being. When he no longer had that he fell apart emotionally. I think it was very much more than a job for Michael Griffith. It was his identity. When he lost that, he really lost his identity.''

Pausing, Zigler added, ''He lost the glue that held him together emotionally.''

''But you know from the interviews with his ex-wives that he committed crimes even while a police officer?''

The doctor had a ready answer. ''This occurred so far in the past, but the fact that he was a police officer at the time served as a check to keep him from going further.''

One or two jurors looked puzzled.

The psychiatrist added, ''It permitted him to be abusive to an extent for reasons which he felt in his mind were acceptable reasons for being abusive. It kept him from going further. Once he no longer had the identity of a police officer he just fell apart emotionally. There was nothing to keep him from going to the extremes which he did eventually.''

Charlton asked, ''The only thing that held him in check was his identity as a policeman?''

''Yes. He told me during my interview that he had lived his entire life—and I read this over sometimes without even looking at [the notes he held]. I think I can quote it verbatim. He had lived his entire life according to a pattern and when his employment with the sheriff's department was terminated as it was, the pattern was gone and he was lost.''

Charlton wanted to make another point to the fidgeting jury

members. "You and I don't need that identity to keep our psychological or emotional stability?"

The doctor added with a smile: "It helps that we enjoy doing what we like to do. You know we think it's important."

Commenting that most people integrate their "multiple dimensions," Charlton asked: "How does that process of integration work for most of us?"

The answer was a long one. "Most of us, or a person with a healthy personality, learns as she or he is growing up that we have different kind of feelings—you know, charitable or uncharitable. We learn to accept different aspects of our personalities. We learn to accept that we have our good side and our bad side. And even though we generally consider ourselves to be good people, that we also have a dark side—that sometimes we have uncharitable or angry thoughts and feelings, and it doesn't blow us away.

"A person whose personality isn't integrated is totally unable to accept the difference or contradictory feelings and contradictory kind of impulses. They have to be just one way all the time."

Charlton asked, "Does the concept of internal controls versus external controls have anything to do with this integration process?"

Dr. Zigler replied, "I think it does. I think each of us have certain moral standards or things which control our behavior, which keep us civilized. And we all have impulses at times . . . the dark side of our natures. We all have impulses to do things that we don't really want to do, and because we are able to accept the fact, we feel like doing things sometimes that we know we shouldn't do. We are able to not do them.

"People who are not able to accept the existence of angry feelings, rageful feelings, who believe that they must be always perfect and can't even accept the fact they might become angry, might become enraged, their internal controls don't function to stop them from behaving in an uncontrolled way."

Charlton asked, "Are you talking about a sociopath, doctor?"

"Sociopath is defined as somebody who doesn't have these internal moral standards. Any one of the jurors may be sitting there thinking, you know, this guy is very boring. And what he is saying is that I'm unnecessarily lengthy and he's using long words. He's really—he's a terrible witness. He's boring—"

Prosecutor Jones interrupted with an objection. "Your honor, he's not answering the question."

Zigler said then, "A sociopath is an individual who has no internal moral standards."

Now came the gist of the psychiatrist's opinion: Griffith was suffering from a borderline personality disorder but was not a sociopath, he told the jury.

The doctor explained: "Individuals with borderline personalities have moral standards, although sometimes they are not able to conform their behavior to these standards."

The most common cause of a borderline personality disorder is either abuse or neglect in childhood, the expert said. That fell nicely into place with the defense contentions that Griffith was an abused and neglected child.

Charlton asked what conclusion the doctor had reached about the childhood of Griffith.

"Most striking to me was not his descriptions of having been neglected as a child. What was most impressive to me was the inappropriate way he told me that he felt about the negligence which he experienced.

"Specifically, he told me about having been neglected. About his mother's alcohol abuse, about her not being at home for days at a time, or coming home and being very intoxicated.

"About spending her money on alcohol and about him and his younger brother not having food, having to take care of himself and his younger brother and occasionally his mother when she was intoxicated.

"But then he went on to tell me that all of that was okay,

that it was even more than okay. If you wish I can read direct quotes, but basically what he told me was that he wasn't upset or angry about all that."

"Why was it good?"

"He said it made him a more self-sufficient person. He said it's good for children to do without even the bare essentials because it teaches them not to expect much."

Boiling it down, Zigler said, "I think it really were as if it wasn't the same person [doing these crimes]. When he no longer was a deputy, not just no longer a deputy but had been fired, he fell apart emotionally. He wasn't the same person is what my tests indicate. He just disintegrated emotionally and psychologically and went into a series of disassociative episodes in which his enraged or primitive part of his identity was governing or controlling his actions."

"So when he lost his identity as a police officer, the Michael Griffith that he knew or wanted to know no longer existed?"

"Right."

Ira Jones launched a scathing cross-examination of the psychiatrist.

"Let's talk about your diagnosis of this defendant. I'll tell you what I'm hearing and you tell me if it's right."

"Okay."

"That something happened between him and his mother that he didn't like. Is that correct? Yes or no?"

"Yes."

"And because of that, some thirty years later he murders people, is that right?"

"I can't answer that question yes or no."

"Let me rephrase it. You state that the only glue that held him together was being a policeman?"

"I believe so."

"Okay, that's your opinion, correct?"

The doctor was getting irritated. "Yes, yes. I said I believe so."

"Let me rephrase it, doctor. Because of some relationship with his mother, some thirty-three years later he goes out and murders people, is that right?"

"I think that is over-simplifying it, but I believe that was the beginning of the chain of events that led to it."

Jones was registering some subtle scorn of the theory: "The only thing that kept him from the killing of people in those thirty-three years was that he was a policeman, the glue that held him together?"

The doctor knew he was under siege, as he undoubtedly expected he would be in the state's cross-examination. "I can't say it was the only thing, but I believe that was the most important thing that kept his behavior and his personalities in control, yes."

"What I hear you saying is that he's not a policeman anymore, not ever going to be a policeman anymore, I'm sure?"

"That's correct."

"Is it too late to treat him?"

"In terms of actually reversing or correcting or basically changing his personality, yes, I believe so."

Jones continued to bear down. "Would it be fair to say this man is dangerous?"

"I think it depends on what kind of context."

"Well, what you're saying to me is that the only thing that kept him from going around hacking up everybody in that thirty-three years was that he's a policeman. Now that glue is gone."

Backed into a corner, the witness hedged a little. "I think I said 'I thought.' I don't know if that was the only thing, but I think that was the most important thing, yes."

"So you know that the glue is gone, right?"

"I think it was gone following his being terminated by the police department. I'm not sure it's gone any longer, no."

The prosecutor probably had a passing thought the doctor

wasn't sure who terminated him, either, though he put it down to a slip of the tongue and didn't press it.

"What put it back?"

"I think being an inmate. I think he has another kind of glue."

"I think, as quoted before, you said to me about his having always lived life according to a pattern and after being fired by the sheriff's department, the pattern was gone?"

"I think he has another pattern."

"What if he should escape—he's dangerous?"

"Yes."

"He'd kill somebody."

"Then he might."

"Sexually abuse them?"

"He might."

"It's probable?"

"If he were to escape, I don't know. I think it's very possible. If he were to, right—I can't refute that."

"Or he could grab somebody and kill them?"

"I don't think that's very likely."

"Possible?"

"Anything is possible. I just don't think it's very likely."

"You're basing your diagnosis upon those two—your ink blot tests and your other test?"

"And also the interview and my interviews with other people, what I've learned about his behavior over the last twenty-five years."

"What about Stella? Did you talk to a person named Stella?"

"No, I did not."

"Why didn't you talk to her?"

"I didn't think it would have added anything to the information which I had. I read statements she had given. I read notes of interviews with her by Mr. Charlton's investigator."

Jones now touched on the shooting incident that happened when Griffith was with Stella Fletcher and her boys in the car and was showing the boys his weapons. When Griffith was wounded in the leg, it had been described by authorities as an accidental shooting.

But now, Jones asked: "Did he tell you who shot him in the leg—did you get into that part?"

"No, he didn't tell me who shot him in the leg. He declined to tell me who shot him."

"Some person other than himself?"

"He indicated that. But also he said that he had taken it upon himself, the responsibility for it in order to not implicate the other person who he chose not to name."

"Did the psychological tests of the defendant consist of ink blots?"

"That's correct."

"What's a sociopath?"

"A sociopath is an individual without moral conscience."

"Would it be fair to say that a sociopath is a person who does what he basically wanted to?"

"I think that's one way—"

"I've heard it described as, 'If I want it, it's right. If I don't want it, it's wrong.' Is that a fair standard?"

"I think that's a good way of saying it."

"Are those persons capable of controlling their conduct when they want to?"

"Yes."

"Okay, from your diagnosis, is this defendant capable of controlling his conduct when he wants to?"

"I think there are two questions there."

"No, it's one. Can he control his behavior? Yes or no?"

"Not all the time, no."

"So just some wild man out there who can't control himself?"

"I believe at times that's what happens."

"Is this a split personality?"

"No, I think I've already said what I think. The term split personality really hasn't been used for decades. I think what you are talking about are multiple personalties. I think I've already answered that I don't believe it's a true multiple personality, but then I believe at times it's like partial dual personalties, if you will."

"Dual—a person can be mean and vicious part of the time and then nice guy part of the time?"

"Uh huh."

"Is he able to control this behavior?"

"No, I don't believe so."

"It's your opinion this man is not capable of controlling his behavior in this other state?"

"I believe when the conditions are such that other side of him takes control of his behavior at these times. I can't—I mean, I've not been there. I haven't seen him at those times. But based upon the evidence that I have, I think there is a significant likelihood that is the case."

The tug of war was about over.

"Well, did you read the offense report as it relates to the murder at the Always & Forever Flowers shop?"

"No, I did not read the offense report."

"Did you read the witness statement as it relates to the murder at the Always & Forever Flowers shop?"

"No, I did not."

"You don't know what he did out there, is that correct?"

"I have a very basic idea of that, but no, I did not."

The defense finished up its testimony with the story of Deputy C. Ontivaro Olvera, the former co-worker and friend of Griffith, and two other deputies who had worked for Griffith when he was a jail supervisor.

Olvera credited Griffith with saving his life when they were scuba diving in Cancun, Mexico. The other deputies testified Griffith had been a good supervisor and friend, had helped them with personal problems and sometimes joined them in basketball games, and was just a "good old boy."

* * *

When the defense team rested its case, state prosecutors called as a rebuttal witness Allan C. Brantley, a supervisory special agent with the FBI at the National Center for the Analysis of Violent Crime, FBI Academy, in Quantico, Virginia.

A member of the investigative support unit at the National Crime Center, Brantley had served as a technical adviser in the filming of the popular movie *Silence of the Lambs,* from the novel about a serial killer.

Prosecutor Ira Jones asked Brantley, "Based on your education, your background experience, and specialized training, have you formed an opinion regarding the future probabilities of dangerousness of this particular defendant?"

Answering that he had, Brantley went on to explain his reasons. "It's my opinion, based upon the totality of everything I had access to and everything I reviewed and all the people I talked to, that the probability of Mr. Griffith engaging in future acts of violence consistent with his past behavior is quite high."

"Do you see any sort of sexual motivation involved in this conduct?"

"Oh yes, absolutely."

"When a person is placed in confinement, if they are, and have been motivated by sexual drives, do those drives just go away or do they find some other outlet?"

"It's my opinion the sexual drives do not go away. It can manifest itself in a lot of different ways. If you are dealing with an individual who is a sexual predator that enjoys not only the sexual features of what he does but also power and control and domination of others that are weaker, then I think you are going to look for outlets that are similar in their backgounds.

"They will look for weaker individuals they can receive their gratification from, or as close as possible to their preferred victim pool. And if you're isolated from females you're going to look for something as close as possible."

"In the male population?"

"If that's what you're limited to, it's going to be another male, yes, sir."

Brantley said the fact that Griffith sought "to limit his viewing from the outside" in two of the crimes showed that "he was very deliberate in what he did."

Premeditation was involved, he said.

Brantley said the McCormick murder was primarily a sexual homicide, with the robbery being secondary. The robbery of the bank and shooting of Sandra Denton was different in that the primary motive was monetary. The FBI agent believed Denton was shot to eliminate her as a witness.

The motive in the attack on Winn Chen was both monetary and sexual, the agent said.

Brantley was of the opinion that Griffith would be a danger to other inmates or employees, female or male, wherever he might be confined and a definite danger to society should he escape.

Chapter 28

The state waived its right to begin the closing arguments in the punishment phase of the trial, preferring to say the final words to the jury just before it began its deliberations on whether Griffith should live or die.

Defense Attorney David Cunningham began. ''Quite candidly, I tossed and turned for several nights wondering what I could tell you to convince you that Michael Durwood Griffith's life is worth saving.

''And as frightened and nervous as I am right now, that can't compare to what you face because the only way Michael Griffith is executed is for each of you to give the State of Texas permission to do that.

''It is your decision whether he lives or dies.''

The attorney said that the defense agreed that Griffith should be punished and punished severely.

''But it is not necessary to take Michael Griffith's life in order to meet those concerns. A life sentence will punish him . . . and protect us.''

Concerning the Special Issue No. 1, whether Griffith would

be a continuing dangerous threat to society—one of two questions the jury must answer in determining punishment—Cunningham told the jury that based on the evidence its answer must be "no."

To answer that issue "yes" would be to ignore the burden of proof that had not been met, Griffith's mental illness and the conditions under which he would be imprisoned for the rest of his life, the defense attorney argued.

"If Michael Griffith were allowed to go out on the street, the answer to the question is a resounding yes," said the attorney. "By your verdict of guilty of capital murder you have decided that Griffith will die, will die in prison. The question now becomes when and how he will die.

"The state on this issue holds that he probably will be a threat to society, the society of prison—fellow prisoners, administrators, and visitors. They must prove to you that he will probably commit violent acts in the strict, regimented, structured environment of imprisonment and of administrative segregation."

Cunningham said the state's claim of his future dangerousness "ignores Griffith's behavior when acting within the confined perimeters of a structured, regimented existence."

"Let's look clearly at what the evidence shows about his kind of behavior within a structured environment," the attorney continued.

He mentioned Griffith's good grades in grade school and how in high school he was an honor student.

"We know that in early marriage to Patricia Manning he worked hard, had two jobs, and supported his kids . . . When he became a peace officer he became a very good one."

He stressed the good employment records in Bay County, Florida, the commendations from officers and citizens.

"We hear evidence of a dedicated, devoted, highly motivated police officer," Cunningham pointed out.

He noted that Griffith had been a model inmate in Harris County Jail since his arrest more than a year ago. Confinement to prison for life would put him in the same structured environment as the jail, said Cunningham.

He also urged the jury to consider how Griffith's violence relates to his "mental illness."

"Now, Michael Griffith may look like you and me and at times he may act like you and me, but he is very, very different from you and everyone else in this courtroom. He is different because he is mentally ill."

Cunningham harped on Griffith's background during childhood, growing up without internal controls on his behavior, without the parental love and care necessary during the formative years of a child.

"Am I saying that because his mama didn't like him that thirty years later he killed somebody? No, that's ridiculous."

The lawyer argued that Griffith gained internal control through his identity as a police officer, "but you can't be a police officer twenty-four hours a day. The police department taught him how to contain his control in the professional relationship.

"It's obvious that the police officers didn't teach him about things that we learned at a young age, about give and take, about compromise, about consideration. Griffith expected perfection at work; he expected quite wrongfully perfection at home. And when he didn't get that perfection in his private life inevitable frustration and disappointment escalated into the violence that you heard described. It's because he can't control his personal life like he can in the jail."

Cunningham reiterated that the structure that had reined in Griffith collapsed when he was fired and "the glue that held him together was removed."

Cunningham continued, "With those reins removed rapid dementia disgraces Michael Griffith, culminating in eighteen days of horror in 1994 with Miss McCormick, Winn Chen, and Sandra Denton.

"Without the control of the sheriff's department, violence was inevitable."

If the faces of the jurors were an indication, the argument wasn't convincing to them.

Defense attorney Michael Charlton told the jury, "These individuals with borderline personality disorders have a pattern of unstable and intense relationships.

"These individuals nurture people only with expectations that the other person will be there in return to meet their own needs on demand. We know because of Griffith's intense courting, his overwhelming them with gifts, his desire to be with them all the time.

"But there was a selfish string attached. He needed that contact with them. He needed that nurturing, and when he didn't get it he was provoked into a rage."

Charlton attacked the state's contention that Griffith was "a sociopath," as the state argued. "One of the psychiatrists told you that people who suffer from a borderline personality disorder and a sociopath often display the same behavior. But there are differences. The sociopath is motivated by profit. The borderline personality disorder subject is motivated by demand and a need for nurturing.

"And the sociopath is inconsistent with those people who would risk their own lives to save someone else. Such as Michael Griffith driving back into the hurricane to rescue that elderly man and also when he rescued Deputy Olvera and got him back safely to shore [when they were scuba diving].

"A sociopath would not do that. A sociopath says you're an idiot if you save someone else's life."

Charlton contested the testimony of FBI Agent Brantley that the murder of McCormick and the attack on Chen were sexual crimes.

"They are crimes of assault," said the attorney. "They are crimes in which violence is directed to women . . . They are crimes to control. They are crimes of violence, not sexual gratification. This anger, this rage, are the result of the disillusionment of his personality, not out of any desires to gratify himself sexually. He was living with women at the time, attractive women.''

In closing, Charlton said, ''There are mitigating circumstances in his background which justify a sentence less than death.''

Chapter 29

Ira Jones, behind his spectacles a precise, methodical, to-the-point lawyer, stepped up to the jury box to start the state's closing arguments.

"You have two questions of law before you," he said emphatically to the jury. "Did the state prove to beyond a reasonable doubt that in all probability this person will commit acts of violence in the future and thus be a continuing threat to society?

"The other question is, taking everything as a whole—all the violence and the crime he has committed, and his moral culpability and everything else you have seen before you—can you make a decision whether there's sufficient circumstances why he should be given life instead of death. Please observe the word sufficient."

Pausing to let his words sink in, the prosecutor declared, "I'm going to ask you to follow the laws the judge has instructed you to do and to base your decision solely and only on the evidence of the case.

"Surely after you have done that you can just let the chips fall where they fall.

"Your duty here is to tell the truth and follow the law and that's it," Jones said. "That's probably the only way you can be able to walk away from your service as jurors with a clear conscience, knowing for all time that under the law justice was done . . . that you've had a tough duty and you did what you had to do."

Jones summarized the evidence, the testimony of Griffith's ex-wives and girlfriends—the same story, life-long pattern of being abusive to women. He spoke of the bank robbery shooting in which no mercy was shown.

"And then there was Winn Chen as a mirror image as to what happened to Deborah McCormick. Some pretext to get into the shop: he wanted flowers with Debbie; he wanted some kind of suit from Winn.

"I submit to you from that last case you can understand how he robbed Debbie.

"Griffith had a gun with Winn Chen. He had a gun with Sandra Denton. I submit to you it's reasonable inference that he was holding a gun on Debbie and marched her down that hallway.

"Winn Chen is fourteen days after the murder of Deborah McCormick and shows a great deal of premeditation. He brought the knife again. Why do you need a knife in a bridal shop?

"He knew what he was going to do.

"He waited for Mildred Beech to leave. More controlled behavior. Robbed Winn. He took the money, then marches her to the back of the store, put that knife to her face while she's on the phone.

"And think about that horrible incidence of Winn standing there, no blouse, no bra, the man standing there with his penis exposed, telling her to do horrible things and holds that knife to her face.

"That shows control. He forces her to perform oral sodomy on him, and then he has to ejaculate in her hair and on her clothing.

"Is this what happened to Deborah McCormick? What kind of person would do that? A person very much in control. He had the choice of killing Winn or not killing her, and he showed you he made the choice. He said, 'You're too young.' Aren't these the words of a person making a decision and a choice?"

Jones mentioned the deputies' testimony about Griffith being a "good old boy" with them.

"So long as you submitted to his power and control, he could be a good guy," the co-prosecutor said.

Jones brought up the opinions of the psychiatrist and two psychologists called by the defense, adding, "And what a wonderful thing about opinion is that we can all have one.

"They might be very nice people and have a sincere opinion, but if it didn't square with the evidence there's probably something wrong with it.

"Their grand theory is because he had a bad relationship with his mother it somehow thirty years later caused all this, and why did it take all those years to do it? Well, being a policeman, he's not to do this, but once he was fired that groove was gone, and after he was an uncontrollable real person in a disassociated state who didn't know what he was doing, the implication for you is he's not blamed for what he's done, right?"

Jones pointed to what he called "the lack of data used by these persons" in making their diagnosis.

He ridiculed the defense conjecture that Griffith's bad relationship with his mother was at fault, that he shouldn't be blamed but his mother should.

"Well, hey, if you're going to follow that theory what you really need to do is blame the sheriff of Harris County. He's the one that fired him and removed the glue, right? Blame anybody but the man who actually committed the crime maliciously, deliberately, mercilessly.

''Griffith was very much in control of his behavior. He picks, he chooses, he selects. One lives, one dies. I can do what I want to do when I want to do it.

''For a person like him it's fun. He enjoyed hurting people. It's in his power to use control. He loves it, feeds on it, hurting people.

''Think about the impact your verdict is going to have on all these other people out there who want to be brutal, who would like to be like him and do mean and horrible and vicious things. A lenient verdict by you is going to send a message to these people.

''I submit to you that criminals need to be convinced what's waiting for them. The only good that this man is going to do is to serve as an example to people that are committed to doing what he's doing.

''It's the only good this trial is going to be. At least when you leave here today you have done everything in your power to stop it. Shouldn't you send a message to anybody that will listen?''

Jones looked straight at the jurors, his eyes scanning their faces. ''People, there's a level of humanity that nobody can sink below. I don't care what your childhood was, you're not going to do things like that. There's a basic level of human dignity that Winn and Sandra and Deborah has, and you're not going to blow it.

''You don't care what your problems are, you're not going to blow it.

''These criminals must know there is something they've got to fear, and I submit that a death sentence will get them the message.

''You know from the evidence he is too dangerous to be loose. How can you bet all those other lives? What if you're wrong? He escapes, he takes a hostage, more blood, more brutality, and you had the chance to stop it and you didn't do it.

"We've had it with this brutality. We've had it with this bloodshed. You commit a crime like this in our time and there's a Harris County jury waiting for you!"

Chapter 30

Prosecutor Casey O'Brien had the last words before the jury regarding the life or death of Michael Griffith.

O'Brien had become close to the victim's mother, Mary Ringer, and to Deborah McCormick's boyfriend Tom Atwood during the weeks of pre-trial work.

He felt the sufferings of these two people, and his heart was in this job of helping to get the maximum sentence for the man who had left the heartbreaking trail of savage violence.

He began "Well, ladies and gentlemen, I thought as we selected the jury I heard repeatedly the phrase 'circumstances of the offense' regarding Issue No. 2. That's why I wrote the word 'society' up there." He indicated the word he had put on the chalkboard.

"The society they chose to argue about is prison. It didn't say prison society in Issue No. 2, folks.

"It says society. It says us. It says prison. It says wherever we find people. If the legislature meant prison they would have put prison in [the wording] of Issue No. 2. If it had, our answer would always be 'no,' wouldn't it?

"We can take the dangerous criminals. We can put them in prison. We can chain them to the walls, put shackles on their feet and hands, and it always will be 'no.' Didn't make any difference if it was Williams in Atlanta or what's-his-name in Oklahoma.

"Whatever it is, folks, the answer is always 'no.' We can design a box for him. We can make sure we spend the time, spend the money, spend the resources that he can't ever hurt anyone.

"This society has chosen not to do that. Therefore, the answer is 'yes' for the protection of society, for protection of the people.

"I'll read you Issue No. 2 again. 'When taking into consideration all the evidence including the circumstances of the offense, the defendant's character and background, the personal moral culpability of the defendant, there's sufficient mitigating circumstance or circumstances to warrant that a sentence of life imprisonment rather than death be imposed.' That's what the line that was drawn in the sand is all about.

"The question is whether or not you see sufficient mitigating circumstances, in the analysis of the picture as a whole, to justify your mercy. I'm going to ask you to look at what's on this side of the scale of justice."

He looked up from his notes. "I don't need to bring out the crime scene photographs of Debbie McCormick again, or get on my knees and stab the rail again for you to understand how brutal, callous, and premeditated the crime against Debbie McCormick was.

"This is cold-blooded. I don't need to pull this sweater again to show you how it was ripped from the body, to show you this was a cold-blooded, calculated crime.

"I thought about something as I prepared to argue this case. I thought about, you know, maybe the jury is upset. Maybe the jury is upset because a lot of people have cried. Mary Ringer cried. Mary almost immediately cried.

"Gee, Mr. Jones, did you have to make her go through that. Why did you make her cry?

"Ira Jones didn't make her cry, folks. He did. He did." He pointed at Griffith.

"Mr. O'Brien, did you have to make Tom Atwood cry as he explained to you the loss of his life-mate? Isn't that cruel? Isn't that cold of you to do that? I didn't make him cry. He did it. He did it on October 10, 1994, and Tom Atwood can't even stand to come back to this courtroom.

"We spent three days focusing on [Griffith] and his background. What the hell made him do this, and these folks right there spend their lives, their Christmases, their Thanksgivings, without Debbie McCormick?

"I didn't make them cry. They cry every time they think about their daughter, their sister, their lover. You are entitled to know the destruction, the wanton disregard for destruction, didn't stop with the death of one person, folks. It goes on and on and on. He killed Billy Ringer, Sr., too, folks. All his ex-wives and girlfriends, all but Patricia I believe, cried.

"Amanda [Lopez] described the incident inside her home as he was straddling her, beating her in the chest, and she thought 'My children are going to find me dead!' I didn't make her cry. He did that.

"Stella [Fletcher] had one of the scariest experiences I believe a woman could possibly go through. Enticed her over to his apartment after he's already beaten her before. I don't know the dynamics of that problem, that the women who have been battered have to go back. I don't know, I don't know why.

"I have never been able to figure it out, but it happens. They go back to the same guy. It happens again and again, and it gets worse and worse. Stella went over there because he promised he would get help and he wouldn't do it again, and she loved him.

"He returns that love in an evil way, folks. Locks her up inside the apartment, plays chicken with a pair of scissors overnight, drives her to work until he gets right down there three blocks from the job, says, 'I changed my mind, you're not going to leave, today is a good day to die.' She cried.

''Every time she thinks about it, thinks that she might have died, she cries. I didn't make her do that. He did.

''In every one of these circumstances, folks, he was wearing a badge, just like that man over there.'' O'Brien pointed to a deputy. ''The pride of patches, the sheriff's department right there.''

O'Brien said that while under the oath of the sheriff's department, ''he would go off to work supervising criminals who had done very much like he was doing at night. He then would go home at night and brutalize women and batter them.''

''Now, you folks said when we selected you that you wouldn't treat a policeman any different than anybody else. I'm not asking you to. I'm asking you to treat him just like anyone else even though he was a policeman, even though he spit on that badge and did it for twenty years.

''Mr. Jones, why did you bring Winn Chen in here? Why did you have to have her tell of the humiliation that she went through? Why did you tell us, in graphic terms, Mr. Jones, she's hog-tied till the policeman untied her? A policeman, a complete stranger, arrives to untie her as she was nude from the waist up. Why, Mr. Jones, did you make her say those things? Why did you make her cry, suffer the humiliation?''

Pointing to Griffith, prosecutor O'Brien said, ''Folks, he did it. He did it to her. He thought about it and he contemplated it, and it was premeditated. I don't care what's-his-name said to you, he knew what he was doing. The whole crime cries to you. He knew what he was doing and he did it.''

O'Brien said he had thought about that testimony of one psychologist who said about Griffith, ''These predators deny, shift blame, excuse, and justify.''

''And we can't blame God, and we can't blame his mother thirty years ago, and we can't blame the sheriff's department for firing him when he beats up women and they catch him.

''We have got to blame him. You can't let him deny. You can't let him excuse it. You can't let him justify. You can't let him shift it to someone else. He did it. He created a room full of victims. Now, as to mitigation. That atmosphere, put it on the scale next to you, see if there are sufficient circumstances that overweigh the moral blame. Should you extend mercy because of sufficient mitigation?

"No, no, no! The answer is no! And the answer to Issue No. 2 is *no.* Please, it's *no.*"

The courtroom audience stirred, as always happens, when a hard-fought criminal case goes to the jury.

Judge Keel said, "All right, members of the jury. You will now retire to consider your verdict, please."

Sometime later in the day, Judge Keel resumed the bench with the attorneys present, and said: "The jury sent out a note asking for the list of exhibits that were introduced into the trial, and the parties are in agreement that my response should be that, because this is true, there is no actual list. But if they want some exhibits they can ask for them, and we will give them to them."

Almost three and-one-half hours after the jury began its deliberations, Judge Keel again was back on the bench. She said to the bailiff, "You say you have a jury panel on its way up?"

"They should be in the basement now, on their way up," the bailiff replied.

Judge Keel then addressed the courtroom at large: "Ladies and gentlemen, let me admonish everyone present whatever the verdict might be, I don't want any outburst made by anybody whether you like it or don't like the verdict. Don't lay a guilt trip on the jury."

The jury filed into the box and was seated. Attorneys and spectators were looking at their faces closely, seeking some indication of their decision.

Judge Keel said, "Has the jury reached a verdict?"

The foreman rose and said, "Yes, ma'am, we have."

"Please tender it to the bailiff."

The verdict was read. The jury had answered Issue No. 1, YES, and Issue No. 2, NO, which mandated a sentence of death be pronounced upon Michael Griffith.

Judge Keel asked if the attorneys wished to have the jury polled on its verdict, and Cunningham said he did. The poll of each juror indicated the verdict was unanimous.

Then Judge Keel asked the defendant. ''Mr. Griffith, do you have anything to say why sentence should not be pronounced against you?''

Griffith, who was standing, showed no emotion. He answered quietly, ''No, ma'am.''

Judge Keel then declared, ''Then it's the order of the court that you, having been judged guilty of capital murder and the punishment assessed by the verdict of the jury and the judgment of the court at death, you shall be delivered by the sheriff of Harris County, Texas, to the director of the Institutional Division of the Texas Department of Criminal Justice, or any person legally authorized to receive convicts, and you shall be confined in the Institutional Division in accordance with the laws of the State of Texas until the day of the execution is received at the date of affirmation by the Court of Appeals.

''This case is adjourned.''

After the verdict, Mary Ringer said she was ''real glad'' and that she had no sympathy for the convicted killer.

''He is sick, that is true,'' she said. ''But he also is a vicious, mean man.''

On January 2, 1996, Grifffith settled up for the other two crimes with which he had been indicted. The ex-deputy pleaded guilty to two separate charges of aggravated robbery in the robbery of Sandra Denton during which she was shot and the aggravated robbery of Winn Chen during which she was sexually assaulted.

Judge Mary Lou Keel sentenced Griffith, who already was on death row, to sixty years in prison.

Casey O'Brien said, "The effect is to ensure that should the worst happen, should he get his capital murder conviction reversed on appeal, he cannot get out until he had served thirty calendar years in prison."

At the time of his conviction, Michael Durwood Griffith was the only former lawman on death row.

However, that is expected to change in the future because there are one or two other former law enforcement officers awaiting trial in Texas on capital murder charges.

ACKNOWLEDGMENTS

I'm grateful to all the people who helped to make this book possible.

Homicide Detective Robert E. King of the Houston Police Department, the primary investigator in the McCormick murder case, was especially helpful, giving me hours of his time in my original research and remaining patient with my dozens of follow-up phone calls over the weeks.

King, and his partner Detective Sgt. Hal Kennedy, their supervisors in the homicide division, and the other outstanding crime scene and laboratory experts of the HPD, did an outstanding job in tracking and bringing to justice the killer of Deborah McCormick—a killer who turned out to be a former colleague in law enforcement.

Thanks also to former Detective Joe Gamino, who once was part of some famous murder investigations himself and now is a member of Media Relations for the HPD.

In the Harris County District Attorney's Office, my thanks go to Assistant District Attorney Dan McCrory in the appellate division, and his courteous and efficient secretarial staff; to

Assistant District Attorney Casey O'Brien, who gave me much of his time in recalling the prosecution of Michael D. Griffith that culminated in the death penalty verdict. Working with the D.A.'s people was a pleasant experience.

I'm grateful for just getting to know Mrs. Mary Ringer, the mother of Deborah McCormick, a woman of extraordinary courage and endurance. My heart goes out to her and other members of her family and friends who suffered so deeply in the tragic loss of their loved one, who was a wonderful person in her own right. Mary, with the help of her beautiful granddaughter Brandy Ridley, who is a daughter of the murder victim, continues to operate the Always & Forever Flowers shop and wedding chapel because she knew that was what Deborah would have wanted.

I appreciate, too, the courtesy extended to me by State District Judge Mary Lou Keel of 232nd State District Court in Houston, and the efficient staff of the District Clerk's Office.

A special note of thanks to Ms. Sherry Adams, chief librarian of the *Houston Chronicle,* a most helpful lady to a true crime researcher, and to freelance photographer Joel Draut of Houston for his expert work.

A special thanks to the courteous staff at the Allen Parkway Motor Inn and especially the helpful shuttle drivers, who daily hauled my wife and me to and from the downtown Criminal District Attorney's Building or Criminal Courts Building.

Bob and Judy Bybee of Port Lavaca, Texas, offered their wonderful hospitality and other courtesies that made our stay in the Gulf Coast area enjoyable.

Thanks go also to the Bay County, Florida, Sheriff's Department for the help of its public affairs officer and secretary.

And as usual, my appreciation for the help of Consulting Editor Karen V. Haas and Editor-in-Chief Paul Dinas, who patiently guided me through the hard spots.

As always, I could not have finished this project without the companionship, encouragement, and editorial help of my wife Nina, who did a large share of recording the trial transcript in this case, offering advice and doing her usual top job of copy-reading the manuscript pages.

This book could not have been written without the help and cooperation of all these individuals.

Bill G. Cox
Amarillo, TX
June 28, 1997